LUCKY MAN

Ken Jackson

Lakeside Outdoors

Copyright © 2024 Lakeside Outdoors

All rights reserved

The characters and events portrayed in this book are fictitious. Any similarity to real persons, living or dead, is coincidental and not intended by the author.

No part of this book may be reproduced, or stored in a retrieval system, or transmitted in any form or by any means, electronic, mechanical, photocopying, recording, or otherwise, without express written permission of the publisher.

*ISBN - 978-0-9975982-2-3

Cover design by: Kenneth George Jackson
Library of Congress Control Number: 2018675309
Printed in the United States of America

Remembering Forest

Wish You Were Here

CONTENTS

Title Page
Copyright
Dedication
Introduction
Prologue

CHAPTER ONE	1
CHAPTER TWO	6
CHAPTER THREE	10
CHAPTER FOUR	13
CHAPTER FIVE	22
CHAPTER SIX	24
CHAPTER SEVEN	41
CHAPTER EIGHT	44
CHAPTER NINE	51
CHAPTER TEN	55
CHAPTER ELEVEN	64
CHAPTER TWELVE	70
CHAPTER THIRTEEN	72
CHAPTER FOURTEEN	82
CHAPTER FIFTEEN	88

CHAPTER SIXTEEN	91
CHAPTER SEVENTEEN	97
CHAPTER EIGHTEEN	99
CHAPTER NINETEEN	107
CHAPTER TWENTY	114
CHAPTER TWENTY ONE	119
CHAPTER TWENTY-TWO	133
CHAPTER TWENTY-THREE	140
CHAPTER TWENTY-FOUR	143
CHAPTER TWENTY-FIVE	157
CHAPTER TWENTY-SIX	161
CHAPTER TWENTY-SEVEN	166
CHAPTER TWENTY-EIGHT	172
CHAPTER TWENTY-NINE	185
CHAPTER THIRTY	190
CHAPTER THIRTY-ONE	195
CHAPTER THIRTY-TWO	200
CHAPTER THIRTY-THREE	205
CHAPTER THIRTY-FOUR	210
CHAPTER THIRTY-FIVE	213
CHAPTER THIRTY-SIX	221
CHAPTER THIRTY-SEVEN	228
CHAPTER THIRTY-EIGHT	233
CHAPTER THIRTY-NINE	237
CHAPTER FORTY	240
CHAPTER FORTY-ONE	244
CHAPTER FORTY-TWO	250
CHAPTER FORTY-THREE	253

CHAPTER FORTY-FOUR	255
CHAPTER FORTY-FIVE	257
CHAPTER FORTY-SIX	259
CHAPTER FORTY-SEVEN	262
CHAPTER FORTY-EIGHT	264
Acknowledgements	269
About The Author	271
Books By This Author	273

INTRODUCTION

This novel is about friendship and beating addiction. Two guys who knew each other in college 30 years ago are reunited through a prank. One man has too much responsibility and the other doesn't have enough. It is a story of learning how to get past tragedy and learning that its never too late to heal.

There are several gruesome parts to the story and the language is adult in many places. Several topics are part of the story. Survivor's guilt, PTSD, alcoholism, and grief are all part of the path that leads to the hope of redemption.

Besides the challenges of the individuals in the story, there is a sense of community and people figuring out what they can do to contribute. There is a lesson that letting people into your life, no matter how old you are, can help you defeat some of your demons.

One of the characters also learns that once you are facing certain death, you can truly find out what you are willing to do to live.

LUCKY MAN

by Ken Jackson

PROLOGUE

We begin in modern day Islamorada, Florida, nestled halfway between Miami and Key West. This is a party atmosphere with the ocean on both sides of the only road. It is a place of live music and good times. It is a place of escape. Even in the modern age of connection and the influences of the outside world, this place seems to be a world of it's own.

This is where University of Wisconsin graduate and lottery winner Jeremy Fine resides as a retired, divorced, drunk.

CHAPTER ONE

The sun was slowly cooking his puke encrusted face. His eyes were shielded by $500 Oakley sunglasses, while his nose was turning as red as a tomato. The smell of bile, fish entrails, and sea salt permeated the windless air. Captain Johnny Price was slowly running the boat out to a patch of floating grass in search of some dorado. Laying in a sorry state on the back deck was Jeremy Fine, millionaire. This was day two of the great Islamorada Dolphin Tournament. Day one finished with Jeremy back at the Dead Animal Bar, otherwise known as the Safari Lounge doing upside down margaritas with a bunch of vacationing nurses that were visiting the Florida Keys. He finished his tequila laced mission around 4 a.m. and Captain Johnny picked him up from the outside deck of the bar, passed out in a beach chair. Jeremy spent the bulk of the morning blowing chunks of slightly digested chicken wings and alcohol into the sea off the side of Johnny's boat. He wasn't merely hungover. He was still drunk.

Johnny was more than a little frustrated. Despite all the planning and anticipation of the tournament, the bite died when the east wind dropped. Also, his main (and lately, exclusive) client barely had the strength to stand on his own two feet, much less fight a big dorado because of his latest bout of binge drinking. The boat smelled, the fish weren't biting, and time was winding down to post a quality fish to the leaderboard. John was truly a professional when it came to this style of saltwater angling. His problem right now was that all the planning and tactics were useless if his boat mate couldn't physically function. Suddenly, Johnny spotted a disturbance at the surface near a patch of floating grass. "Jeremy!" Johnny hollered, "Get your ass up and throw a lure at those fish man!"

Jeremy smiled and lifted his glasses slightly, revealing

horribly bloodshot eyes. "You take this one, buddy. If I set a hook right now, I think I might puke again."

Groaning in disgust, Johnny took a cast past the dorsaling dolphins and worked the lure close to the grass. Suddenly, the water exploded and Johnny buried the hook with a firm hook set. His fish went airborne several times while a drunken Jeremy laid on the deck, giggling, clapping, and obnoxiously cheering for John.

Johnny realized this was a big dolphin and he could use some assistance.

"Jeremy, seeing as this is supposed to be your fish and you are competing in the tournament, would it be too much to ask you to get off your dead ass and give me a hand with this thing?" The sweat was starting to flow on John's brow.

"Hey big J, you da man! You don't need me. Just stay away from those crazy drunken nurses and you can do anything!" Jeremy's voice was wavering as if he was about to doze off again.

After a 20-minute struggle, Johnny put the gaff hook to a 58-pound dorado that was incandescent blue in color. It was the fourth largest dolphin Johnny had ever put in his boat. He laughed as he slid the big fish into the ice storage below deck. Johnny knew this was likely the tournament winning fish. It would be good for his business that it was captured aboard his boat, even though next to the hatch opening lay his drunken, snoring, smelly, millionaire client, Jeremy Fine.

By the time the award ceremony was underway, Jeremy had started consuming cocktails again. He was rosy cheeked and full of stories. A Miami news crew was covering the tournament and saw the animated activity around the bar at Mangrove Manny's, the tournament headquarters. Jeremy sat at the table next to his trophy and large check for $25,000. To Jeremy, this was goofing around and drinking money. The interesting thing about Jeremy's tournament win was that he never ran the boat, picked up a fish pole, or even touched the fish. His only role in the event was telling his accountant to pay Johnny's monthly invoice and pick up the tab at Caloosa Cove Marina for his fuel and maintenance costs. He also added 25% to the invoice as a standing tip.

Paul the bartender opened a beer and set it in front of John.

"Johnny, why do you end up not taking credit for fish that you clearly caught? Everybody knows that clown can't fish and you did all the work. Why don't you claim that prize money as yours?"

John took a long pull off the beer and smiled at Paul.

"That guy is keeping me busy and helping put my kid through college. If I keep him happy, and relatively healthy he'll take good care of me long past what the tournament winnings would've done."

"I know but isn't it frustrating catering to such a dumbass?"

"Yes, sometimes but you got a look at the bigger picture. I'm too young to start over, and if I do my job this could work out for both Jeremy and me."

"Yeah. If he survives the weekend," said Paul.

This was Johnny's attitude towards his relationship with Jeremy. Jeremy, not soon after he had won the lottery three years ago, hired Johnny to take him fishing. Jeremy had so much fun fishing with Johnny and learning about the Florida Keys that they became quick friends. As Jeremy's lifestyle changed with his millionaire status, Johnny's role changed from being just a simple charter captain to being more of Jeremy's babysitter and protector. When Jeremy was away from his wife in Chicago, John found himself getting Jeremy out of jams mostly because of reckless behavior. Drinking became the main problem, as drunk driving arrests, physical altercations, and poor judgment left Jeremy in various states of helplessness. At any time, day or night, Johnny could be called on to "rescue" Jeremy from a series of poor decisions. On a few occasions these decisions even required bail money. While some might look at Johnny as a parasite, simply taking advantage of someone with money, many looked at him as the older brother figure that Jeremy never had. Over two years ago, when Jeremy's behavior got bad enough, his wife divorced him. Since then, Jeremy spent all his available time in Islamorada fishing with John and drinking to excess at all hours.

It was getting to be the end of the festivities at Manny's and the stream of local media trucks were leaving the parking lot. Jeremy was still holding court at the bar, and as long as he was sponsoring shots, he was surrounded by several leathery tanned women actively celebrating the evening with him. By now, Jeremy had built up a hefty $3500 bar tab at Manny's. John had had enough for one day as he still had to clean the boat up and get fuel for the next day's charter. When attempting to exit the bar with a slight wave, Jeremy spotted him and started yelling; "WAIT! WAIT! You can't leave!" Jeremy ran to the entryway and gave John a big hug, stumbling and drooling slightly. "Thanks man! That was fun."

"Which part?" John asked. "The fishing, or the after party?"

"The whole thing my friend. The whole thing." Jeremy hugged him again.

"Ok! Ok! Jer, Jesus, be careful, those blonde bronze beauties are gonna think you're gay or not interested."

"They can't blame me. Big John, you're a very handsome man." Jeremy smiled through his alcoholic fog.

"Paul! "John yelled to the bartender. "Can you make sure this clown makes it to his house?"

The tall and slightly balding bartender came over and took Jeremy by the shoulder and guided him back to his barstool. "No worries, John." Paul assured him. "I'm cutting him off and dropping him at his place when I go home."

It was another hour or so when the crowd finally thinned out and Paul the bartender convinced Jeremy to drink a fourth glass of water to help him dilute the vodka that had invaded his body. It was past sundown and time for people to retreat into their RV's and condos up and down Highway 1. Paul loaded up Jeremy and drove him to his home on the bayside near mile marker 85. It was on a canal with a 38-foot Carver docked out front and a magnificent view to the west for the sunsets. The patio was graced with a pool, grilling area, and small tiki bar for entertaining. It was a place built for a family, but Jeremy rarely had anybody over except for an occasional woman that he could charm at one of the local Keys' watering holes. He spent most of the time in or near the pool nursing hangovers and watching sports on the big screen tv. The square footage and amenities were underutilized. But, with lottery winnings, Jeremy often bought more than he needed. This property was a perfect example.

Paul got Jeremy into the house and made sure he hit the couch. Jeremy mumbled facedown into the couch cushion, "Thanks big guy. You're really earning your tips……" he trailed off. Paul looked around the inside of the beautiful property and shook his head before walking out. "Poor dumb asshole will be dead in a year if he keeps this up…" Paul seemed both sad and amused at the same time. The door closed with Jeremy alone again, mumbling into the couch cushion.

CHAPTER TWO

It was a colder than normal Sunday morning. When Miles looked at his thermometer and it hovered at 15 below zero, he knew several things would happen that morning. First, his one full time employee Carl would be late because his car wouldn't start. Secondly, if the secondary heat pump in the town water plant was acting up, he could count on a frozen water main by noon. Third, if he didn't get some hot coffee in him, and soon, the whole day was going to be a waste of time.

Miles Grogan was a bit of an anomaly. He was a respected mayor and head law enforcement officer of Minaki, a small hamlet in northwest Ontario. He was born in that town 55 years before and had spent nearly his entire life there except for a couple years away at college in the United States. A widower of sorts since he was 22 years old, Miles had a daughter who was the local clinic physician. Miles was also grandfather to a 9-year-old boy. He was responsible for the town, its utilities, his family, and solving the various problems of Minaki's 800 residents. This sleepy little Ontario hamlet was a tourist town in the summer, providing a vacation destination for visitors from the United States. This was late winter. Late March to be exact. The residents and the region itself were looking forward to warmer weather and not being cooped up in cabins and houses any longer.

As Miles pulled his F-150 truck into the parking lot of Ellie's Diner, he glanced over the slope of the hill as it descended to the banks of the partially frozen Winnipeg River. Steam-like condensation rose from it as the open water touched the frozen air. "Spring," muttered Miles in disgust. "My ass."

"Morning, Uncle Miles," the greeting from Pam, his niece who had a hot pot of coffee in her hand as he entered the brightly lit diner. The vintage television had the Weather Channel on, showing the frigid air mass that was invading northwest Ontario. Miles sneered at the television and asked his niece to change the channel. "Here," she said. "help yourself." She handed him the remote.

Miles clicked through several channels before spotting blue waves and sunny views from a fishing program on the Sportsman's Channel. It was a feature about tournament fishing in the Florida Keys. "Oh!" Miles exclaimed with pain and envy in his voice. "Look at that....... waves, sunshine and no ice."

Pam smiled without looking at her forlorn uncle. "Don't worry, Uncle Miles. You'll have your boat out of storage in a few short weeks."

Miles turned his focus on the show for a bit when the overly enthusiastic commentator raised his microphone and gave details of the most recent catch in the Mangrove Manny's Tournament.

"Here we are with tournament champion Jeremy Fine. Tell us Jeremy, this has to be a real treat to be able to celebrate this win despite some tough conditions."

"You bet it's sweet! I did everything I could, but when that 60 pounder came in the boat, I knew it was a special fish." Jeremy was yelling into the mic, obviously drunk and surrounded by several attention seeking bikini clad women around the bar. Music was playing and it looked like a tropical booze festival. Jeremy's hat was crooked, several drinks had spilled on his Blackhawks jersey, and he didn't seem to know where the camera was located. It was clear that in addition to being intoxicated, he was sleep deprived, and blissfully unaware he was being interviewed on television.

"You are one lucky man." The commentator continued, "First you win that 28 million dollars 3 years ago in the Illinois State Lottery and now you pick up this tournament win despite the great competition of all these top local Captains in the Middle Keys."

"Hey, that's not luck. That's skill. John Price runs a great boat and he's an awesome dude. When we put our heads together, there is no tournament that is out of reach." Jeremy loses his balance slightly as he leans on his barstool. "You name any species, at any location, from wahoo to walleye, I can out fish anybody!"

Miles's mouth dropped wide open. He hit the power button on the remote, silencing the television and dropping the diner into an uncomfortable quiet. Pam was wiping down the counter and not looking. Miles silently stood up without his coffee, turned around without blinking, and walked out of the diner. He was transfixed and staring straight ahead. Another car pulled into the lot and Miles never noticed. He quietly opened the door of his truck and got in. After about five seconds the key was turned and the engine fired. Miles pulled his truck out of the lot and turned on the frozen highway towards the town shop.

Miles walked into the office of the Minaki town shop and was surprised to see Carl already there. "Oh, Carl," Miles startled. "You're here."

"Yeah. Where else would I be?" Carl quipped back. "Oh, you were probably thinking my car wouldn't like this weather. I just replaced my battery in Kenora a few days ago." Carl continued droning on about the details of his trip to Kenora as Miles quietly walked past him and into the office, closing the door, and firing up the computer on his desk. The whole time Miles stared at the screen until it booted up and he logged on to Google where he typed in the name Jeremy Fine. Several results came up and he clicked on a headline that detailed a dorado fishing tournament win. He clicked on the photos and pressed his 55-year-old eyes closer to the screen to check the details of the photo. He studied the face carefully. He then clicked on other results from the search. He found several news stories about Jeremy Fine winning a 28-million-dollar lottery drawing a few years before. He did a police search through the Ontario Ministry of Law Enforcement on American citizen Jeremy Fine. It detailed his divorce in Illinois court and several misdemeanor arrests in Wisconsin, Florida, and Illinois. Each arrest included a mugshot. It always showed bloodshot eyes, disheveled hair, and occasionally a bloody nose or torn clothing. It was an embarrassing list that included public urination, disorderly conduct, drunk driving, and one arrest report even gave details of an incident where he was jet skiing naked while drunk wearing a helmet that included drink holders and a tube that ran down to his mouth so he could drink hands free.

Miles sat back in his chair reeling in disbelief at what he had just read. Carl was two rooms away, unaware of the closed door, blathering away and telling stories the whole time. Miles finally uttered the words, "Crazy son of a bitch." He turned off the screen.

CHAPTER THREE

It was about 4 a.m. when Jeremy's eyes creaked open. It was still dark outside as he groaned and rolled over on the cool tile floor next to the couch in the main room of his condo. He had been asleep for over 24 hours and completely slept through Sunday. He slowly rose from the floor to his knees and then pulled himself up using the arm of the couch until he was standing tilted, but nonetheless upright.

His shuffling feet carried him to the bathroom where he turned on the light and gazed into the mirror. He winced at the disheveled reflection that looked back at him. The creases on his forehead looked deeper and the sunburn on one side of his face was peeling. He had a lot of years and rough miles on that 55-year-old face. He looked at the scar under his left eye where he took a hockey puck in high school. His chin had a lump on it that he got when he went off the road driving his Jeep Wrangler Unlimited up in Wisconsin, hitting a tree and banging his face on the steering wheel. It was a face that had been through youth sports, college parties, divorce, lots of scrapes, and hard living that he couldn't remember. It looked like it belonged to a much older man. He slowly slid into the shower and let the water cascade down his face while he tried to clear his pounding head. It had been a rough four days and it was time to clean up and sober up.

By 8 a.m. Jeremy was sitting by the pool, drinking a protein shake, and logging on to his computer. He dropped a couple of emails to his attorney in Chicago and his accountant in Milwaukee. These were both friends from his college days at the University of Wisconsin. Tom Siemens had a law practice that his father started back in the 1970's and now Tom was a senior partner. He and Jeremy had stayed closely in touch since college and saw each other several times a year, with Tom mostly coming down to Florida to visit and escape Wisconsin's cold temperatures. Kurt Schiltz handled Jeremy's money out of his office in Milwaukee. Even before the lottery win, Jeremy knew Kurt to be an exceptional money manager who had coached Jeremy on good investment brokers and real estate opportunities. Despite the divorce, and that fact that Jeremy was a free spender, he had grown his lottery winnings to an even larger war chest. Phone calls, texts, and emails went back and forth to these two friends several times a week. Ninety percent of the contact was friendly and social while ten percent dealt with actual business.

At 9:30, Jeremy's phone rings and he recognizes it's his mom.

"Hello, Mom. Let me put you on speaker."

"Hello, Jeremy. Why didn't you call me back yesterday? I was worried."

"I think my battery died. I was out in the boat." Jeremy lied to his mother. A routine occurrence.

"In that rain and lightning? Good God! What were you thinking?" Jeremy's mom sounded surprised as well as alarmed.

"Ah yeah, it wasn't that bad down here, just a little windy, but we were on the bay side. It must have been worse up by you in Boca." Another lie as he didn't want to explain to his mother that he had slept through an entire day because of his binge drinking. He of course, had slept nearly 30 hours straight and didn't have a clue what the weather had been anywhere.

"Hey, did you hear? I caught the biggest dorado in the tournament with John Price." Jeremy was quick to change the subject.

"No, I didn't hear. I hope that you didn't drink too much celebrating," his mom stated with concern in her voice.

"No, we just had a few beers and ate some lobster tails around the fire afterward," Jeremy was having trouble keeping his story straight.

"Hey listen, Mom. I gotta go, I have another call coming in."

"Ok, Jeremy. I love you. I'll call in a few days. Your father says hello."

"Ok Mom, love to you and Dad."

It was now 9:33. In a three-minute phone call Jeremy lied to his mom six times. Chalk up another reason for self-loathing.

There were exhibition highlights of baseball on the big screen by the pool. It wasn't even 10 a.m. Jeremy thought about building himself a bloody mary, but it was a little too soon he figured. Maybe it was time to get some food. He jumped into his golf cart and went the well traveled half mile to the Ocean View for fish tacos, the breakfast of drunken dorado champions.

CHAPTER FOUR

Miles went over to the hardware store across the street from the town shop and office. It was a family run business with neatly stacked shelves and an elderly couple, Penny and Jim Worth running the store. Penny worked the counter while Jim usually worked in the back, repairing windows, sharpening saw chains, and cutting pipe thread. Miles needed batteries for some of the town's equipment, but found himself distracted by the things he found out since he saw that fishing segment on the television at the diner an hour before. He was deep in thought when finally, a voice broke through his fog and Miles realized that Jim Worth had been talking to him for an undetermined amount of time.

"Miles! Are you ok?" Jim asked

"Huh? Ah, yeah. What did you say?"

"I asked if Carl told you about the Zamboni breaking down again. We have that ice show and the youth hockey tournament coming up to finish the season and we need to keep that ice good for another two weeks."

"Oh, I think Carl mentioned it. Did he order parts?"

"I'm going to see if I can get them, but that old machine is pretty ragged and the parts aren't easy to come by." Jim sounded concerned.

"Ok, well, let me know what you find out." Miles charged his batteries at the counter with Penny and loaded his truck. He had more chores to do and he still hadn't had any caffeine.

Once back at the shop Miles and Carl started working to install the new batteries in the vehicles used for road and trail maintenance. It was an annual affair and there was preparation for each coming season. They were getting ready for the spring thaw along with the mud that would follow. It was a good project to work on during a cold late winter morning. By noon the temperature hovered around zero. The men did not want to think about the wind chill.

It was time to break for lunch and Miles's daughter Gabrielle, or "Doctor Gabby," as everyone called her came by the shop with two carry-out cheeseburgers from The Cider Barn, a local watering hole that had a very good grill with excellent food. It was a weekly treat and Gabby would often join her dad on a Monday for lunch to catch up after the weekend. The first thing Miles enjoyed was his coffee.

"Hi sweetie," Miles said to his smiling daughter.

"Hi Dad. Gosh it's cold outside today."

"Yeah. How was your weekend in Kenora?"

"All I saw was the inside of the motel and the inside of the hockey arena. The boys took second and Robby had two assists. He also had a couple of stupid penalties." Gabby seemed annoyed.

"Well, that's an important tournament and Robby always plays with a lot of emotion. Yeah, it gets him in trouble sometimes, but the coaches seem to love him." Miles beamed with pride when discussing his grandson.

Gabby and her dad talked about small details and were wrapping up their lunch when Gabby asked, "Are you making another run for supplies soon? We're getting low on a few items at the clinic and I was hoping you would be going again before the roads get soft."

"Oh yeah, I was going to ask whether you need anything and have you put together a list. I was thinking about heading into Minnesota by air. The plane needs some routine maintenance and the mechanics at Winnipeg did a crappy job last time and overcharged me to boot. I could get better service in Minneapolis for less even when factoring in the extra fuel costs."

"Well," Gabby exclaimed, "If you're going that far maybe you could get a few other things! Maybe you could...."

"Hey wait. Don't get too carried away I probably will have to get parts for the Zamboni, your clinic supplies, I have to get netting for the tribe, and....."

"Ok! I was just wondering." Gabby seemed annoyed yet somewhat amused.

"Sorry Gabby. I can fly back with only so much weight."

Miles was feeling more like himself after eating lunch and seeing his daughter. The fog from the morning had lifted and he was getting things done. Now he had to put together a plan for an air trip for supplies and maintenance on the Minaki Beechwood Super King Air turbo prop.

Miles called the Beechwood mechanics in Minneapolis and talked to them about working on the town's plane. As it turned out, the 10-year-old model was showing signs of a small oil leak on both engines and it might also require an extended stay. If the engines were losing oil pressure, it would require a prolonged stay to make sure the plane would be air worthy for the upcoming tourist season. It was a necessary aggravation, and it needed to be done.

"Carl! Are you back here?" Miles yelled from his office into the shop area." Has your brother-in-law been sober lately?" Carl's brother-in-law Doug had a pilot's license.

"Yeah. As far as I know." Carl yelled back.

"Good. See if you can have him give me a call. I could use a second in the cockpit for this trip."

Miles finished out the afternoon in the shop and stopped by the Cider Barn on the way home. He wanted to see if Carl's brother-in-law Doug might be there, but he wasn't. There were a few patrons shooting pool and having a drink while the bartender, Kerri was boxing up carry out orders from the kitchen.

"Can I get you something Miles?"

"Large coffee, black, to go." As Miles sat at the bar waiting for his coffee, his mind wandered again back to the morning. The fog gathered around him once again as he kept recalling a painful memory.

Kerri set a covered styrofoam cup in front of Miles and said, "On the house." Miles pulled three Canadian loonies out of his pocket and left them on the bar for Kerri and headed out the door.

When Miles got back and it was dark. He walked into his empty house and lit a fire. He sat in his living room recliner for the rest of the night with just a few lights on and no sound. In the house there was complete and total silence.

In the office the next morning, the phone rang and it was Doug Briever, former local hockey player, fishing guide, and experienced pilot. Miles had known Doug since he was a little kid. Doug was about Gabby's age, but had never finished college. His party lifestyle got him in a few minor scrapes since high school, giving him a bit of a "bad boy" reputation. Miles had to take him into custody a couple times while drunk, but always let him go the next morning with a stern lecture.

"Thanks for calling Doug. I was wondering if you wanted a bit of work?" Miles inquired.

"What do you need?"

"I need to take the Beechcraft to Minneapolis this week and was wondering if you'd fly second seat. The town will pay $300 for each day you're away from home."

Doug worked seasonally and rarely had a paycheck between January and April. The last decent money he earned was cutting and selling Christmas trees, and that was over three months ago. He earned a few extra bucks since then maintaining the ice at the hockey arena but the wallet was reading empty. To be able to fly, get paid for it, and get put up in a nice hotel with food and drinks in late March? It was an offer too good to pass up.

Doug had a one-word answer, "Absofuckinlutely."

"Looks like we leave in the morning. Get packed tonight."

Miles hung up the phone and then dialed his daughter Gabby. He asked her to put together her wish list of medical supplies needed for the clinic. He then called Jim Worth at the hardware store and asked if he wanted to add the part the Zamboni needed. In all, Miles called seven different individuals to create his list of items that would likely have to sustain the residents of Minaki until the spring thaw was over and the frost and mud were gone. All these items were then called in to be delivered overnight to the Minneapolis airport customs hangar. They would need to be inspected by agents prior to flying out of the United States and into Ontario.

Miles spent the morning calculating the weight of the cargo, determining the amount of fuel required, and mapping the route. Next, he would have to file a formal flight plan.

As the afternoon wore on, it looked like the trip was going to go off as planned the next morning. Miles had the plane checked and fueled at the hangar. His manifest was drawn up for the cargo that would return and Miles had all the paperwork for the supplies to be delivered in Minneapolis the following day. His main concern was the oil situation on the Beechcraft engines. The oil was the only thing that could gum up the works. If the plane needed more work, the trip could be a waiting game and Miles and Doug would be stuck in Minneapolis.

The next morning dawned bright and clear. The pilot's term for this was CAVU, short for Ceiling and Visibility Unlimited. It was ideal flying weather and they were ready to get airborne. Doug showed up early and eager to go. After pre-flight checks, Miles cranked the generator and fired the ignition on both engines. Within 5 minutes, they were inflight on a heading of 170 degrees for the hour-long trip to the Twin Cities.

Within minutes of takeoff the frozen spectacle of Lake of the Woods passed beneath them. Miles and Doug felt liberated to be in the air again, away from the gray dreary winter. As they passed over the Rainy River and into American airspace, the snow cover dissipated and bare ground was visible for the first time in four long months. Miles contacted air traffic control out of the Twin Cities and was given a vector for approach. When Miles hit the switch to lower the landing gear, they were 55 minutes in the air.

Upon landing, Miles was directed by the tower to a hangar on the eastern part of the airport complex. It was a long walk from the terminals where commercial aircraft would be, but there was a separate area for pilots, mechanics, and ground personnel to get a sandwich, coffee, shower, or a nap. It was a chance to take a break, so Doug was getting paid to ride shotgun and nap for the day.

Miles met with the mechanics that would inspect the two Pratt and Whitney engines. Along with this check, hydraulics, control cables, wiring, and pressure seals would all be inspected. To save time, Miles hired two teams of mechanics to work on the plane. One for just the engines, and another team to work on replacing tires, batteries, and inspect the electrical wiring.

Within an hour, one of the engine mechanics came back and told Miles some news he didn't want to hear. There might be a propellor shaft seal problem. It would take time to remove the seals and replace them on both engines, but that was only half the issue. The engines would need to be tested after that.

"How long will that take?" Miles asked with a hint of frustration.

The head mechanic, Tim Morton, wiped his greased-stained hands on a rag and delivered the bad news. "Both engines will be tested by us here today on the ground. We'll run them for 30 minutes on the tarmac. If they're ok, you should run the engines for 7 to 10 hours regular flight time and have us check them one final time to make sure there are no leaks. After that, you can fly this thing for quite some time without having to worry about it."

Miles snarled a bit at this news. Not only was he stuck here overnight, he also had to come back here after racking up enough engine hours for the final inspection. It was a pain in the ass, but he knew it was necessary.

Miles went back inside the commons area near the hangar where he found Doug sitting on a couch playing video games with one of the mechanic's kids. Minnesota school districts were on spring break and there were a couple school aged kids milling around the complex with their fathers.

As he grabbed a cup of coffee Miles started to think about the chores he had to call Carl about and what needed to be done now that their return would be delayed by a day. He decided to call Carl back at the shop and check in.

"I'm stuck here until tomorrow," Miles grumbled into the phone.

"Well, you're not missing anything here. The weather is a balmy eight degrees this morning."

Carl had caught up on things around the shop area and was getting ready to fire up some of the vehicles they were going to need this spring.

"Hey, why not put fuel stabilizer in all the snow machines, snow blowers, and anything else you can think of?" Miles suggesteed. "We may not need these much longer this season, and I want that stuff run through all the engines before we put them away for the year." Clearly Miles was trying to keep Carl occupied.

"Yeah, I can do that, but you're just guaranteeing us a good blizzard."

"Go ahead. We can't wait 'til July. Oh, and give Randy a call in Kenora and let the OPP know that I'll be out of the jurisdiction overnight so they can have somebody on call in case you need a hand."

Carl was inquisitive; "Why the delay in getting home?"

"The mechanics must replace prop shaft seals on the engines. It's time consuming. Plus, after about 5 or 10 shuttle runs, I have to come back here for the guys to inspect it again." Miles grew more annoyed just talking about it.

"Why so many trips?" Carl asked.

"It's not the trips Carl. It's engine time. I have to fly for almost 10 hours before they look at the seals again." Miles was getting exasperated at having to explain every detail of the tedious oil drama.

"Boy, it's a shame you couldn't fly those 10 hours all at once. I'll bet you could go somewhere nice," Carl fantasized.

"Yeah, someplace nice, Carl. Like back to work." Miles abruptly ended the phone call and then immediately started dialing again.

"Hello? Gabby?"

"Hi Dad. How was the flight?"

"It was fine sweetie. Hey listen, it looks like I'm going to be delayed until tomorrow because of some repairs. We're going to be overnight here."

"Oh, that's good. Maybe you can have a little fun and have dinner out." Gabby knew this would annoy her dad, but she was trying to put a positive spin on things.

"Dinner out with Doug is not what I had in mind. It'll be all I can do to keep him out of the bars tonight."

"Well do the best you can. This place isn't going anywhere. It'll still be here when you get back."

"Ok Gabby. I love you and I'll see you tomorrow." Miles hung up the phone and now had to sit and wait for the mechanics to do their job. He sat at the table in the commons not far from Doug who had just finished playing video games and was now scrolling through text messages on his phone. Miles found an open computer and decided to sit down and do a search for hotels and restaurants.

After scrolling through some hotel results Miles opened a YouTube page. He typed "Dorado tournament Florida Keys" in the search bar. The search produced several video choices and he recognized the thumbnail for one of the videos. It was the Sportsman's Channel report he had just seen two mornings ago on television. It had over 100,000 views and people had plenty of comments about how drunk the tournament winner was, the inebriated Jeremy Fine. Miles watched the video two more times. The last thing Jeremy said in the interview was, "You name any species at any location. From wahoo to walleye, I can out fish anybody!" This was said with a slur, as Jeremy struggled to hold his balance.

Miles looked up from the computer and saw Doug on the couch. He looked down at the floor, and then up at the ceiling. You could almost see the gears and sprockets spinning around in Miles' head. Suddenly, he looked straight ahead and a sly smile slowly grew across his weathered face. He let out a loud laugh, clapped his hands once hard, rubbed them together, and giggled like a little kid. He closed the YouTube window and got out his phone. He quickly dialed the phone and waited impatiently.

"Randy! Hey! Glad I got you. Can you do me a favor?"

CHAPTER FIVE

It was 11 a.m. and Jeremy was down by his boat when John Price pulled up next to his slip.

"Johnny boy! What's the good word for today?"

"Hey Jeremy. My guests didn't last long today in those waves. I have a little barf to clean up on the deck, but my afternoon just freed up and we found some hogfish this morning. You interested?"

"Hell yes! Let me grab my cooler." Jeremy ran back in and grabbed a couple pieces of cold pizza and 5 beers. Jeremy jumped into John's boat and they took off down the channel.

After a 20-minute ride out on the ocean side, John anchored up a cast length away from some coral. The morning waves had dissipated and the tide was sending their casts close to the fish.

"Do you ever get sick of this?" Jeremy asked as he looked out at the reef behind the boat.

"I never get sick of this place or fishing if that's what you mean. I guess I don't like people barfing on my boat or tangling up lines, or showing up unprepared or hungover."

"John, you just listed four things that I do all the time."

"I know that."

"So why do you fish with me? I mean, beside the fact I pay you."

"Because I don't discriminate." John replied without looking.

"Against who?" Jeremy asked.

"Dumbasses." John replied with a smile.

"You know that sometimes you're a real asshole?" Jeremy quipped back.

"Yeah Jer, but I'm your personal asshole."

After fishing, John brought Jeremy back to his condo by boat. Jeremy unloaded the cooler with three nice hogfish. John took the cooler and went over to Jeremy's fish cleaning table and began to fillet the succulent meat and package the fish for later. Jeremy grabbed the water hose and jumped back into John's boat and began hosing down the deck that had dried vomit from the morning, and various smears of blood and shrimp tails from the afternoon's fishing.

"Hey. You up for a hook and cook? We can take this down to the O.V. and have some dinner. My treat." Invited Jeremy.

"Nah, I have to gas up the boat and I'm supposed to meet up with this girl I met on the boat last week."

"Oh, come on. Get in the golf cart and let's go down the road. There's all kind of girls at the O.V. this time of day." Jeremy spoke from experience.

"Thanks anyway. I'm heading down to the Angler House and meeting her there for a little sunset time." John needed a break from his partying friend.

"What's so special about her? Did she read a book or something?" Jeremy was being snide now because he had to go out alone.

"Well, she's better looking than you. Is that reason enough?"

"Everybody is better looking than me, John. We on for tomorrow?"

"No. Day after tomorrow. I have that family out of Lime Tree Resort tomorrow. I may get into some yellowtail. I'll let you know."

"Ok, I'll meet you at the marina then. Don't be too easy tonight. She won't respect you later." Jeremy said in jest.

John smiled and shook his head. Jeremy had his boat cleaned up and ready to go for the next day. While Jeremy paid his invoices and hired him all the time, John considered him a friend. A friend with a lot of demons, but a true friend. John felt bad that all Jeremy's money couldn't buy him some peace.

Jeremy grabbed the bag of fish, jumped on his golf cart, and headed four blocks down the road to the Ocean View. It was time for happy hour.

CHAPTER SIX

"Good news, Mr. Grogan. It looks like we'll have you ready to go in about 30 minutes."

Miles looked pleased. It wasn't even 1 pm. Lots of daylight left.

"Max fuel if you would, top off the tanks." Miles told the maintenance chief.

Doug overheard Miles say "Max fuel," and turned his head in surprise.

"We have a bunch of cargo Miles. We don't have room for that much gas."

"We aren't loading all the cargo here. And, we need to put on some engine time. I had to add something to the cargo manifest." Doug took the list from Miles and he looked at the printed sheet. Written in pencil at the very bottom were the words, "fresh key lime pie."

"You wanna get a drink? Miles asked.

"Sure," Doug looked at him in bewilderment.

Now airborne, Doug looked unsettled in the right seat. Miles had a goofy smile on his face and it made Doug nervous.

"Where are we going?"

"I promised you a drink, so I'm getting you a drink." Miles was staring out the windshield like nothing was unusual.

"Well, it looks like we're traveling for a bit to get this mystery location for a drink."

"Uh huh." Miles stared straight ahead.

"What are we drinking?" Doug was taking on the role of interrogator as Miles was answering with minimal information.

"How's a Rum Runner sound?" Miles looked at him with a deadpan stare.

"Did you file a flight plan?" Doug's voice raised an octave. His pitch rising along with his anxiety.

"Of course, I did. I had to."

Doug started rifling through the papers on the floor of the cockpit and thumbed through them before his widening eyes landed on a page and then his head turned slowly and looked at Miles.

"Where the fuck is Marathon?" He asked dumbfounded.

Doug and Miles sat in near silence for over an hour as they headed on a southeast course and it wasn't until they were over Kentucky that Doug finally opened his mouth. He was well past confusion and was now wondering if Miles had completely lost it, a casualty of cabin fever and too many frigid Canadian winters.

"Why in the hell do we have to go to Florida to get a drink and some key lime pie?"

Miles calmly looked over at Doug and stated several things in a matter-of-fact tone.

"First off, you're getting paid to sit on your ass. I'm buying the drinks. You get some time out of the deep freeze, and lastly, you may come out of this with a pretty good story. So, why not just shut the hell up and enjoy the ride?"

Doug knew there was more going on but could not get Miles to crack.

"Besides, the mechanics said time is needed on the engines. I can do that better all at once than have to go back to Minnesota after six short trips to Winnipeg. I can have the boys in the hangar take care of this tomorrow and we're back home inside of 48 hours," explained Miles.

Miles seemed pleased that his line of bullshit was seemingly working. But, he realized that Doug was kind of stuck there. He felt like he only needed to dole out information on an as needed basis, so why elaborate?

The Beechcraft sailed along nicely at 30,000 feet, flying directly over Nashville, skirting the heavy air traffic just west of Atlanta. Soon, Doug and Miles saw the Gulf of Mexico out in front of the plane to the right. They were near the west coast of Florida for a bit before going further inland on a heading of 148 degrees south. It was almost 5:30 p.m. eastern time as Miles was given clearance to land at Marathon. Their wheels touched the runway exactly three and a half hours after leaving the ground in Minnesota. Miles taxied to a stop near building number three and got out of the plane. When the hatch door opened, the smell of saltwater hit Doug and the warm humid air surrounded him like a blanket. He relaxed and realized that there might be some fun to be had down here. Miles promised him a Rum Runner and some pie, and he was going to be sure to collect.

Miles met up with Mike Welsh, a transport coordinator for the Marathon airport. Mike directed Miles to a building about 200 feet away where there was a waiting rental car. Mike ran Miles' credit card and Doug walked up while Mike was giving directions to Mangrove Manny's, a 25-minute ride north on Highway 1 in Islamorada.

"Hang on Doug! We're on our way to get you that drink." Miles grinned and got into the driver's side of the white Nissan Rouge. They pulled out in bumper-to-bumper traffic on the busy highway with the sun getting lower in the western sky behind them.

Doug rode in the passenger's seat and grinned about his current situation. He awoke that morning in a frozen Ontario town covered in frost and snow and now he was riding down the highway with the windows down in 78-degree weather on his way to have a tropical cocktail. Overall, it was turning into a pretty good day.

Miles drove with the radio on and a satisfied look on his face. The wheels in his head were turning as plans for the evening lay out before him. A lot of things had to go right for this evolving debacle to come to fruition, but things were looking good and Miles was quite optimistic.

Despite the heavy evening traffic, Miles made fairly decent time and pulled into the parking lot at Manny's. Doug showed excitement as he saw the open tiki bar area with several women sitting together laughing and drinking. Miles wasn't looking at the bar however, as he drove slowly through the parking area carefully scanning the vehicles searching for a particular model.

"Ah, I don't know. This place doesn't look all that happening." Miles was ready to drive out of the parking lot and back onto US 1.

"Bullshit! This looks good to me." Doug jumped out of the car while it was still rolling and walked quickly to the end of the bar closest to the women. Miles hit the brakes and frowned as he realized he couldn't avoid this stop. He would have to divulge the situation with Doug at some point, but it was a little too early in the game. Besides, Miles realized that he might be able to get some information by stopping here.

"One Rum Runner, Sir!" Doug bellowed loudly. "And, I would like to start a tab." He then turned his head towards the gaggle of women to his right, grinning.

Miles went to the other end of the bar away from the noise. He called up the Marathon airport to verify his flight plan and check that the plane had been refueled.

"Take off? Not sure yet. I'll let you know." Miles ended the call when the bartender came over.

"What can I get you? It was Paul, the regular bartender. He looked a little tired from dealing with tourists all evening.

"Club soda and a lime." Miles had to keep a clear head. He had a quiet moment between the laughing and the music to ask a few questions.

"Hey, I heard you had a big dorado tournament here over the weekend." Miles started digging for his information.

"Yeah. It was pretty crazy. TV cameras, sponsors, a bunch of media. It was more than a little nuts, even for here."

"What was the big fish for the weekend?" Miles usually asked questions he already knew the answers to so he could measure response. It was a common practice for people that were in law enforcement.

"A nice big dolphin. It was almost 60 pounds. Beautiful fish." Paul placed the club soda in front of Miles.

"Who won? Was it some local captain?"

"Well, sort of. The fish was caught out of Johnny Price's boat, but the guy that "supposedly" reeled it in was one of our regulars here at the bar."

Miles turned his head at a weird angle as if to ask what Paul meant.

"Yeah, he drank the whole weekend and went out in the boat. He could barely move much less reel in a 60 pounder. He was in rough shape. The guy's a real character."

"I'll bet he's still celebrating." Miles was getting closer to asking more, but backed off a bit. He didn't want to tip his hand that he was searching for the guy.

"Hey, who wouldn't be? Haven't seen him since day before yesterday though."

Miles glanced over towards Doug and saw him in a conversation laughing with one of the girls sitting at the bar. Doug always fancied himself a ladies' man and he went through most of the eligible ones back in Minaki like a brush fire. This was fertile ground with lots of new female opportunities. Trouble was, Miles was on a mission of a different kind. Miles was on the hunt for Jeremy Fine, tournament angler, and Doug thought this night was about tropical drinks and getting laid.

"Hey Doug!"

"Yeah?" yelled Doug across the bar.

Miles motioned him to come over and Doug shot him a nasty look as he was clearly mixing in nicely with his new female friend. Doug finally came over, looking annoyed.

"What the hell, Miles? I'm having fun with Stacy over here and you're........."

"Look Doug, we gotta go. I want to see another place."

"No way. I'm relaxed, this bar is cool, and the girls are fun. Let's stay."

"Come on Doug. We need to get going." Miles grabbed Doug's shoulder. Doug pulled away quickly and raised his voice.

"No fucking way. I'm hungry, I haven't eaten since eight o'clock this morning and I need some food. I'm going to sit at this bar until I get a burger goddammit."

Miles realized he had to calm Doug down because he needed Doug's help if this plan was ever going to work.

"Look, you're right. Let's eat. Except, I want to take you to this other place the bartender told me about that's just down the road. They have great food and if you'd like, you can tell your little blonde-haired friend over there to meet us." Miles smiled at Doug and did his best to calm him down.

"Alright, we can go....... but, if that place sucks, we're coming right back here. OK?"

"Absolutely. That makes perfect sense." Miles caught Doug off guard a bit by being so agreeable.

Miles glanced back at the young woman Doug had been talking to.

"Are you going to let your friend know we're leaving?"

Doug took a last long gulp of his drink finishing it, and put his glass firmly on the bar.

"No. Her tits are too small. Let's go."

Miles fired up the Nissan and turned onto Highway 1 heading towards Islamorada. He had called the Minnesota State Police to do a nationwide search on Jeremy Fine. The background check spit out a vehicle description and address in Florida that was just off Highway 1 in a subdivision on the gulf side. He figured on finding Jeremy in a bar, but there were dozens to choose from. He narrowed his search by going to Mangrove Manny's first as it was the tournament's headquarters and if that didn't work, simply try places that served alcohol that were closest to his address, and then work his way outward. As a last resort, he would go to Jeremy's address, but that would be difficult to explain. This meeting would have to seem like an accident or something by chance.

The next place on Miles's list was called the Ocean View Inn. It was at mile marker 84 on the gulf side and the bar closest to Jeremy's address. He pulled into the parking area looking for a black 2022 Jeep Wrangler Unlimited High Altitude with personalized Florida plates reading JersFine.

Miles was driving slowly through the lot looking for the Jeep, but could not see it. There were several vehicles parked on the highway side of the bar and a couple others around the building along with a golf cart. It seemed like Miles was about to pull out back onto the highway when Doug grabbed his arm suddenly.

"Where the hell are you going? You promised me we'd get some food. I'm starving dammit!"

"Yeah ok, I guess." Miles had defeat in his voice. He didn't see the Jeep he was looking for but was now committed to stopping. Hopefully Doug could eat quickly and they could hit the next couple places before it got too late. Miles was starting to believe he was on a wild goose chase.

"Damn it, Miles. There's a parking spot right there."

Miles parked the Nissan next to the golf cart. He didn't see them, but there were two decals on the golf cart. One for the Chicago Blackhawks and another with a Bucky Badger logo from the University of Wisconsin.

Doug entered the Ocean View first and quickly sat at the horseshoe shaped bar close to the entrance. It was a smaller room, but led to corridor and a larger outdoor bar under an awning where there was a stage for live music along with a fire pit. Doug got a menu right away and ordered a Crown Royal and water while Miles went to the outdoor area to check just in case Jeremy was outside. Unfortunately, he was nowhere to be seen.

"Club soda and lime please." Miles ordered his drink and decided to get something to eat as well. The day was starting to catch up with him and the enormity of this charade was starting to occur to him. He had lied to Doug, used several hundred gallons of fuel for no good reason at all, and was over 2,000 miles from home. He should actually be at home in his own bed by this time, but he was within 84 miles of the southernmost part of the United States. Miles was at a turning point and maybe it was time to come clean and tell Doug what he had originally planned. It was a bad idea and there was still time to call it off. Miles was just about to turn to Doug and let him know what was going on when;

"Hi guys! What can I get for you?" A pretty brunette waitress with a beaming smile had her order book out and pen ready.

"I'll have a steak supreme and some O.V. wings." Doug was hungry.

The cute waitress turned to Miles.

"And you?"

Miles looked up from his menu and he spotted Jeremy Fine coming out of the men's room. His shoulder hit the side of the door jamb on the way out and he nearly fell down. Jeremy caught himself and straightened upright against the back of a barstool. He was visibly drunk and older looking in person than Miles expected. He was caught totally off-guard seeing Jeremy just this second and he stuttered when the waitress prompted him again for his order.

"Sir? Can I get you something?"

Not even looking at her and in a drone-like voice; "I'll have the same."

Jeremy stumbled through the inside bar area and wandered down the corridor towards the outside bar where the fire pit was located. Doug looked at Miles.

"Something wrong? What's up?" Doug was curious about the sudden change in Miles' demeanor.

"I gotta go to the bathroom. I'll be right back." Miles slowly left his barstool and walked towards the outside bar area. He spotted Jeremy sitting at the end of the bar chatting with the bartender, a rough looking woman, about 35 years old with several tattoos. Miles eavesdropped on the conversation which consisted of Jeremy telling the bartender why the Swedish make better vodka than the Russians. The heavily inked bartender nodded her head obligingly, but it was clear she was not particularly invested in the conversation.

Miles now realizing his plan was half-baked, did his best to think of what to do next. He needed to improvise and engage Jeremy to build a rapport. Once he dove into this thing, it would be hard to turn back.

"I prefer Absolut myself." Miles uttered just loud enough to be heard.

Jeremy whipped his head around, looking at Miles and exclaimed to the bartender, "See! My man over here agrees with me. You have good taste sir."

Jeremy slid his barstool closer to Miles. Miles resisted the urge to recoil at Jeremy's breath, which was bad enough to derail a train. He smiled and listened to Jeremy as he droned on about vodkas, but at the same time he was looking at his aged face. Miles had been in law enforcement for many years and had encountered many alcoholics and drug abusers. Their skin looked different. Their eyes looked different. Their senses weren't as keen. Their balance, stamina, and mental acuity were all affected and it was obvious here.

But, as Jeremy continued his monologue, Miles looked closer and could still see the young man that he once knew so well. For a brief moment he could see the face that was fighting off acne. He could see the hairline where it used to be. He could remember the year at school where they got to know each other. He wanted to just say hello at one point and reconnect, but his mischievous side got the best of him. He remembered why they were here. Why he filled a plane with fuel and flew to the middle of the Florida Keys. It was time to get Doug and have him do what he did best, bullshit and drink.

"Excuse me, I have to take a leak. I'll be back in a minute." Miles said as he tried to nonchalantly slide off his barstool and head towards the front entrance where Doug was munching away on his chicken wings that the cute waitress had just delivered.

"Hey man, the sauce on these wings is awesome."

Miles grabbed Doug by the shoulder and said: "Follow me."

"Jesus Christ! I just got my food!" Doug was exasperated.

"Would you just......" Miles was trying to speak in hushed tones but it was louder than he wanted.

Doug got off his barstool and slowly followed Miles to a quiet corner where they could see Jeremy at the outside bar yacking away.

"You see that guy there?"

"The hammered guy in the red shirt?"

"Yeah. How would you like to have a little fun tonight?"

"Miles, what are we talking about here? I wanted to have a little fun with those girls back at the first place we stopped. I'm not going to start messing around with guys."

"No, no, no. I mean pull a prank. You up for something like that?"

"Yeah, I guess. But who is he?" Doug wanted to learn more as he knew something was up and he was finally getting some answers.

"It's a guy I knew a long time ago and I owe him a little friendly payback. What do you say?"

"Sure." Doug said hesitantly. "But can I finish my food first?"

"Grab it and bring it out to the other bar. Tell our waitress." Miles put his face closer to Doug's and looked him directly in the eye. "Two important things. Don't let him know my name and don't tell him where we're from. And, follow my lead."

Doug nodded his head and went to grab his food. Miles walked back in and sat right next to Jeremy. "So, you drinking vodka now?"

Jeremy turned towards Miles and said; "Hey, how was your piss? Any blood or burning sensations?"

Miles feigned a laugh and turned towards the bartender. "I'll have a club soda with lime."

"Bullshit! Have a real drink." Jeremy put his arm around Miles, again the breath was unbelievably bad.

"No thanks, I have to drive tonight."

"No you don't. You can get as hammered as you want and crash at my place. It's like half a click down this street right here. I drove my golf cart here!"

"Well, that's nice but I am taking some high blood pressure medication." Miles had to refuse a drink if he was going to pull this off tonight.

Jeremy looked confused. "Oh yeah? You gotta watch that shit.

It'll make your dick soft."

"Thanks for the heads up. Literally."

Just then, Doug came and sat next to Miles, bringing his food. He set another plate in front of Miles.

"My name's Jeremy."

"Hi, I'm MG and this is my buddy, Doug."

"MG? What kind of a handle is that?"

"It's short for my Indian name."

"What's your Indian name?"

Miles stuttered a bit here. He wasn't ready for this question this early.

"Mannigum Gungahockis." He sounded unsure as he said it.

Jeremy looked him in the eye. "It sounds made up. Like a venereal disease."

"It means loves to fish."

"Well, shit you can call me Magnum Gonorrhea too because I LOVE to fish." Jeremy was slurring his words.

"Doug and I are fishing this week and we're really excited to get out," Miles got the ball rolling.

"What can you tell me about mahi?" Miles was leading Jeremy right where he wanted to go.

"What can I tell you? Everything! You are sitting next to the dean of dorado, the master of mahi, the destroyer of dolphin!"

Doug started laughing out loud.

"What's so funny there, Mr. Cheeseburger?" Jeremy was challenging him. He was also starting to slur his speech a bit more. Jeremy had been at the Ocean View for over three hours and he was starting to fade a bit.

Doug was still laughing. "Can't really put my finger on it, but you look more like a sunburnt tourist than a king of crappie or whatever the fuck you called yourself. And, by the way, this is a steak sandwich."

"Hey, look pal, I live here most of the year and I have been catching fish all over the globe since I was a kid. I just won the damn tournament for mahi about 4 days ago and I am drinking up my winnings." Jeremy proudly raised his glass and took a big gulp, finishing it.

"All in one night?" Miles said with a concerned look on his face.

"No, it will probably take me a week." Jeremy raised his empty glass to the bartender.

Doug was chuckling harder now. Miles motioned for the bartender.

"Ma'am, we need to celebrate our friend's good fortune this week. I would like to buy these boys some shots."

"Fireball MG!" Jeremy was ready for shots and it was right where Miles knew Jeremy would go.

The next hour was mostly Jeremy and Doug swapping fishing stories, most trying to one-up each other. Doug, of course, was talking freshwater mostly while Jeremy talked about fishing the Keys.

"What kind of work do you do Jeremy?" Miles wanted him to reveal his financial status.

"I have the best job in the world MG. I don't have one. I retired about 3 years ago. I am now a professional tournament fisherman."

"You seem kind of young for that." Miles kept after him.

"I left the bullshit behind. I had a job, a wife, a commute to work on the Dan Ryan Expressway. But I was the benefactor of some very good numbers and was able to leave it all behind."

"Stock market?" Miles inquired.

"Better than that," Jeremy answered.

"Inheritance?"

"Better."

"Don't tell me you won the lottery?" Miles sat back trying to seem astonished.

"YES! Twenty-eight million good reasons to tell the world to kiss my ass!" Jeremy slammed his open hand on the bar.

"Gotta piss." Jeremy slid off his barstool and sauntered towards the men's room.

Doug was getting a pretty good load on. Since they walked

into the Ocean View, Doug and Jeremy had done six shots together.

"This guy was hammered when we walked in and he did half a dozen shots with me. This guy is a 'fricken bull." Doug sounded impressed.

"Well, I need you to put the bull down Doug. I want him passed out. Can you finish him off?" Miles was willing to go through with this. Doug still didn't know the scope of things, but he was willing to drink anywhere and anytime. Miles was footing the bill for this party, so he agreed.

"I'm glad this guy started before me."

Jeremy was clearly feeling no pain. He weaved his way back to his barstool and looked at Miles.

"Damn, you look familiar. Where the hell are you from?"

"Up north." Miles needed to be evasive.

"Oh, like the Seminoles. My folks are up north too. They have a place up near Boca Raton."

Miles nodded. Just then, the bartender set two more shots in front of Jeremy and Doug. Jeremy's eyes got wider as he had to decide whether to call it a night or ratchet the evening up a notch.

"Ok, boys. One more for the ditch and I'm gonna head out." Jeremy was willing to call it a night.

"Hey, wait a minute. What are you doing tomorrow?" Miles was doing his best to keep Jeremy with them.

"I dunno. Stuff."

"Why don't you join us? We're going fishing tomorrow and we still wanted to have a little more fun tonight."

"What do you have in mind?" Jeremy needed a good reason to keep this going. He had been at it since before dinner and it was well past sunset now.

"Well, we were just at Mangrove Manny's and there was some nice scenery over there. Doug would like to go back I'm sure."

"Yeah, her tits were kinda small, but I'm willing to overlook that at this point." Doug was fairly wasted and his lazy eye was starting to drift.

"Well shit, boys. If you're gonna be a hero, you might as well be Superman. Who's driving?"

Miles stood up and held up the car keys. "That would be me."

As the three of them cruised back south and west on Highway 1, Miles was laughing to himself. He had forgotten how funny and annoying Jeremy could be. After wondering how this whole debacle started, it was headed in the right direction. Doug and Jeremy were bantering back and forth about fishing. Jeremy had some stories about catching muskies and walleyes in recent years up in Wisconsin with his college buddies.

"I spend a portion of the spring and summer in Chicago. I still have some family there and we catch the end of the Blackhawk's schedule. Sometimes we take a week and fish."

"Hey! You gotta try Ontario man. You wouldn't believe the......"

Wham! Doug's forehead hit the dashboard as Miles slammed on the brakes so Doug would shut up. Doug was drunk enough he nearly let it slip that they were from Canada.

"Yeah! Hey! Wisconsin sounds awesome." Miles glared at Doug. Doug clammed up and rubbed his forehead after he realized what he had said.

"What the fuck, MG? If we wanted Doug to get a concussion, I could drive." Jeremy settled back into the rear seat.

"Sorry. I thought I was going to hit a lizard."

Doug and Jeremy continued to jaw back and forth about hockey teams and fishing during the remainder of the ride back to Manny's. Soon, they pulled into the parking lot. Miles wanted a few drinks here to be the final nail in the coffin for Jeremy. He was close to the edge, but Doug was having a tough time keeping up now. Doug was an experienced drinker with a cast iron liver, but Jeremy brought a whole other level of drunk to the table. Doug and Miles settled in at the bar and Miles stepped to the side and pulled out his phone. He made two quick calls and then joined the boys at the bar where the conversation had turned to women.

"I don't see her." Doug was looking around, disappointed.

"Who." Jeremy asked.

"You know. The blonde with small tits." Doug was getting wrecked.

Jeremy was looking around and spotted three women sitting at a table at the far end of the restaurant area.

"How about them?"

"Too far to walk. I like this barstool. Let's get rolling here." Doug was now solely focused on forgetting the bump on his forehead.

"Paul! Paul my good man. A club soda for my friend here and 2 shots of green tea." Jeremy was getting his second, third, or possibly fourth wind.

It was getting close to 11 p.m. and Miles was watching these two drunkards very closely at this point. Doug was getting just plain sleepy from the day's travel and the amount of drinking he'd done in the last 5 hours. Jeremy was more awake, but making less sense. He was bouncing back and forth on subjects in a manic sort of way.

Jeremy turned to Miles.

"MG! What are we fishing for tomorrow?"

"Oh, we might get into almost anything where we're headed." Miles grinned without showing his teeth.

"Well, where are we headed?" Jeremy raised his hands. He was becoming more animated the more intoxicated he got.

"Up north. I'd hate to ruin the surprise." Miles grinned. Jeremy started laughing.

"I love surprises."

Paul was ready to close by 12:30 a.m. It had been a fairly busy Tuesday, and he was more tired than normal. Three people were left at the bar. Jeremy and two other guys. He decided to make last call. He had wiped down all the tables, cleaned the glasses, and had taken out the trash. Once these guys cleared the place, he could go home. He had given Jeremy a ride back to his place a couple nights before after the tournament, but it didn't look necessary here. He was carousing with two guys he had seen earlier in the evening. Club soda had the keys and appeared sober, so he wasn't too worried about Jeremy. They were laughing and joking as they walked out to the car. As they turned south on Highway 1, Paul wondered where they were headed this late. Jeremy's place was north. He shut off the lights and locked the door. It was time to go home.

"I thought we were fishing up north tomorrow MG. You're headed towards Key West."

Jeremy was speaking very slowly and having a tough time finishing sentences.

"Don't worry. I've got a faster way of heading north. Trust me." Miles was approaching Marathon. He started looking for an all-night convenience store. There was one more thing he needed to get. Miles drove another five minutes before turning left into the parking lot of a Tom Thumb gas station.

"I'll be right back." Miles walked quickly inside. Only a minute later he re-emerged and opened the car door, placing a clear plastic container on Doug's lap in the passenger seat.

"Hold onto this and make sure you don't drop it."

It was a cheap, $5.99 key lime pie. A receipt was taped to the top of the lid.

Another five minutes on the road and they were turning right to the gate of the Marathon air strip. Miles pulled over to building three where he parked the car and found the fully fueled Beechcraft ready to go. He looked over and Doug was having trouble keeping his eyes open.

"C'mon Doug. Let's see if Jeremy wants to join us for fishing."

Jeremy was passed out in the back seat. He nodded off somewhere between Manny's and the stop at Tom Thumb.

"Hey! Jeremy! Dude! Wake up!" Miles shook him by the shoulder. He mumbled the word Fireball and then opened his eyes slightly. He spoke slowly; "Are we home?"

"No, we're headed north to go fishing. You coming with?"

"Well yeah, I guess so. We've been talking about it all goddamn night." Jeremy grabbed Miles by the shirt and pressed his face close. Miles winced at the hot alcoholic breath that slammed into his nose.

"Can we sleep in a little later in the morning before we go out? I've been drinking and I might not be at my best if we go out early." It was a painful sentence to hear through Jeremy's stupor.

Doug and Miles got on each side of Jeremy and had to help stabilize him as he entered the hatch into the airplane. "We're flying? That's AWESOME! I love this trip already!"

Jeremy barely noticed the stairs and stumbled the whole way, eyes barely open. Doug was not in much better shape.

Miles brought an extra seat along to put in the cargo area and he abruptly sat Jeremy into it and buckled him in. He then reclined the seat a bit so Jeremy's head wouldn't fall forward. Miles stood back and admired his project. There sat an incapacitated Jeremy Fine. He was wearing golf shorts, flip flops, and a bright red Hawaiian party shirt. In his pocket was his cell phone and his wallet with $300 in cash with a couple credit cards along with his Florida driver's license. Miles giggled at the sight and turned to walk towards the cockpit where Doug was buckling into the right seat. By the time they taxied to the end of the runway and were cleared for take-off it was almost 2 am. Doug turned with his eyes barely open and said to Miles;

"Why do we have this clown with us?"

"I owe him a ride. I think it's time he collects." Miles grinned as Doug's eyes rolled back in his head and he passed out.

Miles hit the throttles and the engines roared to life. They traveled about two thirds down the runway when Miles pulled back on the yoke and the Beechcraft effortlessly left the ground. Miles took a heading of 335 degrees north and left the lights of Marathon behind him.

CHAPTER SEVEN

In the darkness of the cockpit, Doug's eyes were squinting from the brightness of the instrument panel. His head throbbed as he slowly rose in his seat. He glanced out the window to the right and he could faintly see the light of the coming sunrise.

"How long have we been in the air?" Doug asked while yawning.

"About three hours. We'll be on approach to the cities soon. Check our cargo."

"Cargo?" Doug seemed confused.

Miles motioned with his thumb to the back of the plane where Doug glanced and saw a passed-out Jeremy Fine buckled into a reclined seat with a key lime pie sitting on the floor of the aircraft between his flip-flopped clad feet.

Doug slowly turned around and faced the front of the cockpit as he recalled they had kidnapped the drunk guy from the bar.

"Remind me. Why do we have this guy?"

Miles looked totally serious. "I promised I'd take him fishing up north."

"Not to cause any alarm Miles, but this guy seems like the excitable type. I think he's going to seriously freak out when he wakes up in Ontario during the winter wearing flip flops."

"I wouldn't worry too much about him Doug. I remember him being pretty resilient."

Within an hour, Miles had contact with air traffic control and was given a heading for approach to the runway. His timing was nearly perfect as the Beechcraft mechanics were starting an early morning shift and were expecting Miles for the tests needed to verify the success of the previous days' prop shaft seal replacement. After touching down, Miles and Doug exited the aircraft while Jeremy lay passed out in the seat, still buckled in from Marathon. As the mechanics hooked up a laptop computer to the plane to review the performance data, ground crew members loaded the back of the plane with the supplies and equipment on the manifest for the trip back to Minaki.

"Careful not to wake the guy in the back seat." Miles asked the ground crew as they loaded the plane. "He's had a rough day." The alcohol smell in the plane was pungent and Doug was still technically drunk. Miles had been up for nearly 24 hours straight and needed some strong coffee to finish the last hour of flight back home.

Within 45 minutes, the plane was loaded and sailing down the runway. It was sluggish to lift off with the weight of three grown men plus all the cargo. Miles had just enough fuel to make the trip back home. A very bleary-eyed Doug looked back at Jeremy, still passed out in his seat and now drooling slightly.

"This guy could sleep through an explosion," marveled Doug.

As the northbound Beechcraft continued, the bare ground slowly gave way to snow as they approached the Canadian border. While the cabin was pressurized and heated, you could tell that the outside temperature was dropping.

It was time to descend to the runway at Minaki before long and Miles radioed ahead to have Carl ready with the flatbed truck to unload the plane's cargo and get it distributed to the necessary parties. Doug stretched and yawned hard.

"Man! Some quality sleep is gonna feel good!"

Miles shot him a glare.

"Hey! We're going fishing. Remember!?!"

"What? Oh Christ! We still have to babysit this asshole?"

Doug was perturbed and quite hungover, his head throbbing at this point.

"No, Jesus! Just help me get him into my truck and I'm going to take him out to my ice shack on Pistol Lake."

Doug started to giggle. "On second thought, I think I'll go with you. When this clown comes out of his coma, he's going to shit."

After landing, Carl and his nephew met the plane after it taxied to the heated hangar where Miles' truck awaited. After closing the hangar, Miles and Doug opened the door and stepped out to meet Carl near the back of the plane by the cargo hatch.

"Ok, Carl, you're in charge. Load the truck and get this stuff dropped off." Miles was getting back on the plane with Doug through the hatch.

Carl, confused for a moment grabbed the first few boxes and handed them to his teenage nephew.

"Aren't you going to help?" Carl seemed annoyed and slightly overwhelmed.

"Nope. Doug and I are taking my friend fishing."

Just then, Doug emerged from the hatch of the plane carrying both the legs of a passed out man with shorts and only one flip flop. Miles followed with the rest of millionaire Jeremy Fine carrying him under his arms. They retrieved his wayward footwear and slowly moved down the steps and then crossed the concrete to the open door of Miles' king cab truck and carefully laid Jeremy out on the seat. They closed the door of the truck quietly and smiled as they got in and started the engine. The hangar's door opened and Miles drove out with Doug and the comatose guy in shorts. Carl stood motionless, his mouth open and stunned at what he had just witnessed.

CHAPTER EIGHT

As though something had brushed his head, Jeremy momentarily winced. His eyes were still closed and he felt a familiar dryness in his throat. His lips were parched and the front of his head hurt from pain on the inside, but there was a cool draft on the outside. His ears and feet were freezing. His eyes felt like they were glued shut and filled with sand. He fought to open them while he looked up from a hard wooden bench. There was a window above him, and the sunlight streaming in was bright and blinding. Jeremy rolled onto his back and realized he was covered with a heavy and somewhat musty sleeping bag.

Jeremy felt disoriented and cold. He assumed he was lying on a floor somewhere, but as his eyes adjusted to the light, he glanced around and realized he was in a very small room with plywood walls. There was a variety of hooks and fishing tackle stuck to the walls. The faint smell of propane and fish filled his nose as he rubbed his eyes and tried to get his bearings.

Suddenly, bells started to ring loudly, shattering the silence. Jeremy looked around trying to account for the bells when he realized there was a wheel attached to the wall, spinning wildly. It had fish line on it and the line extended to the floor where there was a small door and a hole filled with murky water.

At that moment, the door swung open wildly and a large man in a heavy jacket filled the doorway. He wore a stocking cap and large bib overalls that were dirty with torn knees. He bellowed loudly, "FISH ON!"

Jeremy swung his legs onto the floor and tried to stand. He was disoriented and still half asleep. He fell backwards into a 5-gallon pail and spilled ice fishing gear onto the floor of the shack. The large man grabbed him by the shirt and got Jeremy to his feet.

"C'mon Jeremy!" he screeched. "This is a big one! Grab the line!"

A confused and bewildered Jeremy, tried to grab the line that was rapidly peeling out of the spool. Instinct kicked in and Jeremy grabbed the line while the man stood over him with a large steel gaff hook. Jeremy began pulling the line and could feel the strong fight of a large fish on the other end.

"Tire him out! Give him line if he wants it!" The large man bellowed to a very shaky and unsteady Jeremy Fine. As the cold filtered in the partially open door, Jeremy glanced out and saw snow and a truck parked outside the door. What kind of frozen hell had he woken up to? He was wearing shorts and flip flops in a climate that required so much more.

"FOCUS! DAMMIT!" The large man yelled as Jeremy turned his head back towards the hole. The two men caught a glance of the tail of a large fish below the hole fighting for its life.

"SHIT! THAT'S A NICE ONE!" The imposing figure bellowed.

The man in the overalls was now moving his hands closer to the hole with the hook in his hand. Just then, the fish went directly under the hole and shook its head in a last ditch effort to escape. The man with the hook then plunged it into the hole almost getting his wrist to the waterline. He then quickly jerked upward as a huge splash hit both men's faces. As the man lifted higher, a large northern pike emerged from the hole, twisting and shaking. Jeremy fell backwards again onto the floor as the large man laughed wildly and held this nearly 20-pound northern pike over his head, slime dripping onto captive's shivering legs.

"Jesus Christ!" Jeremy yelled at the man. "Is that a pike?"

"You bet it is, Jeremy! And she's a beaut!"

"How the hell do you know my name? Where the hell are we, and who the hell are you?"

"We're in Ontario, Jeremy. You finally took me up on my offer to take you fishing. I'm glad you did. Look at this thing!" The large man held the fish up admiring it.

Jeremy, with his eyes wide and mouth falling open, tilted his head and weakly spoke.

"Miles?"

"You bet buddy! Glad to have ya up here!" Miles smiled with a huge grin.

Jeremy crawled to the door of the ice shack on his hands and knees, again losing a flip flop, and promptly threw up.

"Ah, shit." Miles released the northern back into the hole. He then put the gaff hook down and helped Jeremy to his feet. "You city boys always had trouble holding your liquor. Let's get you warmed up."

Miles got Jeremy into the warm truck and loaded up the fishing gear. It helped that Miles brought a thermos of hot coffee so his hungover Floridian guest could get his core temperature up. On the way back to town, Miles explained how he saw the video clip from the tournament and decided to visit Jeremy and pay him back for the prank that Jeremy had played on him so many years ago.

"What prank are you talking about?" Jeremy was confused.

"You mean to tell me you don't remember filling my truck with snow back in Madison when we were in college?"

"Oh SHIT!" Jeremy suddenly remembered. "I forgot all about that. But Jesus! Thirty years nothing and then you kidnap me? What the fuck is wrong with you?"

The two men laughed as Jeremy started to get his bearings. He had been passed out for over 12 hours and was acclimating to a completely different climate while being extremely hungover. Miles pulled into the driveway of his modest home on the bank of the Winnipeg River. Jeremy and Miles entered the house and Miles told him to grab a towel and get a nice hot shower. Miles dug out some clothes for Jeremy and put them on the bed in the second bedroom.

Jeremy asked for a charging cord for his phone as his battery was dead. Miles put the phone on the charger then called up his daughter and caught up with her. She had gotten the supplies from the hangar and Carl got her up to speed on her dad's fishing outing with the stranger from Florida. Milles wrapped up the conversation quickly and yelled up to Jeremy that they should get something to eat.

Jeremy yelled down that he was getting dressed and sat on the bed to collect himself for a minute. The shower cleared his head a bit and he took inventory. He was thousands of miles from home in a foreign country, nobody back home knew where he was, and it was likely that nobody would miss him for several days. There was enough power in his phone to check messages. There were no texts or voicemails. It spooked him a bit at first as he was in essence, kidnapped. But, he was with a friend that he had long lost contact with and it felt good to see him. The last time they were together they were 20-year-old college students with no bigger problems in the world than final exams and research papers. But that was over 30 years ago. Jeremy was curious. What led Miles to bring him here?

Miles and Jeremy got into the truck and headed towards town. They were going to stop at the Cider Barn to get some food and make a couple introductions. Gabriele met the boys at the door and gave Miles a hug.

"Hi Dad. Is this your fishing partner?"

"Dad?" A confused Jeremy looked at both of them.

"Jeremy, this is my daughter Gabriele," introduced Miles, the proud father.

She extended her hand to Jeremy. "Call me Gabby."

"That's Doctor Gabby." Miles corrected her.

"Wow! Your daughter is a doctor. I hope you're a psychiatrist. Your dad got a little crazy on me."

"Yeah. So I heard" Gabrielle looked at her dad with mild disapproval.

"Let's get a table." Miles held the door for them.

After getting settled and ordering some coffee, Miles asked Gabriele how Robby was doing and when his next hockey practice was.

"Who's Robby?" Jeremy inquired.

"Robby is my grandson." Miles grinned proudly.

"Holy shit! You're a dad and a granddad?"

Miles looked at Jeremy and said; "Best two jobs in the world, my friend." Miles got up from the table and excused himself.

"Gotta get these hands clean."

It was now Gabby and Jeremy at the table alone. She wanted to know what had caused her dad to go so far off the rails and see his friend.

"How long have you been friends with my dad?"

"We knew each other for about a year and a half at college. Right before Christmas around finals week sophomore year, he just plain disappeared. He left one night without saying goodbye and nobody saw him on campus again. We had a snowball fight outside my frat house the night before he left and I haven't seen him since. That was over 30 years ago. I think he missed all his finals too."

Gabrielle sat back in her chair a bit and smiled. "Yeah, I knew he left college to come back home."

Gabby sat up in her chair a bit and redirected the conversation.

"What is life like for you?" Gabby inquired.

Jeremy let out a sigh. "I'm retired. I'm divorced. I'm stuck in a different country surrounded by snow. I'm cold." He laughed and Gabby broke out in a smile. Just then, Miles got back.

"Hey! There's the big kidnapper now." Jeremy glanced up as Miles sat down. "What possessed you to come to the Florida Keys?"

"Well, I saw your ugly mug on tv when you won that fishing tournament. I hadn't thought about you or college or anything like that for a long time. I had a half-assed excuse to fly down there, so I guess I just wanted to feel like……."

"Like what Dad?" Gabby asked.

Miles paused a moment before he answered. "Like it wasn't winter anymore."

Gabby smiled but Jeremy looked at Miles with a look of understanding. And then, Jeremy realized what he was looking at when he saw Miles' face. It was a look of emptiness and regret. It was a look that he recognized from his own mirror.

Gabby lost her smile and realized that there was something that was bothering her dad. She knew this wasn't the time or place to talk so she quickly switched the gears of the conversation.

"I'm hungry. Let's get some menus."

After lunch, Miles kissed Gabby on the cheek as they left the Cider Barn. "I'll try to come by hockey practice tonight, but I'm really beat. I have to get some sleep."

"Ok Dad. Get some rest."

"Hey! When is practice? I'd love to see your kid on skates." Jeremy jumped in the conversation.

"Right after school, at 4:00. At the dome. I'll pick you up from Dad's house."

Jeremy and Miles made a stop at the town office to drop off some paperwork for the recent trip to have the plane repaired. Carl was still working around the shop area and was wrapping up some projects for the day.

"Everybody came and got their stuff." Carl reported. Miles locked the office up and headed towards the door.

"Hey! Miles! Looks like your friend is doing better." Carl cracked a smile.

Jeremy looked back at Carl with a slight sneer. "Smartass," Jeremy mumbled quietly.

"Oh! Miles! I put fuel stabilizer in your snow machine too. Its outside behind the shop so you can run the engine a bit."

"Thanks, Carl. Have a good night." Miles and Jeremy walked outside the back door of the shop. They passed by an old Yamaha SRX. It was in mint condition despite the fact it was nearly 40 years old.

"That's your snowmobile?" Jeremy asked. "Looks kind of small for a big guy like you."

"My dad left it to me. And, that small sled is faster than most cars. Don't be fooled by appearances."

Jeremy and Miles got in the truck and started heading back to the house on the river. "I suppose we should figure on getting you back home." Miles was feeling quite tired, but he realized that he had an obligation to his friend.

"I can stay a couple days. I'm in no rush. Besides, how am I getting back?" Jeremy wondered.

"I'll get you to either Winnipeg or Minneapolis and pay for your ticket from there." Miles was hoping he'd be in no hurry.

"Shit Miles. You picked me up, but can't drop me off? You could use some time in the Keys. I know you're an Indian by blood, but even you look like you've been up here drinking bleach all winter. Get some sun."

"I've got too many responsibilities here. I can't be gone for more than a couple days."

Jeremy got a little more serious; "What about it not being winter anymore?"

"Look, I'm going to hit the rack. I've been up for almost 30 hours straight. Gabby is going to be by in a little while if you want to go to Robby's hockey practice." Miles was showing his irritability a bit.

"Ok, ok..." Jeremy needed to make a few phone calls anyway.

CHAPTER NINE

It was getting late in the afternoon and Miles decided to take a shower and go to bed. Jeremy went into the guest room and decided to call up John Price and let him know he was not going to be around for a few days.

"You're WHERE?" John was pretty excited over the phone.

"Yeah! Guess what? I wasn't in Ontario more than a couple hours and I got a trophy northern!" Jeremy was relaying the bits and pieces of the previous evening and left John dumbfounded at his situation.

"That is some pretty serious payback for a prank. This is one guy who definitely waited for you to let your guard down."

"I'll most likely be back in a couple days. I'm going to hang out with Miles and see what town is like. Its still winter here yet, but this seems to be a pretty cool place. I'll call you in a couple days."

"Alright Jeremy. I'll talk to ya later."

After Jeremy ended the call, he wandered out into the living room to see if Miles was there. Jeremy could hear snoring coming from down the hallway as Miles was already in bed. He went into the kitchen to get some water and paused when walking past a wall of pictures. There were photos of Gabby and a small boy. There were also pictures of Gabby and a very tall man in uniform and a beret. Gabby looked quite pregnant in that picture. There was another picture of that man alone in a boat, handsome, smiling, and was holding a fish pole. On his left hand was a wedding band. Along the wall were pictures of a young Miles and an older couple, who he guessed were his parents. There was a picture of a young Miles and a pretty girl and there was also a picture of that same girl alone swinging on a rope over the water in a swim suit. It was an old picture. As Jeremy looked around the house, it seemed like a very empty and lonely place.

Jeremy tried to imagine Miles' situation. He saw the way he interacted with everyone. He remembered what Miles was like back in school. A little quiet, funny, but always playing the role of the responsible one or the older brother. He rarely cut loose and based on what he saw from around town, he had changed very little. That's what made the trip to Florida so shocking to everyone, including Jeremy. It was out of character and seemed like something a foolish man would do and Miles was anything but foolish. At this point, Jeremy was glad it happened.

Just then, he heard Gabby's Jeep pull into the driveway. It was time to go to hockey practice.

Jeremy got into the passenger side of the Jeep and told Gabby that her dad was wiped out and wouldn't be joining them.

"Gabby, I really didn't get much of a chance to catch up with your dad. Is there other family? Is he married?"

"No, he wasn't married. Not even to my mom. There's just me and Robby."

"How about you? Are you married?" Jeremy was trying to understand the pictures he saw on the wall.

"No. I'm a widow." Gabby looked towards Jeremy and weakly smiled. "Robby's dad died in the line of duty in Afghanistan."

"I'm sorry, Gabby." Jeremy felt uncomfortable and stupid for opening this can of worms with a stranger. After an awkward silence, he tried to change the subject and asked how long Miles had lived in Minaki.

"It's ok, Jeremy. You don't have to feel uncomfortable. The thing you have to understand about my dad is that he loved the year and a half he was at Madison. I've heard all kinds of stories about classes, the city, and all about the hockey and football teams. He loved the time there. He also talked about the dorm and going to parties. He talked about his friends, including you. I think it was the best time of his life."

"So why did he leave Madison so abruptly?" Jeremy couldn't make sense of it.

"Because of me."

Jeremy seemed more bewildered.

"I showed up. My mom and dad dated over the summer before his sophomore year and she got pregnant."

Jeremy sat back in his seat in disbelief. "He never said a thing about this back at school. I think he mentioned a girl, but nothing like this."

"That's because she didn't tell him. She was six weeks along and not showing when he left for school. My grandparents told me all about it."

Jeremy was in disbelief. "Why didn't she say anything?"

"She wanted him to return to school and finish his degree. She didn't want to be the reason that he had to quit school." Gabby told the story with surprising matter-of-factness.

"So what happened? Why did he leave so quickly?"

"My mom went into labor prematurely. There were complications and the hospital was too far away. I was born at my grandparents' house. My mom lost a lot of blood and I barely made it." We were taken to Kenora by ambulance that night, and she survived for a couple days, but she died."

There was a stone silence in the Jeep as it turned into the parking lot where hockey practice was well underway.

Gabby parked the Jeep and sat quietly staring ahead. "I haven't told that story to anybody in a really long time. I forget how much it takes out of me emotionally." A single tear rolled down her right cheek.

"My grandparents called my dad at school when the ambulance left for Kenora. They told him about everything over the phone and he jumped on the first available plane and flew home."

"No wonder he left so fast. Nobody knew anything. He even left his truck at school. Just abandoned it."

Jeremy stared straight ahead shaking his head in wonder trying to process the whole thing.

"So, he went from being a college student without a care in the world to being a single father inside of about three days," marveled Jeremy.

"Yeah.... I guess that's what happened. He took care of me, started working for the town and did any job he could while my grandparents looked after me."

"And he raised you to become a doctor?" Jeremy asked.

"No. He raised me to be a Wisconsin Badger. I graduated from med school at UW - Madison. The physician part was my idea. He wanted me to go to Madison in the worst way."

Jeremy sat back in the passenger seat and sighed. "Holy shit."

Gabby looked at him with a tear on her cheek and smiled. "Go Bucky."

CHAPTER TEN

Gabby and Jeremy walked into the arena together. Right away, Jeremy realized he was somewhere unique. The rink was enclosed within a wooden dome that was built back in the 1930's. It was constructed of an intricate pattern of interlocking boards that made a waffle pattern all throughout the structure. It was clearly an early day engineering marvel and the locals did their best to maintain its historical integrity while serving both the hockey and figure skating programs in Minaki.

"This is the coolest hockey rink I've ever seen! Look at this place."

Gabby was in a better frame of mind once she saw her son Robby on the ice. The team was still doing warm-up drills. Jeremy and Gabby both grabbed a hot chocolate and found a spot in the bleachers under a heater.

"I played hockey as a kid growing up in Illinois, but we never had an amazing place like this to skate." Jeremy glanced up at the ceiling high above the lights and saw rows of championship banners for the youth programs all the way up to the high school team. Some of the banners went back as far as the 1970's.

Gabby pointed up at the red and blue banners. "See the two red ones over there from 1980 and 81? Those were my dad's bantam teams, and the 1985 one is from his high school team. He was a heck of a skater."

"Well, he's a big dude. I can tell you nobody ever gave him any crap at Madison. He hit me with a snowball once and I had a welt on my shoulder for a week." Jeremy blushed a bit.

"How about you?" Gabrielle asked. "Any kids?"

"One ex-wife and no kids. Thank God. I'm sure I would have screwed them up."

"So, you're retired, but how did you do that?"

"I was a working stiff in Chicago after college. I did regional sales for a pharmaceutical company and just hated it. I partied from Wednesday night on with college buddies, guys from work, and then acquaintances in cities that I traveled to for work. Little by little, my friends all got married and started having kids. I figured I better do the same. I met this gorgeous woman that worked for Northwestern Hospital and she liked the party lifestyle until the engagement ring."

"She tried to fix you?" Gabrielle inquired.

"Excellent guess! I was going to be her pet project. And, it might have worked if I hadn't stopped at a convenience store one night on the way home from work."

"What happened?"

"I bought a lottery ticket."

"You didn't!" Gabby put her hands over her mouth.

"I did! I sure did."

Gabby turned towards him. "How much did you win?"

"Twenty-eight million dollars." Jeremy said it with a hushed tone as he was sometimes embarrassed when telling the story.

"Oh my God! That's huge. But wait, you said that your wife was trying to fix you and it didn't work? Don't tell me you dumped her after winning that money?"

Jeremy smiled. "No. It's much worse. She dumped me."

"How does that happen?" Gabby asked.

"Well, after quitting my job and encouraging her to do the same, all I wanted to do was party, hang out with rock stars, golf, and sleep during the day. She wanted to continue working, build a home, start a family, and have a husband around all the time. My behavior drove her nuts."

"You couldn't see yourself doing that? The home, the family..." Gabby's voice trailed off.

"No. I couldn't. In my estimation, it was a trap that forced you to grow up, get fat, then old, and eventually die. That's all I saw in front of me."

"That's a shitty attitude." Gabrielle wrinkled her forehead.

"Yeah, that's what she told me. She explained she didn't want to be married to an alcoholic child and that I should take my money and clean myself up. She never wanted a single cent of my winnings." Jeremy looked at the ground and let out a half-hearted laugh. "Truth is, she was a nice girl and she deserved better. I think I just wasted her time."

"Are you an alcoholic?" Gabby seemed serious.

"Hmmmm. That's interesting. Let me see……..Uh, yes. Yes, I am an alcoholic."

"Why? What makes you think that?"

"Easy. Because one drink is too many and 50 drinks isn't enough. I've been arrested, in car accidents, beaten up, lost friends, ruined a marriage, and barely talk to my parents all because of drinking." Jeremy seemed very matter of fact.

Gabby looked onto the ice and watched as Robby and his teammates went through drills.

"So, you played hockey too?"

"Yeah. All through youth leagues and high school. I wasn't very good, but our teams were decent. I'm just a fan now. I see the Blackhawks play whenever I can, but I'm in Florida during most of the hockey season."

Just then, a yell came from the ice as one of the youth skaters went down and grabbed his arm. A puck hit the boy missing the padding. The kid was in obvious pain.

"Excuse me a minute." Gabby got up from the bleachers and headed towards the ice. Jeremy got up with her and followed Gabby to the boards where he stopped.

"I'm also the team doctor." She effortlessly climbed over the bench and shuffled her feet onto the ice kneeling down next to the boy to examine his arm. Jeremy was amazed at her ability to calm the boy down and eventually get him to his feet and back to the bench for a closer look. The boys continued practice as Gabby got an ice pack for the young boy and called his parents.

As practice continued, Jeremy looked around this simple, yet amazing little rink and tried to imagine playing here as a kid. As it got closer to six o'clock, the boys wrapped up practice and left the ice. As Jeremy and Gabby were leaving the bleachers, an ancient Zamboni machine came out to resurface the ice at the end of practice. Jeremy recognized the driver as Doug, the co-pilot from their trip. He hadn't been ice fishing with Miles, but remembered drinking with him at the O.V. back in the Keys, although the memory was somewhat hazy.

Gabby checked her phone after tending to the young hockey player and got Jeremy's attention.

"Hey! I just got a text from my dad. He wants to meet us for dinner after practice." Jeremy was feeling much better and some food sounded like a good plan. Gabby and Jeremy got into the Jeep and headed into town. They pulled into the parking lot of the Cider Barn. The snowbanks were pushed so high that it was hard to see the building in a couple of places. The snow piles that began in early December had a long way to go before melting.

Jeremy and Gabby walked in together and about 10 seconds behind them was Miles.

"Hey you two!" Miles quickened his pace to enter the door at the same time.

"Did you get a nap, Dad?" Gabby knew how long he'd been awake.

"Yeah, I actually feel pretty good."

Jeremy smiled. "Kidnapping can take a lot out of a guy. You need your rest."

Miles brushed off the comment.

"I hope you're hungry." Miles led the way to a corner table where Jeremy and Gabby joined him and shook off their coats.

The mood in the place was light with some old Aerosmith songs playing in the background. After getting waters and ordering dinner from the bar's owner, the three sat and chatted.

Gabby spoke up facing her dad. "Now how exactly did the two of you get to know each other?"

Before Miles could respond, Jeremy's hand shot up, "I can answer that!"

"It was a Tuesday afternoon in November of freshman year. It had snowed about six inches of heavy wet stuff. You know, the kind of snow that makes a really good snowman, the wet packable stuff. We were on Langdon Street not far from our house and noticed there was a snowball fight going on. It was about six or seven guys to begin with, but it escalated quickly. It started moving towards the union and the bottom of Bascom Hill. By the time we were at Bascom, there were over 300 people involved. People started spilling out of the science building, the law building, and the union itself. Some went to the food center and got trays to use as shields and I even saw a couple people wearing hockey helmets. It was off the charts. The close combat saw some people getting facewashes and everything.

At one point, I was at the back of the crowd taking a break. I was standing next to Chad Crosby who got drilled in the shoulder. Nobody knew who threw it. I looked and saw another snowball coming in like a laser. It hit the light pole just above our heads and splattered, shooting snow down our necks and into our collars. I looked and about 100 feet away was this big Indian dude laughing his ass off. Chad saw him too and Chad decided to challenge him."

Miles was laughing hard now as Gabby intently listened to Jeremy's story.

"So, Chad starts to unbuckle his belt and I'm looking at him wondering what the hell he's about to do when he drops his pants and moons your dad here and screams at him to try to hit him. He's yelling, "Come on! Bring it!" I was looking around and everybody sort of stopped to watch what was happening. So, here's like a couple hundred people watching Chad bent over, sticking his ass out and your dad calmly reached down, scooped up a bunch of snow, packed it tightly, and paused like he was on a pitching mound. This whole time Chad is like "Here we go big fella! Try to hit me!" I stood back a little, but I was right close to him like 10 feet away. Anyway, your dad puts his arm back and throws this fastball at us. It was a normal sized snowball, but he threw it so hard and fast it looked like an aspirin tablet. It actually made a hissing sound when it came in. All of a sudden, THWACK! The snowball hits Chad on his right ass cheek. Oh my god! It was horrible and astonishing."

Jeremy continued, "The crowd gasped and Chad let out a

shriek like an old woman before he fell face first into the snow with his pants down. It was surreal because everybody just stopped. They couldn't believe it. Nobody really laughed because it happened so fast and Chad let out this painful cry. I helped Chad stand up and pull his pants. He had tears running down his face. I walked slowly back to the frat house with him as he limped along. Once we made it back, Chad had to lay face down on the couch. He couldn't sit on his ass because it hurt so bad. A day later Chad showed us this huge purple mark. Incredible."

Gabby looked over at her dad who had tears streaming down his face, laughing so hard there was no sound. Gabby put her hand over her mouth. "Oh my god. That poor guy."

Jeremy resumed his story. "Ah, don't worry about him. He was always kind of a jerk. Anyway, about 20 minutes later, we're getting our plans together for that night when there's a knock on our door. I answer it, and your dad is standing there, filling up our doorway. I was completely stunned. I asked him what he wanted and he said he felt bad and wanted to know how my friend was doing. I invited him in, he went over to Chad and saw him lying face down on the couch and asked how he was and Chad went off on him like, "Are you crazy!?!" Well, your dad apologized to him and asked if he could help. Chad was caught totally off guard by this and said I'm going to need to pay you back for this you know, kind of joking. Well, your Dad laughed and we all had a beer. But it was a couple days before Chad could sit at a desk decently in class. Let me tell you. Nobody ever threw a snowball at Miles after that day."

"Dad! I can't believe you hurt a guy like that!" Gabby seemingly reprimanded her father.

"I guess you had to be there." Miles grinned, wiping his tears and gathered his composure.

Once dinner was served, they chatted about Jeremy's house in Florida and fishing. Gabby talked about Robby and how school and hockey were going. Miles sat quietly mostly smiling and enjoying the company for the evening.

"How soon before you need to head back Jeremy?" Miles was ready to move his schedule around to help his friend back to the Keys.

"Not Sure. I called my buddy John in Florida to let him know I wouldn't be fishing with him this week. I don't really know, a few days if you can put up with me." Jeremy chuckled at the thought of being brought up north to Canada at winter's end when he would normally be worried about sunburns and heatstroke.

As the three sat at dinner and talked, Jeremy started to feel uneasy and the noises in the restaurant started to distract him from the conversation. He became shaky and found it increasingly more difficult to concentrate. There was this static inside his head. It had been a while since his hangover abated and alcohol was leaving his system. His jittery mind was now craving alcohol and his body was showing signs of withdrawal. Jeremy excused himself from the table and headed towards the men's room. Instead, he ducked around the end of the bar and ordered a couple of shots of whiskey to settle himself down.

He quickly downed the shots and paid for them without Gabby or Miles noticing. The warmth of the liquid going down comforted him and he immediately felt more at ease. Within a minute the buzzing in his head was gone and he was able to concentrate. As Jeremy sat down, Miles looked ahead and said, "Uh oh."

"What is it Dad?" Gabby inquired.

Miles reached in his pocket and pulled out his cell phone. "This is Miles...... Uh huh......Yeah........Oh man........Where about?.................Ok............. Ok..........Give me about 90 minutes and I will call you for location. Get your gear for a wilderness transport. Ok. I'll call you back."

Jeremy and Gabby could see that dinner was over. Miles had a look of concern and was hurriedly getting his jacket on.

"The medivac chopper from Kenora went down in some bad weather just west of us with a patient on board heading to

Winnipeg. Kenora's OPP office thinks they know the location of the chopper and its radio is still operational. We've got to get the patient along with two crew members out of there by snow machine most likely."

"Should I go with you, Dad?" Gabby was hurriedly getting her coat on too.

"No, there's a medical team coming up from Kenora by truck and I'm meeting them along with all their gear. They have all the people we need. Stay here and hold down the fort."

"Jeremy, can you handle getting back to my place? I have to pick up some clothes at the shop and hit the road right away."

"Yeah, sure. I'll probably head back soon."

"I can give him a lift," volunteered Gabby.

"Ok, Gabby." Miles was almost out the door as their conversation ended.

"Things can go wrong in a hurry, I guess." Jeremy was surprised at the speed in which the evening changed direction.

"Yeah, my dad has been a first responder for most of his life and I've been doing it since I moved back up here with Robby."

"That's gotta be cool when you can make a difference when somebody needs you the most."

"Actually, both the people in need and the first responders wish they were never in the situation in the first place. It can be the worst days for both people."

"I know what you mean. I've had a few scrapes over the years and I was fortunate to have help come." Jeremy was starting to feel more like himself now. The whiskey made him feel normal.

After Jeremy and Gabby talked for another 10 minutes, Gabby was ready to drop off Jeremy and head home and to see Robby.

"Are you ready?" Gabby was putting on her coat.

"Actually, I was wondering if you'd mind leaving me here. I can walk back to Miles' place. The hockey game is on and I was hoping to just hang out and watch for a while." Jeremy claimed.

"I guess so, I mean the house is just a five minute walk down the road. You sure it's ok?" Gabby was a little reluctant, but she was exhausted and ready to call it a day.

"I'll be fine. I'll probably have some dessert and watch the game at the bar." Jeremy was doing his best to put Gabby at ease. Jeremy didn't really care about having dessert or watching hockey. He was actually craving more alcohol.

"Ok. I'll see you tomorrow. Have a good night."

"Thanks, Gabby." Jeremy could now drop the charade and continue the momentum that the first two shots started.

CHAPTER ELEVEN

When Gabby left Jeremy went over to the bar to glance at the hockey game. It was the Canadiens against the Islanders, but it was better than nothing. The Blackhawks were off tonight. Jeremy got in with the bartender and before long two guys in stocking caps came over and sat near him.

"Hey! Are you the Florida guy?" The tall one with a scruffy beard asked. There was a shorter one who was more inebriated blinking slowly while trying to watch the game. He never looked at Jeremy but joined the conversation.

"I heard you were passed out in Miles' ice shack." The short guy gazed at the tv.

"Yes. I was going about my business, drinking at a bar back home and then woke up here." Jeremy's explanation was matter-of-fact and lacking much detail.

The short one finally turned to him, "I'll bet you shit yourself when you saw where you were."

Jeremy looked right at him. "Well, my friend, if you must know I'm shitting myself right this second." Jeremy cracked a devilish and drunken smile.

The three laughed out loud and they finally introduced themselves. Jeremy had stumbled into Billy and Dean Horschel, cousins who worked odd jobs around Minaki and were employed by local resorts during the tourist season. They worked only about five months out of the year, but lived together in a small house near the town shop area. Both cousins were in their mid-20's and had only been out of the area when they played junior hockey years ago.

The three started to drink more and Jeremy was rolling into a good bender while sitting at the Cider Barn watching hockey on the bar's underwhelmingly small albeit flat screen tv. As the cocktails flowed and it approached 11 p.m. the game ended while the bartenders and waitresses were cleaning things up, eager to close the place.

"Looks like we gotta get outa here." Billy slurred and took his grease-stained jacket off the back of his barstool. He stumbled slightly. Dean upended his glass and finished his drink while Jeremy left his glass with a couple sips.

"We did pretty good closing this place." Jeremy walked out to the door and then remembered he had no ride back to Miles' house. Just as Billy and Dean were getting into their rusty dodge truck, Jeremy asked if he could hitch a lift.

"Would you guys mind dropping me off at Miles' house?"

Billy laughed at Jeremy and bellowed "Get your ass in the truck there Florida! Two days in the north and you're still a pussy!"

"Thanks asshole…" Jeremy tumbled into the crowded cab.

Billy drove down the short road past the Cider Barn and the hardware store where Miles' house stood, still dark with no lights on. Miles was still out on the helicopter crash call that came in several hours before.

"Looks like he's not home." Dean was looking through squinted and bloodshot drunken eyes. "You should come back to our place and watch another game. I think the Calgary game is still in the first period."

"Hell, why not?" Afterall, Jeremy was just going to be stuck at the house by himself and Miles could be gone all night. Besides, the wind had increased slightly and snow had begun to fall. He should probably stay up a while and hang out with the Horschel boys until Miles got home. Billy turned the truck around and headed to their house about half a mile past the Cider Barn and right next to the town shop. The party would continue and it was now only Billy, Dean, and Jeremy at the Horshel residence. This meant the music could be loud, and they could even call some of the other seasonally employed locals that had nothing better to do on a weeknight and invite them to join the three new friends in their drunken festivities.

By midnight, several others came to the cousins' residence.

The music was blaring loudly and there were about seven guys sitting around the living room watching the replay of the Calgary Flames' game on tv. Beer cans were thrown at the tv when something unfortunate happened and beer sprayed in the air when something called for celebration. It became more and more chaotic and the level of intoxication was growing more intense.

As the chaos of the night escalated at the Herschel house, Jeremy was losing control of his emotions. The buzzing in his head at dinner had been washed away by several hours of binge drinking and on top of being intoxicated, he now was in an almost manic state. One moment he would be singing along with a song blaring out of the old Jensen speakers, and the next minute he would experience anger at being hauled up to this northern deep freeze. Yelling at no one in particular, Jeremy was acting like a petulant child to nearly every person in the house. These people, strangers to Jeremy, watched him with curiosity, laughing at him one moment and provoking him the next.

Billy, now even more intoxicated, walked outside the house to urinate as the bathroom was occupied. A stiff wind had come up from the southeast and a wet, heavy snow was coming down faster than before. Since leaving the Cider Barn a few hours earlier, over three inches of snow had fallen and it seemed like much more was to come. As Billy continued to relieve himself outside near the back porch, Jeremy stumbled outside and saw Billy. "Hey! What the hell are you doing'?"

"Time to drain the main vein." Billy concentrated on his business, trying not to lose his balance on the icy walkway and fall in his own piss.

Jeremy carried an empty vodka bottle in his hand and started yelling at Billy for some more.

"Hey man, we're out. You drank it all. You should buy me some with all your lottery winnings."

Jeremy, indignant that he was called out for his gluttony, was angry and got in Billy's face.

"Ok, ok, I'll go get some more vodka asshole. Just tell me where."

Billy, annoyed, was thinking it was time to call it a night. "There's an all night grocery store in Red Lake. Why don't you go give that a shot?"

Billy stumbled up the stairs into the house. After banging his shoulder off the edge of two doorways and stumbling past several houseguests, he fell into his dingy room and onto his unmade bed.

Jeremy followed him into the house and started going from person to person asking if they wanted to make a run to Red Lake for more liquor. Everyone looked at him like he was nuts and it became clear that nobody was sober enough to drive anywhere by this late hour. Jeremy grew more frustrated and went outside again where Dean joined him. Dean was clearly drunk, but seemed to be in a bit more control of his faculties than the others at this point.

"Hey Jeremy, let's call it a night. I can run you back to Miles' place. It's late man."

With an astonished look, Jeremy turned to Dean and raised his voice, almost yelling. "What the hell is the matter with you people?!? We just get into a good party and you guys are suddenly limp dicking this. What the fuck? I thought you wanted to party?!? First, I get hauled up to this goddamn deep freeze and then there's no vodka? Now where the hell is Red Lake?"

Dean was getting annoyed at Jeremy's drunken antics and had enough to drink long before. "Well, if you must know, it's about ninety miles straight that way."

Dean extended his arm and pointed directly into a building wind while snow hit him in the face. This was now a Canadian snow storm. It was in tandem with the chaos and violence that was building within Jeremy and it was coming to a head.

"That's fucking great!" Jeremy screamed. His manic state fueled by alcohol was at a boiling point. Jeremy glanced over Dean's shoulder and spotted the town shop just a couple hundred feet away. Jeremy started running towards the building. Dean Horschel watched in disbelief as Jeremy ran through the snow in his borrowed shoes, borrowed jeans, and hooded sweatshirt. Dean shook his head and yelled to Jeremy;

"Where do you think you're going!?!?"

"I'm headed to Red Lake dammit!" Jeremy screamed. "And when I get back, I'm going to show you Canadians how to really fuckin' party!"

Dean started to walk back towards the house, tired of Jeremy's irate tantrum. He figured that Jeremy would eventually calm down and come back inside.

As Jeremy stumbled up to the large metal building, he walked into an overhanging entryway that ran parallel to the long axis of the town shop. Jeremy was looking up and down the long wall when his eyes landed on something that piqued his interest about 40 feet away. He smiled as he stumbled up to Miles' snow machine. It was the 1978 Yamaha SRX that he had seen earlier when he left the shop with Miles.

"Now I can take care of this." Jeremy muttered to himself. He stumbled over to the machine, sat on the seat and saw that the key was in the ignition. He turned the key and nothing happened. Jeremy felt another wave of frustration and anger building within his head. He started to mumble obscenities when he realized that there was a pull start handle on the right side of the machine. He grabbed the handle and gave it a pull, losing his balance, and falling against the side wall of the building. Now even more enraged, Jeremy furiously got to his feet, staggered back over to the sleek Yamaha and grabbed the handle again. This time he firmly planted his feet and maintained his balance. He pulled the starter rope and the engine sputtered and coughed. Calmly, he grabbed the rope again and this time he took a deep breath. He gave the handle a pull and suddenly the engine roared to life. The headlight glowed brightly down the length of the building and Jeremy let out a triumphant drunken howl.

Just then some partygoers were calling it a night walking

down the stairs and exiting Billy and Dean's house. Out of nowhere the sleek old snow machine came flying out of the building's opening and began careening towards the bottoms of the stairs. Jeremy was able to take his thumb off the throttle, squeeze the brake with his left hand and turn slightly to avoid slamming into guests on the stairs.

"Holy shit! Jeremy! You could have killed us! Where are you going on Miles' snow machine!?!" One of the departing guests shouted over the loud engine.

"Making a run to Red Lake for more vodka!" Jeremy bellowed, his hooded sweatshirt now gathering snow as he faced towards the East.

Dean Horschel came out of the house yelling over the engine at Jeremy. "You can't do that! That's Miles' sled and you don't know where you're going! Get off that thing and come inside! You'll freeze to death!"

A girl came down the stairs out of the house with a surprised look on her face. She joined the other departing people at the base of the stairs.

"Where the hell is that drunk guy going?"

"He says he's headed to Red Lake for more vodka!"

Jeremy smiled at the group and yelled loudly, "I'll be back in a while! Don't leave yet! The party is just getting started!"

Dean started to run towards Jeremy so he could pull the key out of the ignition and stop Jeremy before taking off.

With that, Jeremy squeezed the throttle harder, the snow machine kicked up a huge rooster tail of fresh snow, and shot off down the road into a now growing blizzard. The wind had picked up and the snow was falling at a rate of one inch every half hour. It wasn't long before the people gathered outside the party saw the glow from the red tail light disappear and the sound of the powerful engine fade into the darkness. The three departing party goers all shook their heads in disbelief when the girl quietly said;

"That idiot is going to kill himself."

CHAPTER TWELVE

As Jeremy kept the speed of the Yamaha at a furious pace, it was getting harder and harder to see. The snow was hitting him in the face as he sat high on the machine's seat. Getting out into the cold made him feel more sober, but in truth he was starting to suffer the early stages of hypothermia. He didn't have good cold weather clothes, and he was soaking wet from the snow. The heat was escaping faster than his body could produce it. On top of that was his intense level of intoxication. He had no sense of direction and was now out in the open forest outside of town. There was a semi-hard packed road that Jeremy followed for a bit, but it became increasingly harder to tell where the road was due to the growing depth of the newly fallen snow. He had been on the snow machine for only twenty minutes navigating between trees, over a frozen lake, and down a narrow road. Jeremy was already eleven miles from Minaki and impossibly lost.

His damaged judgement had now put him in a position where he was knowingly in danger. He thought he must be near Red Lake, so he would just keep heading in the direction he thought east was. The idea of turning around and following his track back to town seemed too long and he was too cold now. He had made it this far after all. In truth, Jeremy was headed north, hurtling through the woods into an abyss of snow, cold, and certain death. He squeezed the throttle and continued for another mile. His bare hands burned from the cold, the snow was creating near white-out conditions, and he was panicking. "Just have to hurry and get there." He thought......... "Just hurry."

By now, the old Yamaha was going nearly 70 miles per hour along a tree line. The headlight only revealed 50 feet or so at this speed. As Jeremy crouched behind the tiny windshield, he saw a lump of snow directly in the path of the speeding sled.

What Jeremy didn't realize was that this was no lump of snow. It was a large tree stump. He hit the left side of the stump, lifting the speeding Yamaha airborne, and rolling it to the left in the direction of the tree line.

As the snow machine went flying, Jeremy was launched off the seat, high into the air, transforming into a frozen human missile. His body hit a series of branches nearly twelve feet off the ground and snapped through the pines high into the air. The old Yamaha continued to roll like a football, spiraling riderless through the falling snow until it reached the apex of its arc. It slammed directly into one of the pine trees nearly fifteen feet off the ground. The screaming engine suddenly made a horrible sound as metal met wood at seventy miles per hour. Between the heat of the engine, gasoline, and the oil, it exploded into an orange ball of fire high off the ground as pieces of broken snowmobile fell into the freshly fallen snow. The fire illuminated the tree line in an eerie orange glow. Just on the outside of the glow, with half of his body hanging in a tree branch, drunk and unconscious, was Jeremy Fine, precariously balanced millionaire.

CHAPTER THIRTEEN

The old man had just drifted to sleep after having to make a late-night bathroom call. As Dutch Woodson began the second round of sleep for the night, an unusual sound caused him to open his eyes. He heard something, but wasn't sure what it was. He closed his eyes again and then he heard it once more, not quite as faint. It was the unmistakable sound of a snow machine. Annoyed and angry, he tore the covers off himself and grabbed a lantern. He lit the lantern and then trudged out of his bedroom into the great room of his small rustic trapping cabin. He rubbed the top of his bald head and face trying to awaken in the darkness of the cabin. Nobody should be near his remote trapping claim. Dutch stood in the doorway and looked out into the snowy night in an effort to determine the direction of the snow machine's sound. He strained to listen and heard the high revving of the engine. Dutch then heard a high-pitched whine followed by a muffled explosion. His eyes widened as the woods fell silent. Quickly, Dutch went back inside and threw on some coveralls, boots, and a jacket. After going back outside, he laced up a harness with a long tow sled and a wooden box about the size of a small cooler. Dutch took a flash light and trudged off in the direction of the sound.

After wading through the deep snow for about ten minutes, Dutch came across a fresh snow machine track and followed it. As he struggled through the snow for another two minutes, Dutch could finally make out some flickering light. He didn't know what he was looking at initially, but Dutch began to realize it was the remnants of a fire. A snow machine had collided with a tree. When shining his flashlight Dutch could see charred branches.

"Goddamn idiot." Dutch muttered to himself. The shattered hood of the snow machine was visible and he realized the pieces were from a Yamaha SRX. "OH NO!" Dutch anxiously started looking for footprints or anything in the snow. He called out loudly, "MILES! HEY! MILES!"

Dutch frantically shined his flashlight in all directions through the heavy snow seeing nothing. Realizing now from the lack of a track near the fire, the sled had gone airborne before the collision. He spotted the now exposed stump that started the chain of events and then shined the light towards the trees. A limp lifeless body hung up in the branches. Dutch ran as quickly as he could, reached the body, and became confused. He saw an underdressed man with no hat or gloves wearing blue jeans. It was not Miles but the charred rubble was definitely Miles' sled.

Dutch shook his head muttering again, "Who in the hell?"

The body was hung up about four feet above the snow facing the ground. Dutch walked around the right side of the victim, got underneath him, and shined the light on his face. Dutch winced as the light revealed that the rider's right eye was protruding from its socket and his nose was clearly broken. He looked closely and could see a faint sign of breath coming from his mouth. There was the pungent smell of alcohol. He was still alive, but barely. Dutch knew this stranger was badly injured and might not make it.

Dutch went back, got his sled, and brought it close to the tree. He then tried as carefully as possible to extricate this stranger from the branches and get him onto the sled without causing further injury. He used some towels from the box to wrap around the victim's neck to immobilize his head and wrapped tape around those to secure it. He then lowered Jeremy onto the ground. As Dutch lifted him, he could feel the unmistakable crunching of broken ribs. He laid the rider onto his sled and reached into the box for more tape. He took his glove off and very gingerly pulled the right eyelid out and up. The eye made a squishy popping sound. Dutch cautiously pulled the eyelid down and gingerly taped it shut to keep it from coming out again.

He looked at the man's broken face and the put his ear to his chest listening for breathing sounds. The breathing was shallow and weak. The heartbeat was irregular. Between the alcohol, the cold, and the trauma, this man needed medical attention and soon.

"Hey! You! What's your name?" yelled Dutch.

The injured man laid there motionless, before he whispered, "Red Lake."

"Hmmmm. An Irish Indian," Dutch replied.

Dutch reached into the back pocket of the stranger and pulled out a wallet. He found a Florida driver's license with the name Jeremy Fine. The photo was a match except for the bulging eye and broken nose.

"Well, Jeremy, your new name is Dumbass," Dutch declared as he put the leather harness around his chest and turned toward the cabin and started to pull the sled with Jeremy loaded up on it.

"Time to go back to the cabin, Dumbass."

Dutch leaned into the wind gusts and wet heavy snow pulling the sled. It was a difficult route back to the cabin. The wind was increasing and the snow was blowing sideways into Dutch's weathered face. He had a leather sling across his chest that was secured to the front of the sled towing Jeremy. As Jeremy lay in the sled semi-conscious, he made an occasional groan, but clearly struggled to breathe.

Dutch knew that his new patient desperately needed medical attention, but would it occur in time? In the back of his mind Dutch knew that time was of the essence if his sled cargo was going to survive.

It took nearly a half hour to make it back to the cabin. Exhausted, Dutch pulled the whole sled right through the door and onto the floor in front of the fireplace. Jeremy's wet clothes would need to be removed so he could warm up. He was unquestionably suffering from hypothermia. Dutch got a fire going quickly and got on the radio to get some medical assistance.

"Dutch cabin for Minaki central, over." He cued the mic button for a beeping sound on the other end.

Carl had a radio monitor back at his house in Minaki and he oversaw monitoring all radio traffic with Miles not in town. Somebody always had an ear open to make sure emergencies could be handled with the remote area's weak cell phone coverage.

"Dutch cabin for Minaki central." Dutch put the mic down and got a knife out and began cutting the clothing off Jeremy in front of the fireplace's growing heat. A horrible smell hit Dutch in the nose as Jeremy had defecated in his pants because of the accident.

Carl was in bed when the call came in. He heard the long beep and rose off the mattress and shuffled down the hallway to the foyer where the radio was on the antique sewing table. Carl's hair was a mess and he could barely keep his eyes open. He grabbed the microphone and squeezed the button. He coughed slightly, "Minaki central. Receiving you clear. What's up Dutch?"

Dutch was relieved that Carl answered so quickly at such a late hour.

"We need some medical attention out here. I've got a 55-year-old male with blunt force trauma from a snowmobile versus tree. He also has a high blood alcohol level."

Carl was surprised. "Yeah, ok. . . Uh, Miles is out on a call towards Kenora right now and the med chopper is down. Not that they could fly in this crap anyway."

Dutch knew something needed to be done quickly if this guy was going to survive and he was getting annoyed.

"Well Carl, why don't you get Gabby up and see if she can join us on the radio and perhaps shed some light on my little situation out here." Dutch started to snarl as he released the mic button.

"Uh yeah, let me give her a call. Wait just a minute Dutch."

Carl went quickly into the kitchen and grabbed his cell phone and dialed up Gabby's number. It took seven rings before she answered in a bleary voice thick with sleep.

"Hello?"

"Gabby, this is Carl. I just got a radio call from Dutch Woodson and he has a victim of a snowmobile versus tree accident at his cabin. Can you get over here and get on the radio with me? He is going to need some help. It's really bad."

Gabby quickly got out of bed turning on lights and searching for clothes.

"I'll be right there. Tell Dutch to get some vital signs and triage him as best he can. I should be over by you in five minutes." Gabby ran into Robby's room to let him know she was leaving the house for an emergency.

Carl got back on the radio and relayed Gabby's instructions to Dutch.

"She is going to be on the radio as soon as she gets here Dutch. She wants you to triage him and get vitals."

"Already on that Carl. This guy is pretty messed up. I'm going to work on him now. Stay by the radio and get Gabby on as soon as she gets there…. over."

Dutch put the mic down and started to access Jeremy. He carefully removed Jeremy's remaining clothes and looked for injuries. He could see that there were nasty red marks on his torso and could feel broken ribs when he lifted Jeremy into the sled. He had a stethoscope in an old med kit and listened to his chest for breath sounds and pulse. He checked for pulse in his extremities.

"Hey! Dumbass! Can you wiggle your fingers and toes?" Dutch yelled at the naked body lying in front of his fireplace.

Jeremy groaned and despite his condition was able to move fingers on both hands and toes on both feet when instructed to do so by Dutch. After this, Dutch carefully rolled Jeremy to look for any other injuries. Dutch grabbed a pencil and started to jot down the vitals and any other pertinent information.

After loading more wood on the fire, Dutch checked Jeremy's belly by pushing on it and checking for signs of internal bleeding. It was all coming back to him. The training he got before deploying as a young man to Vietnam.

Just as he stood up after finishing his triage, Gabby's voice crackled over the radio.

"Minaki central, Gabby here. Dutch, can you hear me? Over."

"Good to hear your voice Gabby. Over."

"What do you have? Over."

"I have an extremely intoxicated, hypothermic, 55-year-old male. Snowmobile versus tree. Five feet eleven approximately 190 pounds. Blood pressure unknown, pulse is sixty and thready. Likely fractured ribs on right side. Diminished breath sounds same. Possibly tension pneumothorax. Extruded right globe. Fractured nose. Missing one tooth. Chest contusions and semi-conscious. Over."

Gabby was confused. "Extruded globe?"

"He hit a tree so hard his goddamn eye came out of the socket. I put it back in and taped it shut."

"Jesus," Gabby's eyes widened.

Dutch surveyed his patient with the mic in hand. "I checked the belly for rebound or guarding. I don't think he has any internal bleeding, but he's going to need a chest tube. I can give it a shot because moving him in this weather isn't going to happen."

"It's pretty bad out. Dad isn't around because he's at a medivac chopper crash. Our best bet is to try to get him out of there by snow machine when the weather breaks. Hey, do you have a blood type? Over."

"Yeah, it looks like he has a Red Cross donor card in his wallet. Looks to be O positive. Over."

"Dutch, who is this guy? Who would be out by you intoxicated on a snowmobile in this weather at this time of night? Over."

"I was just about to ask you the same thing, Gabby. It's some dumbass from Florida named Jeremy Fine. His ID is in his wallet. I think he stole your dad's SRX. Over."

When this transmission came over Gabby turned white and dropped the microphone. Carl also heard it, and put his hands to his mouth in shock.

Gabby started to walk backwards towards the door and immediately began to tear up. "Oh NO! I'm going up there."

Carl turned immediately and followed her to the door and got

Gabby by the shoulder. "You cannot......go in this weather. You can't see where you're going and Dutch's cabin is way in the sticks! No!"

Just then, Dutch got back on the radio; "Gabby? Do you have any idea who this knucklehead is? He might not make it through the night anyway. Over."

Gabby slipped out of Carl's grasp and bolted through the door. Carl ran frantically outside and yelled to Gabby as she got into her Jeep, "I'll meet you at the town shop! Don't go anywhere without me!"

The radio crackled again. "Is anybody there? What is going on back there?" Dutch was getting annoyed.

Carl raced back to the radio and squeezed the mic.

"Dutch, Gabby is coming out there. This guy is a friend of Miles and he must have taken off with his snow machine. She's heading for the shop now."

"NO! GODDAMMIT! ABSOLUTELY NOT! YOU TELL HER TO STAY THERE UNTIL I TELL HER IT'S OK TO COME HERE!" Dutch yelling into the radio was visibly pissed off.

"I'm going to the shop too, Dutch. We'll take two sleds. I think I can find your place."

"I don't want either of you running around in this godforsaken blizzard. We'll find your corpses in the spring. You stay THERE!" Dutch was adamant.

Carl, exasperated, squeezed the mic, "Dutch, she already left my place and I'm sure she's heading to the shop. Over."

Dutch rolled his eyes and muttered profanity under his breath as he squeezed the mic button. The veins stood out on his wrist and arm with frustration.

"Alright. Listen up. You stay there. Then, you call Doug and wake his ass up. NOW! Tell him to get to the shop and tell him to stop Gabby from going out in this crap. I'll keep this guy by the fire until daybreak and we can figure out what to do then. Over."

"Ok, Dutch. I will get Doug. Over."

Carl got his cell out and called Doug. It rang about 5 times until Doug answered from his bed. Carl explained the situation quickly and told Doug that he was needed at the shop right away.

"I'll be right there." Doug grabbed some clothes and headed out the door.

When Doug pulled into the parking area by the town shop, he saw Gabby's Jeep. The lights were on inside. The wind was strong and the snow was blowing sideways. Visibility with his truck headlights was about 50 feet. He entered the shop and saw Gabby loading up some supplies into a tow sled that had a canopy for transporting patients behind a snowmobile. His eyes widened as he realized she was just a few minutes away from departing into the blizzard.

When she heard the door and saw Doug step in, Gabby was startled. She was frantically checking boxes for supplies and then loading them into the sled.

"Doug! Good. You're here. Can you make sure the Viking sled is gassed up and ready? I've got to get out to Dutch's cabin."

"Gabby, this weather is crazy. You can't go out in this. I know Jeremy is out there with Dutch, but you can't take a snow machine way out in this crap tonight. Let's wait until daybreak and see if the wind drops."

Gabby turned with a hard look in her eye and clenched teeth.

"I am going up there. I am leaving in two minutes. I am not discussing this with you or Carl or anybody else. Now check the gas or get out of here." Her eyes were like daggers.

Doug was not going to be able to talk Gabby out of this and she was about to bolt. He realized the best thing he could do was help and try to keep Gabby safe. He would prepare the sled and go along with her.

"Give me a minute Gabby."

Doug ran into the locker room off the main shop area and grabbed some cold weather clothes including insulated coveralls, a utility pack, and a snowmobile helmet. He exited the locker room and re-entered the shop area where Gabby was putting on some insulated bibs and boots.

"I'm going with you."

Dutch continued to keep an eye on Jeremy while waiting by the radio. It looked like his breathing was becoming more labored. Dutch knelt next to Jeremy and listened to his chest again and realized he couldn't wait any longer. Jeremy had a collapsed lung and needed a chest tube.

Jeremy was barely conscious and Dutch needed to do a lifesaving surgical procedure in front of his fireplace. He retreated to his galley area of the kitchen and retrieved a fillet knife used for cleaning fish. He then put the blade into the edge of the fire to heat the blade up. He then took a syringe from a first aid kit and removed the plunger. After a moment, he took the hot knife out and set it on the table above him. He poured some alcohol on Jeremy's side where his broken ribs lie beneath bruised skin. Proping a flashlight up to illuminate Jeremy's side, Dutch then carefully probed his side looking for a specific spot. He then reached for the knife and took a deep breath. Dutch smoothly and quickly pushed the hot, razor-sharp blade into Jeremy's rib cage and cut a slit approximately two inches long and then pulled the knife out. Jeremy let out a muffled groan as Dutch retracted the knife from his torso.

Next Dutch carefully grabbed the shaft of the syringe and inserted it into the hole, creating the change in pressure needed for the lung to reinflate. He could hear air going out after guiding the tube of the syringe into Jeremy's chest cavity. He then taped gauze around the hole. He cut and secured the shaft of the syringe with tape. Then Dutch listened to Jeremy's chest and could now hear breath sounds from both lungs as his breathing visibly improved. Jeremy's heartbeat seemed stronger as well.

Dutch turned back to the table where the radio was and grabbed the microphone. "Minaki central this is Dutch. Over."

Carl had just hung up the phone a moment before. He talked to Doug at the shop. He walked slowly over to the radio and picked up the microphone. He keyed it, "Minaki central here, Dutch. Over."

"Can you get Gabby back on the radio soon? I think I bought us some time with the patient. Over."

Carl was quiet. He slowly keyed the mic and sat in his chair. "Doug tried to stop her Dutch, but she wouldn't listen. They are both heading your way."

Dutch wanted to yell at Carl, but he knew it was useless. He knew Gabby and when she was focused on something, nobody could talk her out of it. He felt a little better that Doug was with her, but this was a bad storm with poor visibility and it was the middle of the night. Doug had a good sense of direction and knew the location of the cabin, but these were horrible conditions.

With a sense of resignation, Dutch keyed the mic, and spoke slowly and quietly. "Roger…… Minaki central…………. message received……. Dutch out."

Dutch dropped the microphone on the desk, got up slowly and walked towards the fireplace. He stood over Jeremy as he still lay in the sled, naked, with a chest tube sticking out of his right side. He looked down at him with a look of disdain and muttered, "I hope you're worth it, asshole."

CHAPTER FOURTEEN

Doug jumped onto an idling Yamaha snow machine outside the open garage door of the town shop. Gabby then emerged from the open garage door with a larger Yamaha, a Viking, which had a longer track base and a cargo area behind the seat. She was also towing a rescue sled that had a clear plastic canopy for the transport of patients.

In their helmets were two-way radios so communication could take place while in route. As the door of the garage closed, Doug could make out a faint SRX track in the snow from when Jeremy grabbed the machine earlier and drove past the Horschel house. Doug wondered if he should follow the track or just take the quickest route to Dutch's place.

"What do you think Gabby? Just head for the cabin?"

"Yes! We know he's there. Forget the sled track. Just get to the cabin!"

Doug was still trying to grasp the enormity of the situation. It was the middle of the night, in a blizzard, and it was up to him to find a cabin that was over 10 miles away in the middle of dense Canadian woods in late winter where there was extremely deep snow. He needed to make sure to not get stuck, lost, or injured. He needed to get medical help to a drunk man that hurled his body into a tree at seventy miles per hour. There was no formal trail and the sled that Gabby was pulling had a high probability of getting stuck. The shortest route would require them to cross two lakes, and he was wary of getting stuck in the slush on the lake ice in these late winter conditions. He took a calculated risk and decided to take a route further north that would take them into steeper hills and less swampy areas, but the slush on the lakes could be avoided.

"Let's go Gabby."

Doug squeezed the throttle and adjusted his mirror so he had a clear view behind him and could watch Gabby's progress. He knew that Gabby was an excellent rider and had traveled by snow machine thousands of miles in her life with her dad. She was smart enough to know that the tow sled was a necessary liability and that staying in the trail that was already broken would be crucial.

As Gabby fell in behind Doug, she was feeling frantic and felt tremendous guilt. She didn't take Jeremy back to the house like her dad suggested and now he was badly injured, possibly dying, in a remote wilderness. This guy should have been home safe in a warm bed, sleeping it off. She could never have known the chaotic and drunken circumstances that put Jeremy on that Yamaha hurtling through the woods during a late season Canadian blizzard. She only knew that he was at Dutch's cabin and that he needed help. She fought back tears thinking about her dad's friend and tried to force it out of her mind. She had to focus on getting there safely and staying in a safe track behind Doug.

It was slow going for the first few miles, but Doug located an old logging road that was more open where they could travel faster and avoid the low hanging branches from the snow-laden pines that stood in the way. They could have gone slightly faster, except the wind and blowing snow kept them from out driving their headlights. They seemed to be making good time considering the conditions and before long, Doug and Gabby intersected the shoreline of Beaver Lake where Dutch's cabin was located. They carefully followed the shoreline of the lake, avoiding all the deep slush pockets and water that would surely halt their progress.

Doug felt a wave of relief when they reached Beaver Lake and knew that they were within reach. As they travelled along the last half mile, Gabby was grateful Doug led the way and found the cabin. It was nearly an hour later when the two Yamaha machines pulled up to Dutch's remote secluded residence.

Dutch was once again checking Jeremy's vital signs and respiration when he heard the engines as Gabby and Doug pulled into the yard area. It was a huge relief knowing that Gabby had arrived safely. When Gabby and Doug shut their machines off, Gabby quickly instructed Doug to grab several boxes from the tow sled. She grabbed a box herself and hurried to the cabin door where she was met by Dutch who promptly hugged her.

"Thank God. . . you're alright." Dutch pulled her inside the cabin and grabed the box from her.

Doug quickly followed carrying several items in and a gear bag containing medical supplies. Dutch and Gabby got together and stood over Jeremy where they discussed his condition.

"His pulse has improved and he seems to be breathing ok now." Dutch knew she would be checking his vitals first.

It looked as though Gabby did not even notice that Jeremy was naked. Carefully, she inspected the location of the chest tube and Dutch's tape job. Doug was unpacking boxes and pulled out an oxygen tank along with some IV bags.

"Doug, get me that tubing over there and bring me that tank," ordered Gabby.

Doug handed her the items and she quickly set up an oxygen line. She then started working to get an IV running on Jeremy. Dutch stood back and let Gabby work. As she worked, she talked very little and made sure that the lines were clear and not encumbered.

"Doug, get me that tacklebox over there."

Doug handed her the box and she got out an oral thermometer.

"Probably want to stick that up his ass." Dutch said in snide voice.

Gabby tried to ignore the tone of his comment. "I don't want to roll him over right now."

"Remind me Dutch, what's up with the eye?" She peered at Jeremy's face and forehead.

"When I found him, it was sticking out of the socket a bit," Dutch explained.

Gabby looked up at Dutch. "How did you put it back in?"

"Like you're supposed to, I extended the upper lid out and it sucked back in by itself."

"Good idea taping it up for now." Gabby looked carefully at the tape.

"Yeah. Good chance it comes out again if he coughs or sneezes." Dutch took a sip of coffee.

In little more than twenty minutes, Gabby had checked over Jeremy. His oxygen level was up, and he was now stable on IV fluids. She caught her breath, sat down at Dutch's dining table and started to make some notes. Dutch had been watching Gabby work the whole time, but also shot several nasty looks in the direction of Doug. As all this was all going on, Doug stood silently in the corner and merely watched. Dutch quietly walked over towards Doug and looked him directly in the eye and in a low voice said, "Come out to the tool shed. I'd like to have a word with you."

Doug was a little apprehensive, but he had successfully led Gabby to the cabin safely after all, and it looked like Jeremy might survive. He couldn't imagine what the problem could possibly be.

Dutch walked out first into the wind and snow as Doug followed. They turned around the corner of the cabin and walked into another smaller log building where Dutch lit an old dented Coleman lantern. After Doug entered, Dutch closed the door and turned towards him. He spoke in a calm and deliberate voice with a menacing tone.

"Doug. Did Carl call you?"

"Yes, he did."

"And, what did he say to you?"

"He said that Gabby was heading up your way and that Jeremy was in trouble and needed medical attention."

"Hmmmm, I see. Did he say anything else?"

Doug paused because he knew what was next. "Yes, he did. He said I should stop her because you said it was unsafe and that we should wait until morning."

Dutch took a step closer and looked Doug directly in the eye. He spoke quietly. "Then why are you here right now?"

"Gabby was leaving no matter what I said. I figured that she needed my help to get here. It seemed..."

Dutch interrupted and yelled loudly at Doug, "YOU HAD ONE GODDAMN JOB AND THAT WAS TO STOP HER! YOU GOT LUCKY THAT YOU FOUND THIS PLACE OTHERWISE I'D BE OUT THERE LOOKING FOR THE TWO OF YOU IN THIS FUCKING STORM!"

Dutch flew into a rage and was backing Doug up against the wall of the small shed when Gabby swung the door open wildly and jumped between the two of them. Gabby got right in Dutch's face and yelled.

"DUTCH! IT WAS MY IDEA! MINE! I WAS COMING UP HERE WITH OR WITHOUT DOUG. WE MADE IT HERE SAFELY BECAUSE OF DOUG!"

Doug was backed up against the wall and his eyes were wide. He knew that Dutch was about to kick his ass. Despite the fact that Dutch was over 70 years old, he scared the hell out of people when he was angry. Doug was relieved that Gabby intervened just as things were boiling over.

Dutch turned away in disgust. He was mad at Jeremy because of his foolish behavior. He was mad at Gabby for taking such a risk going out in the storm and he was mad at Doug because he didn't stop Gabby. Dutch loved Gabby like she was a member of his family. He looked at Miles as a nephew. Dutch and Miles's father were like brothers. The fact that this stranger had made the people closest to him take such risks was infuriating.

Dutch stood against the wall, facing away from Gabby and Doug. He calmed down for a moment and paused.

"Who is this asshole anyway?" Dutch inquired.

Gabby spoke with a soft voice, "He's a friend of my dad's."

Dutch spun around and raised his voice.

"A FRIEND!?! Yeah! Some friend. Let's go out in blue jeans and tennis shoes in a blizzard and total my friend's snow machine, that is a family heirloom, while trying to kill myself. Oh yeah, and also, let's have people go out in the middle of the goddamn night in a blizzard to try to save my sorry ass and put them all at risk! Some friend!"

Gabby stepped up to Dutch and pressed her hand to her chest. "DUTCH! I'm ok. Doug is ok. That man is probably going to be ok because of what you did here tonight. That man owes you his life."

She stepped closer to Dutch and looked him in the eye. She softened her voice and spoke calmly, "You saved his life."

Dutch looked at her and gave her a look of resignation. He knew Gabby was right.

"C'mon." Gabby said. "Let's go back in where it's warm."

Doug and Gabby walked out of the dark shed and left Dutch in the dim light of the lantern.

Dutch looked out the door and towards the cabin where Jeremy lay badly injured in front of the fireplace. He snarled quietly to himself, "Fuck him."

CHAPTER FIFTEEN

It was approaching five am and Miles was exhausted. He was within the last few minutes on the road and driving was difficult. The blizzard had made the road hard to maneuver and forced Miles to drive extremely slow. Rolling the window down a few times helped keep him awake as the cold air hit his face and kept him alert. He spent most of the night helping locate and evacuate the victims of the chopper crash. The operation was successful and the prognosis for both the crew and patient was favorable. Miles spent a good part of the night helping carry gear in to the site through the deep snow and then slide the victims out with sleds over the snow. It was extremely difficult and grueling work in horrible conditions. His fifty-five year old body was in top shape, but two hours in the truck had allowed his body to stiffen up and he was growing very sore.

As Miles approached Minaki, all he could focus on was his bed and the coming sleep that his mind and body craved. Relief finally came when he saw the opening of his driveway. It appeared that fifteen inches of new snow had fallen overnight and it seemed as though the wind was finally starting to abate. As Miles pulled into his garage, he grabbed his cell phone and sent two text messages One message went to Gabby to let her know that he was home safely,and another to Carl.

"Carl, back at the house and exhausted. I'm going to bed now. Don't bother me until noon at least. Miles."

As Miles entered his house through the garage, he shuffled his feet slowly and his legs struggled to make it up the three steps into the kitchen entryway. He assumed that Jeremy was likely sleeping in the back bedroom and didn't want to wake him up by making a lot of noise. Normally, after this kind of night Miles would jump in the shower before going to bed, but he was too exhausted and just wanted to sleep. Miles went into the bathroom, set his phone on the vanity, and began brushing his teeth. He looked in the mirror. There were dark circles under his eyes and his hair was matted against his head from dried sweat. Miles thought again about walking down the hallway and checking on Jeremy, but decided he needed sleep and didn't wake him. He walked into the kitchen, wrote a note for Jeremy, and left it on the table;

"Jeremy, got home late and am sleeping until noon. Go ahead and make yourself some coffee and I'll catch up with you when I get up. Miles."

As Miles entered his bedroom and collapsed half-dressed on top of his covers, he knew nothing of Jeremy's condition, or of Gabby and Doug's trek out to Dutch's cabin in the middle of the night. He had no idea his father's snowmobile had been totaled. Miles had absolutely no reason to believe anything was wrong.

Carl received Miles' text message and was wide awake in radio contact with Gabby at Dutch's cabin.

Carl immediately wanted to text Miles about the situation, but paused for a moment and then decided to radio Gabby at the cabin first to let her know that her dad had arrived safely home.

"Minaki central, Gabby? Over."

"Gabby here, Carl. What's up? Over"

"I just got a text from your dad that he's home. He said he's sleeping until noon. I don't think he knows what's going on. Do you want me to talk to him or do you want to call him? Over."

Gabby looked at her watch and knew what kind of night her dad no doubt had. He obviously hadn't been to the shop to notice that the snow machines were gone. He must have assumed that Jeremy was asleep at the house. Miles had been out of radio range of all the earlier transmissions as Dutch reported in when the accident first happened. Jeremy's condition was relatively stable and there was nothing else that could be done until daybreak when a new trail could be broken. Gabby carefully considered the situation and knew that the bad news could wait. She squeezed the mic button.

"Carl, just send him a text back that you'll call him at noon.

That's it. I'll call him when we get the situation here figured out. Over."

Carl knew her reasoning, but he knew that this was the kind of thing that Miles would want to handle personally.

"Gabby, your dad is going to want to know what's going on. Over."

"I know Carl. But he's going to be very upset and exhausted. Plus, he's going to want to come up here right away. That's not going to do anybody any good. Just do what I said and I'll be the one to explain what happened. Over."

Carl knew she was right, but he knew that he was going to catch a wrath of shit from Miles for this eventually.

"Ok Gabby. Noon it is. Minaki central out."

Miles had already collapsed on his bed as his phone sat on the counter next to the bathroom sink. Carl sent a text to Miles that simply read, "I'll call you at noon." It flashed on the phone unnoticed as Miles began snoring in the adjacent bedroom.

CHAPTER SIXTEEN

As dawn broke, Dutch peered out the kitchen window of his cabin and could see that the storm was over. It was an unusual kind of winter storm. It wasn't followed by strong northwest winds and plummeting temperatures. This was a storm of March and the high pressure that was arriving ushered in some southern winds and warmer temperatures as it slid in from the south. The sun was going to be out and all of this was going to start melting within 24 hours.

Doug walked towards the window and handed Dutch a cup of coffee.

"It looks like it's going to be a decent day." Doug looked out the window and then turned to Dutch.

"That had to be scary, you know, putting in a chest tube like that under those conditions."

Dutch took a sip of coffee and looked straight out the window.

"It was a hell of a lot easier than the first time I did it." Dutch had a faraway look in his eye.

Doug had a tough time picturing the immense pressure of doing something like that in the first place.

"What was different this time?" Doug inquired.

Dutch kept his gaze out the window but you could see his eyes darting back and forth remembering a difficult past.

"This was easy. I was in a nice dry cabin with enough light and it was just the two of us. The first time I put in a chest tube it was at night. It was raining and I was in ankle deep water on the edge of a rice paddy while the north Vietnamese were shooting in our direction."

Dutch turned to Doug and gave him a steely look directly in his eye. "This was a piece of cake."

Gabby began to pack up some of the gear she and Doug brought that was no longer needed. As daylight began to stream into the cabin, Jeremy began to stir and make some moaning sounds. The alcohol was wearing off and the pain of his injuries was starting to take a foothold. Gabby knew he had a large amount of alcohol in his system, but wasn't sure exactly how much. She was reluctant to administer pain meds because they could cause more problems than they would solve given his level of intoxication. But it was now clear that Jeremy was in a growing state of pain and it was only going to get worse. They needed to stabilize his broken ribs with a wrap of some kind and then safely get him out of the woods and back to the clinic where she could better assess his injuries with x-rays and proper monitoring. It appeared that he had no internal bleeding, but the true extent of his injuries was not yet known.

Gabby decided to radio Carl back in Minaki and start figuring out what to do next.

"Minaki central, this is Gabby. Over."

"Minaki central reading you loud and clear, Gabby. Over."

"Good morning, Carl. The weather looks better here. Did my Dad contact you yet? Over."

"No Gabby. Not a peep. I think he must still be sleeping. I wasn't going to contact him for a few hours yet."

"Ok, that's fine. I think we're going to want to bring the patient back in an hour or so. We need to pack the trail to ensure as smooth a ride as possible. This is not going to be a fun ride back. Over."

"Alright, Gabby. Let us know if you need anything and we'll get it out to you. Let us know before you leave. Over"

"Will do, Carl. Gabby out."

Gabby then turned to Doug. "Hey, start thinking about a route back to town that would be fairly flat and smooth. We can take a little extra time, but we should avoid hills and uneven terrain. With his injuries, Jeremy is going to need a smooth ride back."

Doug put his coffee down. "I have a few ideas."

Dutch turned to Doug, "You were smart last night not to cut across those lakes. You would have gotten stuck in that slop for sure."

That was the closest to an apology that Dutch was ever going to give for going after Doug the night before. Dutch still regarded Doug as an immature kid in many ways, but he was ready to step up here and Dutch realized that he was looking out for Gabby. After his initial anger subsided, he appreciated what Doug had done.

Jeremy let out another groan from under his blanket by the fireplace as Gabby was putting an ace bandage around him tending his damaged rib cage. The IV was still connected and the chest tube remained in place. His right eye was still taped shut and dried blood was smeared on his face and neck from his facial injuries.

"I wish we could better assess him for a concussion out here, but I guess that will have to wait."

Dutch took a sip of coffee and shared his idea.

"Well, based on my experience, one of three things could be going on. One, he could have a concussion. Two, he could still be affected by the amount of alcohol in his system. But the third scenario is most likely."

Doug turned to Dutch. "What's that?"

Dutch stepped closer to Jeremy and looked at him laying on the floor and tilted his head.

"He probably wasn't all that bright to begin with."

As Jeremy lay on the floor, he was beginning to hear voices. It was dark and he had trouble recognizing the voices of the people talking. Everything seemed dark and unfamiliar. He could see a wooden ceiling and a stone fireplace hearth with a large animal head hanging above him. Was it a moose? He couldn't be sure. There was a heaviness in his chest and his head was throbbing. He thought he was just hungover at first, but this was unbelievable. His skin hurt. His tongue felt like a piece of wood in his mouth. He realized there was tubing on his face and could hear air going through the tube and into his nose. His vision was diminished and Jeremy realized he could only see out of one eye. He had trouble moving his head since it was immobilized with a neck collar that Gabby had fixed on him during the night.

He tried to adjust himself to relieve the discomfort. Jeremy turned to his left slightly when a stabbing pain in his right side instantly stopped him. He let out the sound of a wounded animal.

Gabby realized that Jeremy was becoming increasingly more conscious. She didn't want him to move suddenly or do anything to displace the chest tube or otherwise hurt himself. She walked over to him in an attempt to see if his cognitive response was there.

"Jeremy. This is Doctor Gabby. You were in an accident. Can you understand me?"

Jeremy took a breath in to respond, but it hurt. He quietly whispered through his dry mouth and damaged lip.

"I understand." He responded in agony. It was barely audible.

"Your right eye is taped shut. That's why you're having trouble seeing. You also have a serious chest injury. If you had to rate your pain on a scale of 1 to 10, where would you put it?"

Again, Jeremy was barely audible but his answer indicated he was clearly miserable.

"About fourteen."

Gabby smiled slightly. She knew he was in pain and was relieved that he could respond.

"Listen up Jeremy. You are in a cabin quite a ways from town. We are going to have to transport you by tow sled and get you back to the clinic so we can get you treated. Do you understand?"

Again, it was little more than a whisper.

"Yes."

Gabby smiled and turned away in order to resume packing up the gear needed to move her patient.

Jeremy took a breath and tried to get her attention.

"Gabby." It was slightly louder, but more painful.

She turned towards him.

"Yes Jeremy?"

He took another labored breath and fought to get the words out.

"What happened?"

She realized that he had no recollection of the accident. It could have been the alcohol that gave him a blackout or it could have been that his brain erased it. When the body is traumatized in such a way, this is not uncommon.

"You were riding a snow machine and you hit a tree. Now try to get some rest. We're heading out soon."

Jeremy was completely confused. All he could remember from the night before was watching a hockey game at someone's house. That was where his memory ended.

Doug decided to leave the cabin and scout out the best route to take back. He started along the lake shore and then cut further south where the terrain was flatter and less bumpy. Doug got nearly halfway to town and was confident that the trail would be packed down enough to haul Jeremy back safely. The snow from the night before was causing the pine branches to sag and many tree limbs snapped under the weight of the heavy snow and strong winds. It was late morning now and the sun was out and the wind was nearly still. The sunshine hitting all the newly fallen snow made the morning almost blindingly white.

When Doug got back to Dutch's cabin, Gabby had her gear packed up. It was time to figure out how they were going to load Jeremy into the sled. The transport sled had a litter with a glass canopy they could put a battery-operated heater in to help. That, coupled with the blankets should help to keep the temperature warm enough for the 45-minute trip through the woods back to the clinic in Minaki.

Doug and Dutch brought the litter into the cabin and set it next to Jeremy on the floor. Gabby lined the tow sled with blankets to prevent the cold from seeping in underneath the sled chilling the patient. Gabby held the IV bag above Jeremy as Doug and Dutch carried him out to the sled and gently laid him down on the blankets. The cool air felt good on Jeremy's face and the sunshine nearly blinded him in his one good eye.

As they covered Jeremy with blankets and rigged up the heater, Dutch pulled Doug aside.

"Listen, based on what Gabby told me, Miles is going to have a shit hemorrhage when he finds out about this and it's going to happen as soon as you get back. You tell Miles to either call or radio me when he starts to lose his shit. I will talk to him. Got it?"

"I understand." Doug got his helmet and gloves on as Gabby came over and gave Dutch a hug.

"Thank you." She kissed him on the cheek.

"Your dad is probably going to have a rough time hearing about this. You know, his sled and all on top of his friend getting hurt."

"I know. But I think Jeremy is probably going to be ok."

Dutch nodded.

Gabby got her helmet on and fired up the Yamaha Viking with Jeremy in the tow sled. Doug pulled out and Gabby fell in behind him and headed towards the lake. The two sleds disappeared down the shoreline and back towards the town of Minaki. Dutch retreated into the cabin and fired up the radio.

"Minaki central. This is Dutch. Over."

A 20 second pause occurred before Carl replied.

"Minaki central here Dutch. What's going on up there? Over."

"Gabby and Doug are bringing the patient back to town. They just left. I'd give them less than an hour and they should be there. Over."

"Thanks Dutch. I will be waiting for them. Over."

"Hey Carl. Have you talked to Miles yet? Over."

"No. I was going to call him in about an hour. Over."

"Ok Carl. Just wondering. Dutch out."

CHAPTER SEVENTEEN

Miles could see light coming into his bedroom window through his tired aging eyes. He slept on his stomach all night in his clothes and his back ached from the hard labor of the night before. The smell of dried sweat in his clothes and matted hair hung in the air. It hurt to move. His shoulders, back and thighs all ached from wading through waist deep snow during the night as they pulled the victims of the chopper crash to safety and transported them to the hospital in Kenora. As Miles sat up in bed, he looked in the mirror over his bedroom bureau and saw a man that looked years older than he should. He winced as he reached for his socks and pulled each of them off slowly. His back creaked as he then stood up and removed his dried-on blue jeans. Miles grabbed a towel and walked slowly into the bathroom, past his phone, and turned on the hot water for the shower. Steam began to fill the small bathroom and the heat felt good. The warm water seemed to loosen up his aching muscles and the smell of soap replaced the stink of dried sweat. As Miles began to feel like a human being again, he realized that he was going to need most of the day to rest and recoup.

Miles got out of the shower and began to dry off. He noticed his phone next to the sink and checked to see if anything happened since he got home. He noticed the text from Carl and saw that he would be calling him around noon. He felt so much better after the shower and was ready to get something to eat. He figured on stopping by the shop and checking in with Carl.

Carl had the plow truck out and was clearing the last of the new fallen snow from the lot in front of the shop when Miles pulled in and parked. Carl had been up all night monitoring the radio and then got in the truck and began to plow snow as soon as he knew that Gabby was on her way back with Doug and Jeremy. As soon as Carl noticed Miles pull into the lot, he parked near the door and got out. Miles parked next to him. The look on Carl's face had Miles instantly concerned. He could see immediately that something was wrong.

"What's going on?" Miles had a look of confusion.

Carl sighed. "Come inside. I have to talk to you."

CHAPTER EIGHTEEN

It was a relatively smooth ride back from Dutch's cabin, in large part due to Doug who cut a fairly straight and level trail that made all the difference. Jeremy was in the tow sled with a small amount of pain meds helping him, but he was extremely stiff and still somewhat confused and disoriented. His faculties were starting to return, but he was having trouble remembering why he was staring up at the sky surrounded by snow covered pine branches.

The last mile was on the same road that Jeremy had taken nearly 12 hours before when he absconded with Miles' Yamaha in a drunken rage. The Horschel residence and the town shop were passed on the way to the clinic in town. As Doug and Gabby pulled up to the door of the clinic, they could see Miles' truck parked there. As soon as the engines were quiet, Miles and Carl burst through the door and came up to meet them. Miles looked especially flustered as he hugged Gabby when she removed her helmet.

"You took a hell of a chance." He squeezed Gabby hard.

"I'm ok, Dad. C'mon let's get him inside."

Miles removed the canopy quickly and he and Carl grabbed the stretcher from the tow sled. Doug held the door while Gabby grabbed a few boxes and followed them in. The group went through a few wide doorways and into an exam room with a hospital bed and monitoring equipment. Miles and Carl then got Jeremy transferred from the canopy stretcher to the bed smoothly. Jeremy was semi-conscious, and made few sounds. Gabby immediately started to hook up blood pressure, heart and breathing monitors to keep an eye on his condition.

"I'm going to get some chest film and see how that lung is doing. Let's wheel him in through here."

Gabby led the way and saw to his placement on the bed for the x-rays.

While Gabby was taking pictures of Jeremy's chest, Miles pulled Doug aside.

"Thanks for leading the way up to Dutch's place."

"I tried to talk her into waiting, but there was no stopping her. You know how she gets."

"Carl explained everything to me about the accident except how he got up there. Whose snow machine did he take last night?"

Doug gulped and realized that Miles didn't know, and he really didn't want to be the one to tell him.

"He, uh, grabbed your SRX from the shop." Doug reluctantly answered.

Miles stared straight ahead looking through the window into the exam room where Gabby now had Jeremy's bed wheeled around. Miles realized the SRX was now destroyed, but he had other more pressing concerns. It was as if he didn't hear Doug. He didn't want to hear it.

Jeremy opened his eyes fully and started to open his mouth.

"I'm sorry," He muttered as he looked into Gabby's brown eyes.

"You're lucky to be alive Jeremy," She lectured.

"Where are we now?" His mouth was dry and his words squeaked as he talked.

"We're at my clinic in Minaki. We just got back from Dutch's cabin."

The fog from Jeremy's brain was starting to lift. He was in quite a bit of pain, especially his side and shoulder. Gabby asked several questions so she could assess him further before they moved him.

Gabby walked out of the room and then saw her dad. "I want to draw some blood to see his intoxication level. We need to get his eye checked and replace the chest tube that Dutch put in last night. I think he should have a head CT as well. But, for now his vitals are ok, and he seems stable. "

Miles was curious how the night got so out of hand. "How did he get so drunk last night? I thought he was heading home."

"He wanted to stay at the Cider Barn last night when I went home. He was watching a hockey game at the bar and seemed fine. I don't know what happened after that. Carl called me after midnight when he heard from Dutch. I'm not sure what happened at the Cider Barn."

Miles would normally be more upset with Gabby, but he knew she had a long night and deep down knew that this wasn't on her. He felt more responsible because he left his friend and things went sideways while he was out at the chopper crash. Miles had been unable to anticipate just how out of control Jeremy could get. Jeremy being in a strange environment and then losing control of himself was a telling sign for Miles. It looked like bringing him here turned out to be an enormous mistake.

Doug met Miles in the hall outside Jeremy's room. He looked extremely tired. He had been up all night with Gabby.

"If you don't need me anymore Miles, I'm going to hit the rack. I'm beat."

"Yeah, thanks Doug. I'll catch up with you later." Miles appreciated what Doug had done and gave him a slap on the shoulder as he headed towards the door. Carl waited next to Miles.

"Good news." Gabby spoke up from the exam room. Miles entered as she was looking on the computer screen at the chest film that she shot.

"Looks like two rib fractures, and more importantly, his lung is reinflated and things look good. His blood pressure is a little high and there are no signs of other internal injuries. He just asked to go to the bathroom and I gave him a jug. Remarkably, there's no blood in the urine."

"Wow. It seems like this could have gotten a lot worse." muttered Miles while shaking his head.

Gabby looked at her dad and saw the worry on his face. "It looks like he's going to be ok. He wants to talk to you."

Miles took a few steps towards the room and Jeremy turned his head.

"Hey buddy." Miles looked down towards Jeremy and felt guilty.

"I don't know what happened. I must have blacked out. I was at some cabin and this old grouchy guy helped take care of me. I don't know much else." Jeremy's voice cracked as he spoke in whispers and muffled tones.

Miles looked down and squeezed Jeremy's hand.

"Don't worry about that now. Just get some rest and try to heal."

Jeremy closed his unpatched eye and turned his head. Miles walked out the door and met up with Gabby and started to ask her questions. She stopped him and signaled for him to follow her down the hallway so they could speak without the possibility of Jeremy hearing them.

"What's up with him? Is he in trouble?" Miles asked Gabby.

"He's stable right now, but I don't know how. He has a blood alcohol level of .18, two broken ribs, a punctured lung, a damaged eye, broken nose, numerous contusions, and a broken off tooth. Given what happened to him, and the speed of the accident, I really don't know how he's alive. The only reason he's here on this earth is because of Dutch."

Miles knew that his friend was in trouble physically, and he also knew that a very rough stretch was ahead. Jeremy would be confined to a hospital bed and would not be able to drink alcohol. Withdrawal would start and serious consequences would follow when he stopped given his condition.

"Gabby, you know what he has ahead of him, right?"

"I think we can manage it, but I'd still like to get him out of here to a bigger facility for a CT of his head. His cognitive function has improved, but who knows what's going on in there. If his heart rate changes significantly, or if he starts to get the sweats, hallucinates, or worse, begins having seizures, we will have to treat him medically." Gabby seemed to have things in hand, but was concerned nonetheless. She knew enough about alcohol withdrawal to know what Jeremy might face on top of his injuries.

Miles knew that Jeremy needed to just rest and try to start healing. There was no sense in worrying about what was going to happen beforehand. They would deal with that later. In the meantime, he wanted to find out exactly what happened the night before. Carl filled him in on the situation as it transpired at Dutch's cabin. What he wanted to know was how Jeremy seemed to be handling a normal dinner out the night before and then ended up in the remote wilderness and near death by Dutch's cabin on Beaver Lake.

Doug waited outside as Miles exited the clinic door.

"Hey Miles, Dutch said you should give him a call. He wanted to talk to you."

"Way ahead of you Doug. He started to get into his truck and suddenly stopped. He turned back towards Doug and walked up to him.

"I know what you did to help. With Gabby and bringing my friend back. I appreciate it, Doug."

"No problem, Miles." Doug almost felt uncomfortable with Miles as he never saw him get emotional like this. It was out of character for him, to express gratitude. It was something Doug wasn't used to seeing in this respected, almost father figure.

Miles turned out of the parking area and headed back to the shop. As he went through town, he thought about stopping at the Cider Barn to ask about the previous night's activities and get a handle on what had happened there to Jeremy. But he decided against it and instead just went to the shop. The new snow had drifted and the road was still a mess, but Carl had started to plow the driveway and parking area of the shop. Miles got out of his truck and stopped Carl.

"When you came in this morning, did you see the tracks from my snow machine from last night?"

Carl put the truck in neutral and pointed towards the shop.

"There was a big snow drift right up to the door. I didn't see anything. No track, no footprints, no anything. There was just too much wind and snow last night."

Miles turned and saw the Horschel house and realized that

by early afternoon, there were no footprints or tracks of any kind leading to or from the house. That could mean nothing or something. He would find out later. For now, all he wanted to do was get on a snow machine and get up to Dutch's place to find out what had happened overnight. He went to his locker, and found some heavy clothes to wear along with a helmet. He jumped on the last remaining sled in the shop and pulled up by Carl who was still plowing snow.

"I'm headed up to Dutch's place. I should be back before dark." Miles squeezed the throttle of the snow machine and disappeared down the road before turning into the woods towards Beaver Lake.

As Miles traveled through the woods in the brilliant sunshine, he couldn't help but wonder about Jeremy's path that led him into the woods. It didn't make sense. He kept asking himself what he had gotten his friend into. Was Jeremy so bad off that he couldn't function? Was he so bad that he couldn't be left alone? It left his head spinning. As Miles got closer to Beaver Lake, he was impressed with the depth of the new snow and what the wind had done. There were many broken branches and snapped off tree limbs. The heavy, wet snow and wind had altered the woods overnight. The fact that Jeremy was out in this last night made no sense at all.

It was about 25 minutes later when Miles pulled up next to the cabin where Dutch lived. Dutch could hear the snow machine coming from a quarter mile away and was standing in the doorway with a cup of coffee in his hand.

When Miles stopped the machine about 20 feet in front of the door, he simply killed the engine and looked at Dutch. Neither man said a word. Miles let out an exasperated breath of air and slumped on the seat. He looked whipped. The stress of the morning and the guilt was weighing on him. Dutch let out a half smile and nodded to Miles to enter the cabin.

As he walked through the large doorway, Miles's eyes had a hard time adjusting to the darkness of the cabin interior after being out in the blinding sunshine and newly fallen snow. Miles sauntered over to the rustic looking dining table and sat in one of the two mismatched chairs. Dutch poured a cup of strong, hot coffee and set it in front of Miles.

Dutch sat on the other side of the table directly opposite of Miles and after a few seconds of additional and somewhat uncomfortable silence, he spoke in a gravelly, hushed tone.

"I'm not real impressed with your friend."

Miles stared at the steam rising from the coffee and didn't look up. He just shook his head.

"I had no idea things were this bad. I had no idea."

Dutch nodded in agreement.

"Gabby told me about your little flight down to Florida. How long has it been since you saw this guy?"

"Over 30 years. I hadn't seen or talked to him since college." Miles paused and took a sip and setting the mug back down.

"I was hoping that we could sort of pick up where we left off, you know. Like guys do."

Dutch smiled and almost laughed. "Well Miles, let me tell you. You are not the same guy from 30 years ago and I'm sure that your buddy isn't either."

"This guy is laying in a bed with tubes coming out of him and I can't help but feel responsible."

"NO." Dutch interrupted him as soon as the sentence was completed. "This is NOT on you. We are talking about a grown ass man here. He made his choices. Those choices resulted in some unintended consequences, but it was him. He is all busted up because of his behavior, not yours."

"I know that's the logical thing to think Dutch, but I gotta ask myself, what situation did I create here?"

Dutch thought for a moment because he wanted to choose his words carefully. He knew that Miles was worried about his friend, but he didn't want him to carry all of this weight. True, Jeremy was in a bad spot, but it was because of his choices and his heavy drinking.

"Listen, you reconnected with an old friend. He ran off the rails. Once he's healthy enough to travel, get him on a plane back to Florida and wish him well. Send him a Christmas card. But don't think that this is as bad as it will get for him. You and I have both seen guys like this. Drama follows them like a dark cloud. It's always raining and its never their fault. Just get him back where he belongs."

Miles and Dutch sat at the table for a few moments and took a few sips of coffee. Then Miles realized he had forgotten about something.

"Do you know where the SRX is?"

Dutch nodded. "Yeah. It's a little bit of a hike from here."

"I should go get it." Miles looked up at Dutch. "How bad is it?"

Dutch let out a sigh. He knew what that sled meant to Miles.

"Bad. Maybe that's a job for another day."

"Yeah. I probably don't want to see it right now."

Miles took a last sip of coffee and got up from the table. They both stood up and walked to the door. Miles turned to Dutch as he walked outside.

"I appreciate what you did last night. Thanks."

Miles' gratitude made Dutch uncomfortable and he didn't say a word. He merely nodded as he stood in the doorway.

"I think this is going to melt quick." He said awkwardly changing the subject. "Maybe spring is closer than we think."

"We can always hope."

Miles turned to Dutch. "You need anything up here?"

"Just peace and quiet."

Miles let out a slight grin. He knew what Dutch meant.

CHAPTER NINETEEN

Back at the clinic, Gabby watched Jeremy carefully and tried to anticipate any upcoming problems. An assistant was called to come in and help with monitoring Jeremy and administering medications. Gabby was exhausted. She had been up most of the night and now that Jeremy was resting comfortably, she felt like she could go home and grab a shower and something to eat. For now, Jeremy was sleeping and under the spell of some meds to thwart off the potential of seizures along with something to handle the pain of the accident. She left instructions with her assistant Kaitlyn to call her if any changes occurred and then headed home.

By the time Robby came home from school, Gabby was lying on the couch taking a nap. Robby went to the refrigerator and grabbed a quick snack before hockey practice. As he gulped a glass of milk, his grandpa Miles pulled into the driveway and walked stiffly towards the door. As he entered, Gabby heard his voice and rose slowly off the couch. She was bleary eyed, groggy, and not totally awake.

Both her and Miles sat at the kitchen table while Robby made a sandwich. Robby turned towards them, saw they were both exhausted, and wondered what had been going on.

"Where were you guys? Did something happen last night?"

"Yes Robby, Grandpa's friend got hurt in a snow machine accident."

"Is he going to be ok?"

"We think so. He got hurt pretty bad though."

Robby shrugged, "Glad he's going to ok. I gotta get to practice. See ya."

"Bye kid." Miles let out a slight grin and then turned towards Gabby.

"So, what's going on with Jeremy?"

"Well, he seems stable right now, but he's got pain meds helping him and I gave him some Benzo to help ward off seizures as the alcohol leaves his system. He's going to be dealing with withdrawals as we detox him. I think we should be able to handle it, but he will need more help."

"What kind?"

"He needs to get sober. If he doesn't, his liver is going to go, or he'll die doing something asinine like this again. He also needs a dentist for his busted tooth, and an eye doctor to check him out. We should try to fix his nose once the swelling goes down. We might have to rebreak it for it to heal properly."

"How about his ribs?"

"All we can really do is stabilize them and try to get his lung to heal. Dutch really saved his life by putting in that chest tube. If he had waited for me to get there, it may have been too late."

Miles was still unclear as to how Jeremy got so drunk after he left for the scene of the chopper crash. He wanted to retrace the events of the night and find out what put Jeremy on such a reckless path.

"Did you see him with anybody when you left the Cider Barn last night?"

"No, Dad. He was sitting at the bar watching the hockey game. Jeremy said he would walk back to your house."

Miles then looked at her closer and realized how exhausted she was.

"Get some rest, Gabby. You look like you need it."

"Yeah. Kaitlyn is keeping an eye on things there right now. She's going to call if she needs me."

"I'll swing by and check on her and see Jeremy. I've got a few chores to do as well."

Miles stood up and kissed Gabby on the forehead and then went out the door. He was still wondering what had happened during the night. He drove his truck over to the Cider Barn and saw that it was open.

He walked in and saw that the owner, Pat Creedy, was cleaning up behind the bar and restocking items.

"Hey, Pat. Did you work last night?"

"No, Miles. I left around 5pm and Ronny was bartending last night. He closed around 11. What's up?"

"I was trying to figure out what happened to a friend of mine last night. We had dinner, but he left after me and was in a snow machine accident."

Just then Pat spotted Ronny's car pull into the lot.

"Here's Ronny now. You can check with him."

As Ronny entered the Cider Barn, Miles approached him and knew that he had served Jeremy the night before. As frustrated as he was because of the accident, Miles tried to control his emotions because he needed information about the previous night.

"Yeah, your buddy was in here. He was laughing it up and watching hockey with the Horschel boys. They stayed until closing and your friend left with them. I think I overheard him ask Billy for a ride back to your place."

"Did anybody seem out of control or anything?"

"No. They were a little loud, but not overly crazy. It was an average night. Nothing special. What's the matter anyway Miles?"

"My friend ended up almost killing himself. I'm going to see him now. Thanks for your help."

Miles set his jaw and wanted to pull Billy and Dean Horschel out of bed and beat the shit out of both of them. He knew them as a couple of classic underachievers who spent a lot of time drinking, out of work, and wasting time. It seemed like Dean and Billy had worked for most of the business owners in town at one time or another and were let go because they pulled no shows, or were late, or did a crappy job. They bounced around from odd job to odd job after they were unable to fulfill their hockey dreams. Their main focus was partying, getting girls back to their house, and video games. Jeremy couldn't have met a worse couple of guys on the front end of a bender and Miles knew it.

It was Miles' instinct to go see Billy and Dean, but he knew that he needed to calm down first. It was getting close to dark and

Miles figured he would stop by and see Jeremy. As he pulled into the clinic parking lot he sat in his truck for a bit and realized that his friend was in a lot of pain from the accident, but also realized that Jeremy's biggest nemesis was himself. He only knew Jeremy as a cocky, fun-loving 19-year-old kid that liked to play sports and spend time with his friends. In the over thirty year gap, he had obviously had financial success, but did not have close family. He knew very little of Jeremy's life back in Florida, or the path that steered him away from having a wife and family. In short, he saw that Jeremy had done little to grow up. He wasn't that different from the Horschel boys. He just had more money, substantially more money. It made him realize that blaming Dean and Billy probably wasn't the right thing to do although, kicking their asses would feel good in the short term.

Miles walked into the clinic and saw Kaitlyn at a desk writing down some information on a chart.

"Hello, Kaitlyn. How's the patient doing?"

"Oh, hi Miles. He's doing ok. He's been sleeping mostly. His vitals are good. So, far I haven't had to call Gabby. She said that she was going to come in around midnight to check and see how things were going."

"Well, if it looks like things are good, why don't you knock off and head home. I can sit with him until Gabby comes in."

"Are you sure? I know you had a rough couple of days."

"I can sit here and if something comes up, I can call Gabby, same as you. Besides, I'd rather be here anyway."

Kaitlyn could see that Miles was worried and being with his friend might make him feel better.

"Ok, Miles. Just give me a call if you need a break."

"I'll be fine. Have a good night, and thank you, Kaitlyn."

With that, Kaitlyn finished her notes, put on her coat, and headed out the door. Miles quietly pulled up a chair next to Jeremy's bed. The light was subdued in the room at this point, but it was still easy to see Jeremy. Kaitlyn had cleaned the dried blood off Jeremy's face. His eye patch had been replaced and his good eye was developing a handsome shiner. The right side of his face was swollen and his loose gown revealed a dark contusion on his right shoulder. He was on an IV and his new chest tube seemed to be clear. He still had some dried blood stuck to his matted, thinning hair, but he looked a lot better than when he first arrived at the clinic. He was sound asleep.

Miles knew that when Jeremy woke up, he would likely want to transfer to a bigger hospital and receive more intense care. Gabby was insistent about seeing a specialist for his eye care. Jeremy also needed a dentist to look at him. These were services that Minaki did not have.

Miles figured that Jeremy would be leaving soon, so he decided to stay at his bedside. He still felt guilty about leaving Jeremy that night and Jeremy falling in with a rough crowd. Miles really didn't know that Jeremy was so prone to binge drinking and losing control. Miles was tormented by the thought that his prank set the wheels in motion that resulted in Jeremy nearly killing himself. Miles thought to himself; "What the fuck was I thinking?" Prior to flying to Florida with Doug, Miles looked up his arrest records and did a background check. Miles knew that Jeremy had problems, but this was something he didn't anticipate. Miles blamed himself for that. If he had known that things were this bad, he never would have brought him up north and made him vulnerable. This weighed heavily on Miles.

As Miles sat next to the bed. He reminisced and replayed several moments from long ago in his head. He recalled going to Madison for the first time and seeing the campus. He remembered the smells of the tailgate parties before the Badger football games in the autumn outside Camp Randall Stadium. The lights of State Street and the glow of the capital at night after walking down Bascom Hill. He was a young First Nations kid in the big city on a big campus and he felt so small. But, at the same time, it seemed like so much was possible. It was exhilarating. He was attending classes with students from all over the United States and countless other countries. All those different personalities, customs, and accents. He was treading water in a big place and it was energizing to him. Miles remembered meeting Jeremy and the infamous snowball fight. He thought about the parties they attended and how comical Jeremy would be around girls. Jeremy was always talking up a different girl each week and Miles would just shake his head and laugh. It was all about school, girls, and parties. It seemed like a hundred years ago.

A low voice spoke softly. Barely audible at first, but distinct.

"Hey.........Miles." Jeremy whispered in a hoarse voice.

Miles had not realized it, but he had dozed off for a while. The only sound was the oxygen machine that provided a humidified stream of air to the tube hanging on Jeremy's face. It was quiet otherwise.

"Miles......wake up."

Miles turned his head and could see that Jeremy's eye was open and his head was turned.

"Hey, Jeremy. Look who's awake." Miles sat up in his chair. "You want some water or ice chips?"

"Water please. I'm really dried out."

Miles grabbed a cup with a straw and held it for Jeremy at his bedside. Jeremy took a couple pulls off the straw and swallowed slowly and painfully.

"That is good. Man, my face hurts. I have a bandage on my eye too? I must have really done it this time."

"You are pretty banged up buddy."

"What happened?" Jeremy spoke slowly and with a scratchy, low voice.

"I don't know everything yet, but you got really drunk and took a snowmobile out about 10 miles from here and slammed it into a tree. An old trapper pulled you back to his cabin and saved your life."

"Jesus. I don't remember a damn thing. I was watching hockey at this house and we were yelling and then I don't know....." Jeremy's voice trailed off.

"Have you done anything like this before?" Miles quietly asked.

"You mean blacked out and almost killed myself? Well, not

like this bad, but in the neighborhood."

"You can't do this man. You keep doing this, you're gonna die."

"You're right. I know," admitted Jeremy.

"Should we call anybody? Your fishing buddy in Florida? Your mom?"

Jeremy thought for a moment.

"Let me talk to them tomorrow. I don't want you to call them because that will freak them out and I can't really talk right now. I'll call them when I sound a little better. Do you know where my phone is?"

"No, you came wrapped in a couple blankets. No clothes. I can find out if Dutch has your phone at the cabin."

"Dutch? He's the guy who saved me?"

"Yes, and Gabby. She came out in the middle of the night to take care of you at the cabin. She put her own life in danger."

"I couldn't figure out if I saw Gabby, or if that was a hallucination. Man, this whole blackout thing really sucks."

"She's going to be here in a few hours to check on you. You need your rest. I'll stick around until she gets here."

Jeremy tried to re-adjust his position in bed and settled back in, closing his good eye. Without making eye contact with Miles, he spoke slowly and deliberately. "I've drank myself into some bad situations over the years, but this one really hit me. I shouldn't be here now. I should be dead."

Miles stood up and squeezed Jeremy's hand, "Hang in there buddy. We're going to help you."

CHAPTER TWENTY

Gabby woke up and saw that Robby was already in bed. She thought about calling Kaitlyn to see if anything changed since she left the clinic, but figured that if she didn't call, things must be ok. At around 11 p.m. Gabby got dressed and made herself some dinner. By 11:30, she decided to go in a little early and relieve Kaitlyn. When Gabby's Jeep pulled into the clinic parking lot, she saw that her dad's truck was there and Kaitlyn's car was gone. She figured out what had happened pretty quickly.

As she entered the hallway and took off her coat, Miles came out to greet her.

"Did you get some rest?" he asked.

"Yeah Dad. I slept good and just ate some dinner. How's Jeremy doing?"

"He was awake a few hours ago and we talked briefly. He seemed better than I expected."

"I'm going to go in, check on him, and update his chart."

Miles went by the front desk and poured himself and Gabby some coffee while she entered his room. She checked Jeremy's vitals and went around the bed to check the condition of his chest tube. It had to remain clear and could not have any obstruction, or the lung could collapse again. As she moved around the bed, Jeremy opened up his eye and spoke in a quiet tone.

"Hi Gabby. How am I doing?"

"You seem to be stable Jeremy. How do you feel?"

"Like there's a truck parked on my chest. But I think I've got another problem."

"What's that Jeremy?"

"I'm getting this buzzing in my head and I'm getting the shakes and the sweats. I think I'm going to need a drink for this to go away."

"Jeremy, I knew this would be coming and you cannot drink under my care. The withdrawals are starting. I have some medication to help you through this but it won't be easy. There's going to be a rough period that could last a couple days. It's called detox. Now, have you ever detoxed before?"

"Yeah. And, it really sucks. I tried it twice before during rehab stints and I really struggled. The last time was about 9 months ago and I was so sick. I wanted to die."

"Jeremy, do you want help? I can help you, but you have to want my help. Do you want me to help you?"

Jeremy had been put in this position before by his wife, his parents, even some of his college buddies, but this time, it was different. He seemed to have cheated death and was lying in a hospital bed all busted up because of his drinking. He was backed into a corner because of his own poor decisions. He knew he needed to stop, but had failed twice already. Jeremy wondered if he just had to learn how to live with his alcoholism. He was in no position to bargain at this point, so he let out a sigh.

"Yes. I could use your help."

"Good Jeremy. Now I want you to tell me your symptoms, and be completely forthcoming. Don't leave anything out. If you hear voices, tell me. If you start to see things that don't make sense, tell me. This is going to be a crazy roller coaster, but know that I will do my very best to help you through it.

"You going to dry me out?"

"Yes, Jeremy, but that's just the start. We're going to get an eye doctor to come to Minaki and look at that eye and then you're going to need to see a dentist about your tooth."

"What tooth?"

The broken tooth on your right side. Didn't you notice it? Move your tongue. Can you feel it?"

"Oh. Jesus. I didn't even realize that I had a busted tooth."

Jeremy paused for a moment and got real quiet. Gabby was checking his covers and adjusting his bed when he spoke slowly again.

"Gabby?"

"Yes, Jeremy?"

He spoke slowly again. "Can you do me a favor and get me a mirror?"

Gabby knew that Jeremy hadn't seen himself since the accident. It was going to be a shock when he got a good look at himself, but she knew that this kind of thing would be beneficial. He would be able to see the consequences of driving drunk on a snow machine.

"Yeah Jeremy. I can do that."

She reached over to the cabinet and pulled a small hand mirror off the shelf. She slowly carried it back to Jeremy and then held it in front of his face. As the image in the mirror looked back at him, Jeremy could see the swollen jaw, the bruises, his broken nose, and the scrapes. The dried blood in his hair had matted it down pretty good, but it was mostly wiped clean. The patch over his eye made him look like a criminal. He stared straight ahead and almost through the mirror as he didn't recognize himself. He muttered in a hushed voice.

"My God."

Miles stood outside the doorway of the room and overheard the exchange. He retreated to the desk area when he realized Gabby would be coming out soon. He handed her a coffee as she reached the desk.

"Thanks Dad."

"How are things going?"

"Well, the good news is, he wants to get sober. I think the best thing to do is detox him here at the clinic before we think about transporting him. A bigger environment and a larger hospital may be too much stimuli for him. Keeping him calm will be the key. That's where you come in."

"Me? What can I do to help?"

"I want you to stay away from here for a couple days. At least until he gets through detox. This process can be a little crazy. The least amount of outside contact, and the fewer people he has to deal with the better. I know you want to help, but keeping this place serene is going to be the best thing. You understand?"

"I do. But shouldn't I be here to help?"

"I might need you here, but for now, go in and tell him that you're going to be busy the next couple of days and tell him you'll see him later. Make up something. If we need you in the meantime, you can come in. But my gut tells me that you should stay away for now."

Miles was understanding, but disappointed. He felt that he had to make up for the fact that he bought alcohol for Jeremy in Florida before bringing him on the plane that set this whole chain of events into motion. Miles nodded, walked down the hallway, and entered Jeremy's room. Jeremy was awake and turned his head slightly to Miles as he walked in.

"Hey buddy. How you feeling?" Miles was standing at the foot of the bed looking at Jeremy's chest tube.

"Like a failure."

"Don't think like that. Gabby told me that she's going to help you with drying out. That's not failing."

"I've been through it before and you're looking at the results of my success."

"I've heard that sometimes it takes a couple tries. I'm glad you're doing it again."

"Let's face it, Miles. I'm out of choices. Look at me. I'm a fucking mess. I should be dead right now."

"Yeah. But you're not."

There was an uncomfortable silence as Miles didn't know what to say. He was about to speak up when Jeremy spoke instead.

"Hey Miles. Can you do me a favor?"

"You name it."

"Give me a couple days here before you come back. I'm starting to feel this booze leave my system and its rough. I've been through it before and I turn into a real asshole when it gets bad. It's best if you let me get through the hard part before you come back. Can you do that?"

A wave of relief went through Miles and he couldn't believe what he was hearing. He didn't want to be the one to abandon his friend, but Jeremy realized it was probably for the better. Miles stepped up to the edge of the bed, and Jeremy raised his hand, and Miles gave it a squeeze.

"Anything you need, buddy. Just let Gabby know and I'll get it. If you need me, just let her know."

Jeremy nodded and gave him a forced smile.

Just then Gabby came in and Miles met her at the door. "I'm headed home Gabby. I'll give you a call later." Miles kissed her on the forehead.

"Ok, Dad."

Gabby walked towards the edge of Jeremy's bed and could hear the footsteps moving down the hallway and then the door opened. She could see his truck lights go on as he backed out of the parking spot and pulled out onto the road towards his house. She turned towards Jeremy and he looked right at her.

"It's starting. I think it's going to be a long night."

CHAPTER TWENTY ONE

Miles was just leaving the building when Doug called to him from a parked truck in the lot.

"Hey, Miles."

Miles turned, walked over to Doug's truck, and Doug handed him an iPhone.

"This was left at the Horschel house last night. I think it belongs to our buddy."

"The Horschel boys told me a little bit about what happened. It seems like Jeremy just snapped. Everybody was ready to call it a night and Jeremy wanted to get more liquor. That's why he grabbed your machine and took off."

"Where the hell was he headed? There isn't a place near here to buy liquor at that time of night."

"Billy said that he was headed for Red Lake." Doug was shaking his head.

"Jesus Christ. How in the hell………." Miles' voice trailed off, too frustrated to continue.

Doug knew that Miles was having a tough time handling this, "Look, I'm heading home. I'll be awake for a while. If you want, stop by."

Miles felt like for the first time, somebody understood. Doug understood that Miles needed somebody to lean on about this.

"Thanks, Doug."

Miles decided to head home and get some sleep. He felt good that Gabby was taking care of things with Jeremy overnight and that he would get over there to check on things in the morning. Miles realized that in order to be good for anybody, he needed to get some rest. When he got home, he took Jeremy's dead phone and plugged it in the charger. He hit the mattress and turned on the tv where he slowly closed his eyes and nodded off.

Gabby was checking on Jeremy throughout the night. One

moment would find him awake watching television and just a short while later he would be snoring. As she occasionally checked on him and took vitals, Gabby would try to gauge Jeremy's anxiety level. It was important that he remain somewhat calm as to not physically harm himself because of his injuries. But his mental state was her biggest concern. As the detox process continued, his body would react in different and sometimes violent ways. He would tremble slightly and at times he would sweat profusely.

Gabby knew the second day would be the toughest psychologically because the amount of time and sheer volume of intoxication was so pervasive. It would be a long hard road to reset Jeremy's brain and to teach it how to think sober.

As the detox process went into the second day, Jeremy appeared to be having conversations with someone in the empty room. These hallucinations included people that he hadn't seen in years. Conversations with his dead grandparents occurred several times and he even saw his favorite childhood pet, a black labrador retriever named Sassy. He helped bury her when he was 11 years old.

As the sweats and trembling subsided, the mind games became more of the issue. It was a challenge for Gabby as she tried to keep Jeremy on an even keel. Not really acknowledging the conversations was a way of trying to keep things calm. As Jeremy spoke with an unnerving clarity with his conjured-up visitors, Gabby would listen and try to gauge the temperament of what was being said. This was in an effort to keep Jeremy from becoming too upset and even needing restraints. She commented to Jeremy at one point that "visiting hours" were over and his subjects would have to come back tomorrow. It was exhausting for Gabby, and Kaitlyn came in a number of times over the two-day period to give her a much-needed reprieve.

As the third day broke, Jeremy had been asleep for nearly ten straight hours. Gabby came into the room around eleven in the morning and used a damp washcloth to wipe Jeremy's forehead. He was still hooked up to several monitors and needed a catheter to expel urine. She checked the condition of his chest tube and checked his vitals.

When Gabby was just about to turn to the door, Jeremy whispered, "Am I dead?"

Gabby could barely hear him, but it was unmistakable. "No, Jeremy. You're not dead. You are very much alive."

His mouth was dry and he still struggled to see out of only one eye, the black patch and bandage covering the other.

Gabby looked at his good eye and asked him several questions. "Do you know where you are?"

"I think I'm at a little hospital," Jeremy was slow to respond.

"Can you tell me what happened to you?"

"I think I hurt my chest. My whole body hurts."

"Jeremy, you've been in a bad accident. You were intoxicated and we've had you here for three days. I have to run a few tests, but I think the alcohol is out of your system. How does your head feel?"

"Confused...My head is confused. I saw a lot of stuff that doesn't make sense. People I haven't seen in years. Things I haven't seen in years."

"We've been trying to dry you out. We need to remove your chest tube. It's going to be painful. Then we need to get you to a bigger hospital and get you sober." Gabby explained. "Do you remember talking to me about that?"

"Yes. I remember. Is your dad around? I'd like to see him."

"Sure Jeremy. I'll give him a call. He wanted to wait until you were ready."

"I was wondering if you could do something for me."

"Sure Jeremy. What is it?"

"I'm really hungry. Can I get something to eat?"

"Yes, Jeremy. We'll get you something to eat." Gabby smiled as this was a good sign.

Jeremy appeared to be more lucid. His reaction to pain was normal and the color of his skin was better. Considering what he had been through, he looked amazing.

Trying to take inventory of the situation, Jeremy was

opening his good eye. His memory was really jumbled and his confusion was heightened by the near completion of detox. The hallucinations of dead relatives and pets had Jeremy bewildered to the point he thought he was dead. How else could he be seeing these people?

At the same time, he came to realize that his head was clear for the first time in a long while. Months even. Probably since he had spent the better part of a week with his parents at their place in Boca Raton. He wasn't able to drink as much there and resumed his binge drinking when he returned to his home in Islamorada.

Gabby called up her dad to let him know that Jeremy was ready for a visitor. She hung up the phone and went back into Jeremy's room to talk with him about his continued treatment. He would need to get up and move around and start using the bathroom on his own. The chest and rib injuries appeared to be on the right path of healing and it was time to remove the chest tube.

Miles arrived about a half hour later. He had worked the previous couple of days to try to reconstruct the events that led to Jeremy's crash in the woods. He absolved the Horschel boys of any wrongdoing as it was Jeremy who had apparently lost control and took off. It was Jeremy's own doing that caused him to nearly lose his life.

As Miles walked into the room, he was amazed at Jeremy's color. He looked much better and Jeremy even let out a smile when he spotted his large college buddy enter the room.

"How's the patient doing?" Miles inquired.

"It was a pretty rough couple of days, but I'm still alive and improving."

"Gabby said your appetite is coming back. That's a good sign."

"Yeah, I haven't really eaten since we had dinner the night of the accident. Just these IV bags to keep me going."

As Miles pulled up a chair, he took off his jacket, reached into a pocket, and pulled out Jeremy's fully charged phone.

"Here ya go. You left this behind at the Horschel house that night. It looks like you have a few messages. I'm guessing you need to make a few calls."

"Thanks." As Jeremy reached for the phone he winced slightly when he put pressure on his damaged right side.

"Gabby said it looks like you can get that tube out today."

"Yeah. It looks like I will have to check into a place to get sober too. As soon as I can though, I'd like to thank that guy for saving my ass out there in that godforsaken blizzard. From what I hear, I'd be long gone without him."

Miles knew the trip to Dutch's cabin would have to wait. He smiled, "That old crusty guy wanted to string you up like a dead deer. I think you better postpone your plans to go and see him."

"Maybe so, but I've got to stop putting things off and start doing things differently. The first thing I want to say is how sorry I am for wrecking your snowmobile. I'm going to try to replace it."

Miles dropped his head and spoke softly, "Let's not worry about that now. I owe you an apology for bringing you up here. I had no idea things could go sideways so quick. I just wanted to bring you up here, see you again, and have some fun reconnecting and reminiscing about our days in Madison. I put you in a bad spot."

"Hey buddy. This was my own fault. I've done a bunch of stupid shit. This time I just happened to do it around you."

"Listen, I've got to run a couple errands and then I will come back and grab a bite with you, ok?"

"Alright. I'm not going anywhere. Besides, I've got a few important and awkward calls to make."

"See you in a little while."

As Miles left the room and walked down the hall, he knew that Jeremy would be leaving soon and Gabby would help with the transfers. "What's his schedule looking like?"

"Well, I'm doing a chest x-ray soon. If things look good, I'm removing his chest tube. Jeremy also needs to get looked at by an eye doctor so we can see if he needs treatment for any cornea damage. We need to discuss with him his rehab treatment and where he wants to do that. Apparently, he's been through the process before and Jeremy might want to go to another place with a different approach given his multiple relapses."

Miles understood that once Jeremy had a plan in place, he'd be leaving soon and Miles wasn't sure if he'd see him anytime soon or, for that matter, ever again. He felt a responsibility to continue what he had restarted as a friendship, but was uncertain about how to do it. Staying in touch with people wasn't something he had a lot of success with.

Jeremy grabbed his phone and looked at his voicemails and text messages. Several were from John and one voice message had come in yesterday from his mom. He decided to call her first and try to explain what had happened. After a half hour of explaining things, Jeremy had to talk her out of coming up to Ontario to get him. He assured her that he was in good hands and that he would maintain better contact with her. After that, he called John up and explained his situation. During that call, he broke down for a moment and realized just how close he came to dying. He ended the call with John after about 15 minutes and then discussed a few things with Gabby.

"After the eye doctor, I need to check in to somewhere for rehab. I have been to a place in Minnesota before, but I'm not sure going back there is the best choice for me."

"Do you have a primary doctor back home?" Gabby inquired. "Maybe he can help you decide."

Jeremy laughed a bit. "My primary doctor is the one that happens to be standing in front of me at any given medical moment. Currently, you're first in the running to be my main doctor."

Gabby sighed, "We don't have to decide this right now. Why don't you talk with some of your family members and then make some decisions? I can get you some info in the meantime."

"Ok Gabby, that sounds like a plan. I do have one thing to talk about with you and your dad. I will need some help with this."

"Sure, Jeremy. Name it."

"I want to go out to the cabin and thank that old guy for saving me. I mean, in person. I can walk to the bathroom in some pain, but I'd need help going out there to see him. You know, the right way."

"I don't think that's such a good idea. First of all, I know Dutch personally and a note to him will suffice. I think he'd appreciate that. Secondly, that would be a bumpy ride out there and you're in no condition to take a trip through the woods. In my opinion, you should put that off for a while."

"Well, maybe you're right." Jeremy conceded.

Jeremy was starting to get a clear head as the alcohol had left his system. His appetite was returning, he could go to the bathroom unassisted, and despite the aches and pains of his ribs and shoulder, he was able to manage an occasional smile. Gabby took Jeremy into another room to get a chest x-ray and look at the damaged lung to see if it had progressed properly. After this, Jeremy was back in his room and Kaitlyn brought in some food for him. The meal was easy to digest, a small protein shake, mashed potatoes, and chicken soup. Just as Kaitlyn left the room, Miles came back in with a paper bag and some sandwiches that he had picked up.

"There he is." Jeremy brightened as Mile stood tall, filling the doorway. "Looks like you robbed a restaurant."

Miles grinned. "I got these from the Cider Barn. I told them these were for you and they didn't charge me. I guess the owner felt guilty because you drank there on the night of the accident."

Gabby entered the room and saw her dad with the sandwiches and put her hands on her hips. "Who are those for?" She had a judgmental tone in her voice.

Miles took on the innocent look of a small child and in jest retorted, "Anybody who attended the University of Wisconsin?"

Gabby let out a small smile and looked at the patient. "Well, Jeremy, I have good news and I have bad news."

"I have had plenty of bad news this week so far. What's the good news?"

"The good news is we can remove your chest tube."

"And?"

"The bad news is those sandwiches will have to wait a day or two until we see how your system handles bland food first. So, eat up your spuds and soup and we'll see how it goes. I'd like to see you have a successful bowel movement before we start dumping all kinds of spicy food into your system."

Miles laughed as he now saw the drastic change. He realized that Jeremy would have to treat his body differently while he recovered. It would not just be what he drank, but what he ate as well.

Jeremy looked inquisitively at Miles. "What's so damn funny about me being stuck on a diet of porridge and gruel?"

Miles chuckled, "It looks like all those days of devouring food at the Red Shed has finally caught up with you. You are now paying for your dietary transgressions."

"Oh my god! I would destroy a Shed burger right now. Or, a gyro from the Parthenon?"

Gabby winced at the thought of a gyro. "Those were so gross! You could smell the spices and garlic coming out of your skin for two days!"

Both Miles and Jeremy looked towards the ceiling with food fantasies from 1980's Madison dancing through their brains. They couldn't help but smile.

"I don't know how you guys ate that stuff. Lay off the sandwiches for today and let's see how this goes. I'll give you some time to rest and I'll be back later to take that tube out."

As Mile dug into the bag and Jeremy picked through the potatoes on his plate, Jeremy stopped and looked at Miles.

"Let me ask you something. You left school so quickly. And now, I know why. But, at no time during those 30 years did you call, reach out, or try to visit any of us from the old house. It was like you disappeared and never wanted to rejoin us. Then, suddenly, you fly down to Florida and scoop me up like we were twenty years old again. Why? What happened? I don't get it."

Miles stopped chewing and listened to Jeremy. He paused, grabbed a napkin as he swallowed, and wiped his mouth. He let out a sigh as he knew at some point, he had to try to explain his actions.

"After I left Madison and returned here, I was terrified. I was just a kid and I didn't know what I was doing. My girlfriend was dead, I was a single dad, and I didn't have any money except what my parents had set aside for my schooling. I had enough to do the four years in Madison and graduate. That was all. My parents saved and worked for every penny. But all of a sudden, it was all about Gabby, and being a good dad. Providing for her future became my main objective. It was my whole life. I had to forget about Madison, school, parties, and you guys. I had to focus all of my attention back home. It scared the shit out of me. I didn't know what I was doing. My parents were a big help. My girlfriend, Julie, her parents didn't like me at all. They resented me for getting her pregnant and then when she died, I think they blamed me for that too, although they never said so. They helped a little bit with Gabby when she was very little, but eventually they retired and moved away. Gabby has had some contact with them over the years, but actually, her only real grandparents were my folks. All of them are gone now. Julie's parents and my folks. School and you guys just seemed so far away and so long ago. The thought of going back just seemed unattainable, so I just blocked it out. After a while, it seemed like that whole year and a half in Madison happened to someone else. Like, I had never even been there."

"Jesus. I guess you were busy back here." marveled Jeremy.

"Yeah. I worked with my dad at first, doing construction and maintenance at the resorts and homes around here, then I got the job with the local police department and worked for the town. My mom helped raise Gabby throughout her school years when I was working. When it came time for Gabby to go to college, all the money that my folks had saved for me had grown enough to help put her through school. She did a wonderful job at Wisconsin as an undergrad and opted for medical school there. That's where she met her husband."

"Didn't you go back even once?" Jeremy couldn't believe what he was hearing.

"I went to Madison one time. It was when Gabby earned her bachelor's degree. I went to the ceremony and I cried like a baby. I thought of her mom, Julie, my parents, all the people that had played a role in her success. Julie's parents didn't go. I was always pissed at them for that. I realized that leaving Madison had left a big hole in me. It was like ripping a big scab off and I bled. When she graduated from medical school, my folks went, and she had her husband there. I didn't need to go through that anguish again. I just wanted to block it out."

"So, after all that, why come and find me? Why now?"

"I don't know. I think it was seeing your goofy face on national tv after you won that tournament. I realized how much fun everybody had at college. All of you guys had gotten under my skin. It took decades to realize that I was lucky to have gone there, even for just a short time. I turned my back on it for too long. I wanted to feel like a kid again. I guess I was just sick of always being the grown up. I got nostalgic. Being an adult and in charge of everything is a pain in the ass."

Jeremy smiled, "I can see that here. Everybody looks at you like you're their dad or big brother. Who do you hang out with?"

"I go fishing with Robby as much as I can."

"That's grandpa stuff. I mean your friends. Or a woman. Didn't you spend time with anybody after Julie?"

"Well, that's a long story. There was a woman I met when Gabby was just finishing high school. She was from Winnipeg. She didn't like it here and wanted me to move. I thought she was great and all, but I couldn't leave Minaki. I was responsible for too much here."

"So, what you're saying is that you decided to just live here and work?"

"No. I guess I figured that things would be fine eventually. I'd be able to work less and spend time with Gabby and Robby. Eventually everything would be fine," Miles explained.

"But, you have found, eventually hasn't really happened?" questioned Jeremy.

"No. I guess not."

"So, kidnapping me seemed like your only option? Sort of a way to relive your youth and glory days if you will?"

Miles grinned again, "Yep."

"Since we've reconnected, I'd really like to see you man. Are you going to come down to see me in Florida?"

"If I can."

"Dude. You gotta get out of here away from the sticks. This place is great for a while, but there is a whole other world out there and you need to see it."

"Yeah, but my daughter is here. My family, nieces, nephews, they all live here. My job is here."

"Listen. I know that my life is clearly not a blueprint for success, but you seem to have taken this responsibility thing too far and it will kill you faster than my drinking could kill me. They say that one day you'll wake up and you're fifty. Well Miles, fifty already happened a few years ago and you didn't seem to notice."

"Alright Jeremy. If I promise to come down to your place for a visit, will you let me up for some air on this?"

"Yeah, yeah. But I'm going to hold you to it. Besides, I'm good for you."

"You are? How's that?"

"I got you to fly to Florida to play a prank on me. If I were to actually provoke you into some real fun, there's no telling what we could accomplish…..sober of course."

"Of course," Miles shook his head with a smile.

Gabby reentered the room and delivered some welcome news.

"You've got a big day ahead of you Jeremy. The eye doctor is going to be here in half an hour to check you out and after that in a couple hours, we'll pull your chest tube."

Jeremy smiled. "That's great news. Is it going to hurt?"

"Yeah, some, but it will pale in comparison to your fractured ribs. How did your food go down?" Gabby inquired.

"It tasted good. I haven't been this hungry in a while."

"It figures. Based on your bloodwork, you were slightly malnourished when you came in. Your drinking and lack of food was causing all kinds of problems with your systems. Honestly, given your trauma, I'm surprised you were able to survive the accident."

"Well, it looks like I'm probably ready to make plans for my rehab."

"Yes. I found a couple of places. One is in Indiana, and the other is in Georgia. I talked to their intake people about your case and they are both prepared to help. They have outstanding reputations. Their staff and facilities are first-rate. I think it comes down to a choice of geography."

"Thanks. I guess I would lean towards Georgia because that's closer to my folks and home. I'll talk to my parents about it later today and then we can make more definite plans."

Miles and Jeremy talked for a little while longer. Soon, the eye doctor came in and carefully removed the patch and gauze that protected Jeremy's damaged eye. There was a big shiner below the eye and at first, it was difficult to open. Finally, the doctor managed to check things out and do some reactive tests to the pupil. He seemed surprised.

"The optic nerve seems intact. There is a significant abrasion on the cornea, but given the nature of the injury, I think it's remarkable?"

"English Doc. How is the eye?"

"What can you see?"

"It's blurry, but I think it still works."

"It will take some time, but in a few weeks, your vision should be back to normal. You'll have drops to use several times a day, but in time, it should heal. Just don't do a lot of physical things for a bit. You don't want that eye to slip out again. Even a hard sneeze could cause a problem."

Not long after, Gabby came in with a tray of bandages and tape. She gloved up and prepared Jeremy for the removal of his chest tube.

"Hold your air firm in your lungs Jeremy. Nothing in or out while I do this. Don't move until I tell you." Gabby instructed.

Jeremy nodded. As he lay still, Gabby had prepared four-by-four bandages with tape and ointment to seal the hole. With one motion, she slowly, but smoothly pulled the tube from his side and then strategically placed the bandage over the small hole. She pressed the tape firmly down. Jeremy let out a muffled shriek as she had to apply slight pressure to a damaged rib on that side, but he held the breath firmly in his chest.

"Ok, Jeremy. You can breathe now."

Jeremy turned toward Gabby. His red eyes had tears running down as the pain flowed from his body out the top of his head. He tried to control his breathing, but it was tough.

"Oh……oh…………….oh……………..oh." Jeremy wiped the tears from his eyes as he fought to regain his composure.

"I need to add a bit more tape to the dressing. Can you handle it?"

"Give me just a minute. I…………I………. wasn't ready for that. Just a minute."

Gabby finished the dressing and then began updating Jeremy's chart.

As Jeremy settled down and started breathing easier, he started the giggle a bit. Real quiet at first and then progressively louder until his laugh was unmistakeable.

"What's so funny?" Gabby smiled.

"How the hell am I going to tell this story? I mean kidnapped, drunk, basically dead in the woods and then brought back to life by my college buddy's daughter." He chuckled. "Who's going to believe this whopper?"

"Well, honestly. There wouldn't have been much to work with if it wasn't for Dutch. He's the one who actually saved you. If he hadn't been in the picture, you wouldn't be here."

"I really don't remember much about Dutch. I was so messed up between the drinks and the accident. I remember laying by a fireplace and there being a brown dog. Beyond that, I don't recall much else."

"He found you in the woods, brought you back to the cabin, called us, put in your chest tube, and cleaned you up. He did all the complicated stuff." explained Gabby.

"Who is this guy? Some kind of superman?"

"He's a trapper, and a retired US Army vet. He was a combat medic in Vietnam. About as crusty as they come. He's like family to me. He was my grandpa's best friend."

"Wow. He must be kind of old if he was in Vietnam. And he did everything during a blizzard." Jeremy shook his head in amazement.

"I don't know how old he is. He must be in his 70's, for sure. You'd never know it by talking to him. He still thinks he's twenty-five."

"When do you think I'll be ready to head out?" Jeremy asked.

"In a day or two. There is no rush with your busted tooth. I talked to a dentist by phone and that can be handled whenever it's convenient. The main thing is getting your rehab spot set up in Georgia. Dad will coordinate and fly you to Winnipeg or Minneapolis to connect. Do you want someone to travel along with you?"

"Gee. I never even considered that."

"It wouldn't be a bad idea. They could check you in and make sure you make your connecting flights and all. Dad could probably do that."

"Actually, I think my fishing buddy in Florida might be the right man for the job. He's a super guy. I talked to him on the phone yesterday and he was kind of freaked out when I told him what had happened. I can buy him a ticket and have him fly into Minneapolis so we can travel together."

"What's his name?"

"John Price. He's a charter captain and one of my closest friends. He sounded relieved that I was going to rehab."

"That's good. We want people who are a positive influence with you now. I'll let dad know we should start making some travel plans for you."

Gabby felt a sense of relief that Jeremy's strength was gaining and that his focus was on getting sober. His brush with death scared him and she was relieved that things seemed to be headed in the right direction now.

CHAPTER TWENTY-TWO

Gabby called her dad and began figuring out the logistics of Jeremy's journey. It proved to be quite a process. She wanted Miles to hand Jeremy off to John at the airport, and to make sure Jeremy had a constant traveling companion the whole way to the rehab center in Georgia. There would be the rendezvous in Minneapolis and then Miles would turn around and fly home. It looked as though it would take a couple of days before Jeremy was stable and could travel safely. Gabby had to contact the rehab center to make sure they knew Jeremy's current medical condition and the limitations he would have while recovering from his injuries.

Later that afternoon, Jeremy and Miles were sharing a snack in Jeremy's room. By now, Jeremy was sitting in a chair next to his bed and wearing scrubs instead of the hospital gown with the ties and the open back. Kaitlyn was around to help, and Gabby had gone to Robby's hockey practice. As the two sat with the tv on, Jeremy turned to Miles.

"I need your help with something."

"Sure. Anything for you, Jeremy."

"I need you to help me go see that old guy who saved my life. I want to thank him in person."

Miles sat back in his chair and sighed. He knew it wasn't a good idea for a couple of reasons. First, Miles knew Dutch would never want to see Jeremy again. Second, it would be a rough ride by snow machine for a guy with broken ribs. So much of the snow had melted in the last week since the storm and there were spots of bare ground starting to show. Spring made travel harder in some cases and going by four-wheeler or ATV did not seem like viable options. Overall, Miles just didn't want to do it. What would Gabby say?

Jeremy could see the reluctance in Miles's face, "What's up? Why not?"

"You don't have to do any of that now. It would be a rough ride and the timing just isn't right. Dutch is a bit of a hermit and doesn't welcome visitors. I don't think it would be a good decision. When you've healed a bit and come back for a visit, you might be able to thank Dutch then."

"I know I could put it off, but I really want to do it before I leave for rehab. I owe this guy my life. I just want to start doing things the right way and I know this is the right thing to do. I need to make amends. Isn't there something in the twelve steps about making amends?"

"Jeremy. I know this guy and I'm telling you that you should wait," Miles answered, a bit more emphatic.

"Miles, please. Just do this favor for me."

Jeremy and Miles stared at each other for at least 10 seconds with neither of them blinking. Finally, realizing that Jeremy was trying to do the right thing, Miles relented.

"Ok. As soon as Gabby says you are strong enough to leave here, I'll run you up to Dutch's place. For a ten minute stop. That's all. I need to take some batteries up there anyway. I'll do it sooner than I'd planned so you can come with."

"Good. Then it's planned. After we get back, we can fly out and I can hook up with John in Minneapolis for the trip south."

"Ok, Jeremy. We'll do that."

Miles slowly began to see the logic of Jeremy's idea, but still didn't like the idea of hauling his friend all the way out in the sticks. Gabby would definitely not approve and it would be risky just getting Jeremy out there, bouncing around with a bad eye, broken ribs and a long alcohol rehab stint hanging over him like a big dark cloud. An unscheduled trip out to Dutch's place was not definitely what Gabby had in mind for Jeremy's recovery. Despite this, Miles understood Jeremy's position. He would follow through with his friend's wish.

After eating, Jeremy had some time to make a few phone calls and get his plans in order. He called John in Florida first to let him know about the rehab center in Georgia. John agreed to meet him in Minneapolis in a couple of days. Jeremy volunteered to pay him for the days he would miss on the water, but John declined.

"You can pick up the cost of my plane ticket buddy, but the rest is what I would do for you anyway."

This made Jeremy realize even moreso what a good friend John was. He wasn't just a meal ticket to John. He was John's friend. The clarity of sobriety gave this realization more weight. He got a taste of a feeling he hadn't had in a while, the feeling of being thankful.

Jeremy awoke the next morning to the smiling face of Gabby as she was filling out some information on his patient chart. It was the best sleep he had since he'd arrived at the clinic. The chest tube had been very uncomfortable and no longer having it meant he had slightly better angles to lie in bed at night. His ribs still ached, but it was a dull pain and not the searing feeling he experienced when he first arrived. It had been a week in total since the accident, and his head was clearing up a little more each day. His sense of smell was better. Food had more taste, and even his hearing had improved, or so it seemed.

"How would you like to get outside and see some sun today? It's really nice outside," Gabby urged.

"Sounds good. Are you kicking me out?"

"I am seriously considering it. Your numbers look good but, I want to check your chest and hear your breath sounds. We want to make sure your breathing is good before you exert yourself in any way. That lung has been through some serious trauma."

"I'll be careful." Jeremy promised.

"Dad is coming over in a little while. He is going to want to coordinate the flights so you and John can connect in Minneapolis for your trip to Georgia. If all goes well today, you can leave tomorrow."

Gabby left Jeremy's room and he looked around. He only had the medical scrubs he was wearing, his wallet, and his iPhone. He had no regular clothes to wear since Dutch needed to cut them off his body at the cabin.

Jeremy picked up his phone and dialed up his parents in Florida.

"Hi Mom. I just wanted to let you know that it looks like I'm getting out today. I will leave here tomorrow and be in Georgia by tomorrow night for my rehab stint."

"Your father and I were hoping you could do your rehab closer to us. We'd like to see you."

"I don't think I'll be able to have any visitors for a while. That's how it works to start with anyway. I will be able to write you. That I do know."

Jeremy explained some of the medical issues and briefly Jeremy's dad got on the phone and spoke to him.

"We need you to get well Jeremy. Do whatever you have to do to get through this."

"I will, Dad. I love you."

"Same here."

After using his phone to book a plane ticket in John's name, he called John and gave him the flight info. Key West to Minneapolis followed by two tickets from Minneapolis to Atlanta. Then, one ticket from Atlanta back to Key West for John to get home.

After Jeremy finished the flight details, Miles strolled in with a plastic bag containing blue jeans, shoes, a t-shirt, and a Cider Barn hoodie.

"Your new wardrobe is here." Miles was in a good mood. When Jeremy arrived here a week before, it was hard to imagine this moment.

"Get dressed. Then, let's check with the clinic warden to see if you can get paroled."

Jeremy was pleased to have regular clothes again. As he lifted his arms to take off the medical scrubs, he winced in pain as his damaged side barked at him. It was a pain that went deep into his chest. He realized his movements needed to be slower and more deliberate. Jeremy felt tears begin to well in his eyes from the pain, but he managed to hold it together. As he gingerly slipped on the new shirt that Miles brought, he leaned slightly to guard his damaged right side.

A smaller dressing covered the healing hole in his side from the tube. It needed to stay in place for a time. It would be a couple weeks before the hole would completely heal. Wound care was part of his new existence.

Jeremy had a few documents to sign for Gabby. Since he was the only patient for the time being at the clinic, and he would be checking out shortly, Gabby could close the doors and take a little time off.

For lunch, the threesome decided to go to Miles' house. He had a big pot of chili going on the stove. It was a sunny day with a slight south breeze. It was almost sixty degrees, a veritable heat wave for Ontario in March. Perhaps spring was on its way after all.

Jeremy felt ok riding in the front seat of Miles' truck. The few bumps in the road were a little uncomfortable, but Jeremy knew it would be some time before he knew what he should feel like. Jeremy exited the truck in Miles' driveway and walked cautiously up the stairs to the door. All of a sudden, he felt tired. Not out of breath, but sleepy. His eyelids grew heavy.

Gabby and Jeremy sat at the kitchen table where Miles set a hot bowl of chili in front of each of them. There was a heaping pile of bread and crackers along with onions, sour cream, and shredded cheese.

"Dig in everybody." Miles grabbed a bowl for himself and sat with them.

"I sure wish I would have had enough brains to just come back here after we had dinner that night."

Miles grinned as he looked at Jeremy across the table. "Next time, you'll know better."

After the three finished eating and chatted good naturedly at the table, Jeremy felt even more tired. Gabby could tell that he needed some rest.

"I'm going over to the arena for a bit before the boys start practice. Let me know if you need anything."

Gabby went over to her dad, speaking quietly out of earshot.

"Let Jeremy get a nap. Healing takes a toll on your stamina. Needing rest is a good sign."

"Ok. I'll let him get some rest."

"Dad, is there any alcohol in the house?"

"Yes. There's some wine in the cabinet next to the pantry."

"Let me take it. No sense tempting fate this close to Jeremy's departure."

"Ok. Grab it on your way out."

Jeremy retreated into the living room and laid down on the couch. He closed his eyes and almost immediately fell asleep.

It was a little after three o'clock when Jeremy opened his eyes. He had been asleep for about an hour and a half when he rose slowly and deliberately off the couch while protecting his damaged side. He shuffled out to the kitchen where Miles sat at the table, writing out a few checks and paying some bills. He looked up over his reading glasses when Jeremy entered.

"Hey, sleepy head. How was your nap?"

"Wow. I was wacked out. I haven't been this tired in a long time."

"Yeah. Your body is playing catch up. It's going to be like that for a while. According to my daughter, you are going to need your rest to heal properly."

"Hey, if we are leaving tomorrow, when are we going to be able to go up to that old guy's cabin? I still want to talk to him before I leave."

Miles let out a deep sigh and responded slowly. Choosing his words cautiously, Miles looked at Jeremy and said, "I was hoping you had forgotten about that. I still think it's not a good idea."

"But, you said you'd help me."

Miles looked at the clock, and against his better judgement told Jeremy, "In two and a half hours it's going to be dark. If we leave now, we can be up there in a half hour, forty minutes tops. But, we gotta go now. You up for that?"

"Yeah. Let's go."

With that, Miles grabbed his coat and hat, he reached into the closet and grabbed a coat and hat for Jeremy.

"Here. Put this on. It will be cold by the time we get back."

CHAPTER TWENTY-THREE

The two men left in Miles' truck and headed to the shop. There was an ATV inside the garage. It had a large cargo tray on the back. Miles quickly loaded up the three large 12-volt batteries he was supposed to bring Dutch, and strapped them on with bungee cords.

"Come on. You ride behind me."

Jeremy looked at the machine and knew the step up and onto the seat was a bit much for him in his weakened condition. His hip was still sore and it hurt like hell to lift it or put any weight on it.

"Can you help?" Jeremy asked, feeling somewhat defeated but still determined.

"Jesus Christ, Jeremy. If you can't even get on an ATV, maybe you shouldn't go into the woods for 10 miles."

"Dammit Miles! Help me!" Jeremy's anger and frustration were showing through. He was in pain, but insistent about seeing the old man at the cabin.

Miles muttered under his breath but grabbed a small footstool next to the work bench. Jeremy was able to step on a rung and then reach his right foot to the machine before swinging his stronger left leg over the seat. Between the pain of the movement, and the exertion since they left the house, several beads of perspiration had formed on Jeremy's brow and upper lip.

"Get me up there before I chicken out," he grumbled.

Miles strapped an extra gas can on the back and fired up the engine. The sun was casting late afternoon shadows and there was a lot of mud forming on the road as the warm afternoon sun cooked away the remnants of the blizzard. Miles and Jeremy traveled past the Horschel house and down the very road that Jeremy had followed that fateful night during the storm. As they entered the woods, the motion and bouncing of the vehicle made Jeremy uncomfortable. As they traversed the woods, Miles would anticipate the larger bumps and slow down while Jeremy tried not to wince in pain. The melting snow revealed some bare spots in the woods on the trail. Water flew to the sides as the tires splashed through the muddy areas.

After about fifteen minutes, the two men came to a long straight patch of road. It was still covered in snow, but was nonetheless hard packed and smooth. Next, the ATV came to the edge of a frozen lake where giant pools of standing water could be seen. Miles went slower as to not get the both of them totally soaked from all the water. The engine was noisy and they spoke little. Jeremy didn't have the lung capacity to do a lot of yelling anyway.

After they got to the other side of the lake, they could see a beaten trail that led up a hill. In the distance, a small bit of smoke could be seen rising up from the trees. Miles stopped the engine and got off the machine. Jeremy stayed on the seat as it was difficult for him to move and he had found a somewhat tolerable position. Miles faced away from Jeremy and stood up near a tree. He unzipped his pants and began to urinate. He turned his head slightly over his shoulder and began to speak.

"Jeremy, when we get to Dutch's place, I want you to stay on the machine while I go inside. He's not used to visitors. When I think the time is right, I'll bring him out so you can talk to him."

Miles shook once and zipped up his pants. He turned towards Jeremy.

"You understand?"

"Yeah, I get it. Is he some kind of hermit or something?"

"I suppose……well, he…….yeah. Something like that. "

Miles jumped back onto the ATV and continued up the bumpy trail and soon the log cabin was in sight. Miles parked about 30 feet from the door. A brown dog came around the corner of an adjacent shed wagging its tail.

"Hey Jake! Come here boy!" Miles rubbed the dog's neck as the large animal pushed against Miles' long legs. "This thing is a big baby."

Miles turned to Jeremy. "Just wait here. I'll be back in a few minutes."

Jeremy nodded as the dog walked over and put his front legs in Jeremy's lap as he stayed seated atop the ATV. The dog wagged his tail as Jeremy carefully pet the large hound on top of the head. Jake licked Jeremy's face appreciatively.

Miles entered the dark cabin and saw Dutch over by the kitchen counter cutting up some onions as the smell of venison stew overtook his senses. There was a large pot was bubbling on the stove. Dutch was making a sizeable feast.

"Boy that smells good," Miles said as his mouth watered.

"I heard ya pull up. If you stick around for a while, you can help me sample this batch."

"I don't think I can stay long. I've got to get back. But I did bring you those batteries you needed."

"Good. I was hoping you had them with you."

Miles hesitated, "Oh, and there's one other thing."

"Yeah, what's that?" Dutch continued to cut on the counter without looking.

"You up to seeing a visitor?" Miles inquired cautiously.

Dutch stopped cutting and turned towards Miles with an inquisitive look. Without saying a word and with the knife still in his hands, he walked towards the door and stood in the opening. Astonished, he saw Jeremy petting Jake as he sat on the rear of the ATV.

CHAPTER TWENTY-FOUR

"What the hell are you doing here?" Dutch barked at Jeremy.

Jake jumped down and got low to the ground at the terse tone in Dutch's voice. Jeremy's eyes grew wide as he saw the old man standing in the doorway with a large knife in his hand. Dutch stepped forward with a confused look on his face. Miles quickly exited the cabin and got past Dutch so he could take a position between the two men. Dutch turned towards Miles.

In an angry tone, Dutch asked, "What is he doing here?"

"He's leaving tomorrow and he wanted to talk to you before he left."

Dutch turned back towards Jeremy and shouted.

"You're an asshole. You know that?"

Jeremy slumped and stared down at the ground.

Miles tried to diffuse the situation as Dutch was visibly agitated. "Please Dutch. He appreciates what you did."

"Oh. Really?" Dutch stuck his knife in a wooden fence post next to him, causing Miles to let out a sigh of relief.

Jeremy lifted his head and looked at Dutch. "I want to thank you for saving my life."

Dutch looked at Jeremy with a glare of contempt. "You're welcome. Now take off."

Jeremy, confused by Dutch's response, looked to Miles for some guidance, but even Miles didn't know what to say.

"ON SECOND THOUGHT, NO! WAIT A MINUTE! DON'T GO!" Dutch raised his voice and quickly stormed back around the back of his shed to a large garbage can. He hoisted the heavy lid, dug around with a stick, and lifted out a pair of heavily stained and ragged blue jeans. He carried them with the large stick and came back around the building towards Miles and Jeremy. The two men were dumbfounded and confused as the irate old man returned carrying a stick with what appeared to be blue jeans hanging off of it. He flung the jeans on the ground in front of the ATV's tires.

"I meant to send these back with you the other day when you left, but I just plum forgot. These are the shit-stained blues jeans I had to cut off your body when I found your sorry ass hanging in that tree."

Jeremy, totally confused blurted out, "Wait, shit stained?"

Miles eyes got wide as he looked at the disgusting mess on the ground.

Dutch sort of shook his head as he continued his tirade, "Yeah, there was quite a bit of shit there. There is some blood mixed in as well, but that turns sort of brown when it dries, so it's easy to confuse the two after the dust settles a bit. Anyway, your pants were stinking up my property, so I'm glad you came by to pick them up."

The two men stared at Dutch, their eyes and mouths wide open. There were no words.

Dutch continued on, "Yeah. It's amazing how much shit comes out of a person during an accident. One minute you're blissfully intoxicated and sailing along. The next minute, you're half dead and your bowels let loose. Suddenly, there you are, ready to meet your maker and to your embarrassment, your pants are full."

The three men sat silent. Dutch paused for a moment, glared one more time at Jeremy, then turned around, marched back into the cabin and slammed the door. Miles walked around, found the stick and picked up the jeans with it. He took them around back to the garbage can.

For a moment, Jeremy sat on the ATV stunned and then mumbled slightly, "I didn't know I shit my pants. Nobody told me that."

Jeremy waited for a moment, then winced as he raised his leg to get off the ATV. He maneuvered slowly to avoid any sudden movements. He was able to dismount and get both feet planted on the ground. Just then, Miles returned and saw Jeremy.

"Let's just go. I'll talk to him later for you," Miles offered.

"We can go in a minute. I just have to tell him something."

Miles, exasperated, stared up at the sky and shook his head. He knew bringing Jeremy here was a mistake, although he did not anticipate the blowback that occurred.

Jeremy slowly strolled over to the door and knocked gently.

Dutch's raspy voice barked from the other side, "Now what!?!"

Forlorn and pitiful, Jeremy timidly entered the room. His eyes had trouble adjusting to the darkness. When he could see, his eyes landed on Dutch, who had his arms folded across his chest and was leaning against the cabinet by the stove.

"I know you're upset with me and I think I understand a little bit why. I know it doesn't mean much to you, but I am so very sorry for disappointing everyone and I want to thank you for helping me, for saving my life."

Unimpressed, Dutch looked at Jeremy with a judgmental glare before asking, "Did Gabby get you dried out?"

"Yeah. It took a little over four days."

"I'll bet that was fun."

"Oh yeah. It was little slice of hell."

"You know you shouldn't be here right now. How long have you had your chest tube out?"

"Gabby pulled it yesterday."

"Where exactly does she think you are right now?"

Jeremy sighed because he would be admitting to more lies. He hated admitting to lies. Lies were something he was a little too good at. Lies kept things on an even keel. By lying, he could avoid disappointing people and making them upset, or so he thought.

"She thinks I'm resting at Miles' house." Jeremy reluctantly admitted.

"So, Miles is in on your bullshit too."

"Yeah. I'm afraid he's in on it too."

"Well, he's a great human being. He'll do anything for anyone, and then some. Only trouble is, a guy like you brings a guy like Miles down. He can't make up for the trouble you've caused. The shitty kids always bring down a classroom. More than the good kids can elevate it. One bad apple spoils the bunch."

Jeremy was visibly frustrated. He just wanted to show his

appreciation and he was getting a lecture instead. He was tired, sore, and in no mood to get bitched at. He was trying to do the right thing.

"Look dammit. I'm trying make amends. To own up to my mistakes. Starting now!"

Dutch headed towards the door and grabbed his coat.

"C'mon Dumbass. Let's go."

Miles had been eavesdropping and stepped away from the door as Dutch quickly shot past him outside. Jeremy followed with a confused look.

Dutch mounted the ATV and started it up.

"Miles, Dumbass and I have to go for a short ride. We'll be back in a little while."

Jeremy's eyes got big as he looked questioningly at Miles and then back at Dutch. He then reluctantly hobbled towards the four-wheeler and attempted to step up and onto it. Dutch could see Jeremy struggling and then hopped off the ATV. Next, Jeremy tried to step up, but couldn't get his leg high enough. Miles decided to get involved and reached for a big chunk of wood that was lying next to the shed. He brought it over so Jeremy could use it as a step to get a little higher. Dutch looked down and shook his head as he saw how weak Jeremy was when he was finally seated.

"Great idea bringing the cripple out here, Miles. Both of you should have your heads examined."

Miles had the look of a small admonished child as Dutch then easily slid onto the seat and revved the engine.

"Don't worry Miles. I won't kill him. Not just yet anyway."

Dutch and Jeremy sped off as Miles nervously stood by the cabin with no idea what was going on. As Dutch drove the ATV he carefully navigated around trees and onto level spots, Jeremy's mind was racing. Where was Dutch taking him? What was the reason for this? Why hadn't he listened to Miles? They traveled about a quarter mile when suddenly, Dutch rolled to a stop and cut the engine. Quickly, Dutch got off the machine and started walking at a brisk pace up a slight incline and into a group of trees.

Dutch glanced back at Jeremy, still seated, "Are you coming?"

Jeremy did his best to swing his leg over and slide slowly and carefully off the machine. Dutch had disappeared into the woods in the meantime and Jeremy tried to follow his path around the thick trees. After walking about fifty feet, Jeremy was completely lost. He looked around and couldn't see Dutch anywhere.

Suddenly, Dutch let out a yell, "Over here!"

Out of breath, Jeremy walked even more slowly towards Dutch's voice.

"This way!"

Just then, Jeremy followed the voice and could see Dutch standing by a line of trees. Dutch was strolling around and looking at the ground, walking back and forth. Jeremy then realized. This is where it happened. The accident that would have taken his life had it not been for Dutch. A cold chill went through him as he grasped the enormity of it. He had nearly died here.

As Jeremy caught his breath, Dutch looked up in the tree. Jeremy gazed up as well. Neither spoke at first.

The late afternoon shadows had made the woods darker and more foreboding. The sky was still clear, but the lack of sun made the charred remains of the tree an eerie midnight blue where the SRX had slammed into it. Bare wood was exposed from the bark being ferociously torn off in the violence of the collision. As Jeremy looked down, he could see all the different colors of fiberglass and plastic pieces from the shattered hood. Bent metal was sticking out of the partially melted snow. It was hard to comprehend that the rubble was a snowmobile at one time. It was a collection of blackened junk at the base of a barbequed tree.

Dutch looked at Jeremy, "This is not your tree. Yours is over here."

Jeremy snapped out of his trance and followed Dutch over to

an exposed stump. It had a freshly torn chunk of wood taken out of it on the left side. Dutch walked Jeremy slowly over to the stump.

"See here. This here stump set everything in motion. You hit the left side of this stump slightly. That sent the whole shit airborne and to the left. But you were lucky."

Dutch paused before continuing in a sarcastic tone. "If you had hit this thing straight on dead center, the sled would have crumpled and your chest and rib cage would have been opened up on the handlebars. Your guts would have been splattered out all over the snow. Death would've taken only a few seconds. If you hit the stump's right side, you might have done the same thing, but you could have gone airborne and rolled with the sled landing on you and killing you. Or, you might have been thrown free and landed in the powder without a scratch. Then you would have wandered off in your drunken state and died of hypothermia. But you hit the left side and I guess we'll never know."

Dutch walked ahead and stood next to another pine tree with several broken branches.

"See, now this one here, this is your tree. The branches look busted off about 10 feet up. You hit the trunk with your head and chest, but I think the branches must have slowed you down. Then, you fell through to these other branches about six feet to this spot here." Dutch showed a slight opening in the branches about 4 feet off the ground.

"Right here is where you and I met. You were caught up in the pine boughs, bloody and unconscious, facing the ground with your eyeball hanging out of your skull."

Jeremy paused and sat down. The gravity of what had happened seemed to overwhelm him for a moment.

Silent and bewildered Jeremy said, "I don't remember a single thing. Just nothing."

Next Jeremy sat on the ground humiliated with his elbows resting on his knees. His head was down.

Jeremy then looked up at Dutch. "I sure wish that that stump wasn't there."

Dutch chuckled. "Hey, that stump probably saved your sorry ass."

"What are you talking about?" Jeremy was totally confused.

"If you would have continued, you would have been further from my cabin and let me tell you something sweetie, there is nothing out there but more snow and an assortment of wild animals. For one hundred goddamn miles. You would have hit something else, run out of gas, or just passed out cold. You. Dressed like a stupid child. In a blizzard. Drunk!"

Jeremy's head was down again. He knew he had this coming.

"I hate the fact you brought me here. But I think I needed to see it." Jeremy admitted.

"You're damn right you needed to see it." Dutch sat next to him staring straight ahead.

"If I don't get up to take a piss right then, I wouldn't have heard the machine and more importantly, heard the crash."

"What would have happened then? If you didn't hear it?"

"Hmm. Well, you would have died here for sure. Most likely, the cold would've gotten you first, but your lung and chest injuries would have caused too much stress on your heart and cardiac arrest would have resulted. It might have taken twenty minutes or two hours. Hard to say."

"I can't ever drink again for as long as I live." Jeremy commented in a flat tone.

"No, at least you shouldn't." Dutch paused for a bit, letting things sink in. "You know what pissed me off so much is that people so close to me care deeply about you. I mean, they got up in the middle of the night in a blizzard, risking their own safety to save your pathetic ass. Doug and Gabby both risked their lives to save you."

Jeremy was sitting silent, not sure of what to do or say next.

Dutch looked at Jeremy sitting overwhelmed on the ground, "What's next for you?"

"I leave tomorrow. Heading to a rehab place in Georgia."

"Oh yeah? Been down that road before, have you?"

"Yes, can't you tell? I'm one of their biggest success stories."

"Well, next week when you're sitting in one of your air-conditioned meeting rooms in a bath robe talking about your traumatic childhood, I want you to remember this spot. And, remember the fact that you're goddamn lucky five different animals aren't digesting and shitting out parts of you in these woods."

"AHHHH, DAMMIT! There was nothing wrong with my childhood!" Jeremy screamed out.

Dutch got calm as Jeremy lost his cool.

"You mean, everything was perfect? Your daddy didn't beat you as a child? Your mother didn't abandon you?" Dutch was intentionally provoking Jeremy.

"NO! My parents loved me and still do!" Jeremy was nearly raging.

"Oh, your dad is still alive?" Dutch asked softly.

"YES! YES! My dad is still alive!"

"Is he a good man?" Dutch goaded.

"Yes……. He is a good man."

"Well, I guarantee that he thinks you're an asshole."

"AAAAAAHHH! FUCK YOU, DUTCH!" Jeremy screamed as loud as he could, then got to his feet and faced away from Dutch.

Dutch began laughing at Jeremy's rage. He wanted to break Jeremy. He wanted to force Jeremy to face the truth and acknowledge what he had become. Jeremy was an accident waiting to happen, and his death could have happened right here. Dutch felt a sense of validation when Jeremy cursed at him. Dutch needed to rip away Jeremy's false bravado. Jeremy needed to hear that he was a failure. He needed to hear the raw truth and Dutch was more than willing to serve it up.

"Your biggest problem is that you still think you know what's best for you. Guess what? The truth is, you don't. You don't belong here right now. Somehow you convinced Miles to drag you up here, hoping to thank me and feel better about yourself. You're half busted up from the crash. You can't get out of your own damn way."

Dutch and Jeremy sat silent for a short time. It was an uncomfortable silence. Jeremy then spoke quietly.

"What's going to happen to me?" He asked, fighting back the tears filling his eyes.

"Well, if you pay attention and do all the right things, you have a fifty-fifty chance of surviving. If not, you'll be dead within a year."

"You sound like an expert on the subject."

"I stayed sober today. That's how much of an expert I am."

"When is the last time you drank?"

"December 24, 1983."

"You remember the date?"

"Yep. It was a Christmas present to my son."

"How did you do it? I mean, did you get help?"

"I stopped drinking for a while, but I was just dry. I didn't really get sober until I had a sponsor and went to meetings. That's when I became ready to listen to others and take advice."

Dutch looked at Jeremy and said in a somber tone, "You're a long way from that point. A long way."

"Listen, I'll do anything to beat this."

"Shit, you should hear yourself. You'd say anything to get your way."

Jeremy felt a scared rage building within him. Seeing the accident scene brought on a wave of anxiety and heat traveled through his whole body. It was like a fever that began in his legs and extended slowly to his neck.

Suddenly in a calm and manner of fact voice, Jeremy turned back towards Dutch. "I know. Keep me here."

Dutch heard Jeremy but it didn't register. "What did you say?"

"Keep me here. At your cabin. Teach me how to listen. Keep me from killing myself."

Dutch started chuckling. Trying to process such a ridiculous request. How did this guy become his responsibility?

"I am not in the sobriety business. And, I am NOT looking for a roommate."

"Ok, hardass, thanks for hauling me out of the woods

and then telling me how I'm going to fail and probably die. Appreciate it."

"I built this cabin out here to avoid assholes and somehow you still managed to find me!"

Dutch was losing his cool and his agitation level was rising. Meanwhile Jeremy was a sweaty mess. He spun around and stared at Dutch screaming at the top of his lungs, "I DON'T WANT TO DIE!!"

Dutch surged at Jeremy, grabbed his jacket, and pressed his face up to Jeremy's. Their noses were almost touching. Their eyes met. The veins in Dutch's forehead stood out. His face was beet red. He barked back at Jeremy, "THAT'S NOT GOOD ENOUGH!!"

Dutch's physical strength was surprising. He seemingly lifted Jeremy off the ground by his jacket collar. He continued tearing into him with a sharp and taunting tone.

"Why don't you want to die Jeremy? Are you afraid you're going to miss something? Are you afraid of what's next? What if there is no next? Ever think about that?"

Jeremy's eyes were red. He was broken. The tears he had managed to fight back earlier began to fall. His posture sagged and a feeling of defeat seemed to overtake him. He barely had the strength to speak, but had enough air in his lungs to mutter quietly, "I just want to live."

Jeremy tried to hold it in as best he could, but he began to sob uncontrollably.

Dutch was shocked by what he heard. His head recoiled. He instantly loosened his grip on the collar of Jeremy's jacket. His eyes widened. He took his hands and smoothed out the wrinkles in Jeremy's jacket. He then turned and gently slapped Jeremy on the back of the shoulder.

"C'mon. Let's head back to the cabin."

Together, they walked back to the ATV without a sound. As they walked, Jeremy slowly regained composure. As they arrived at the machine, Dutch found a piece of wood that he set on the ground alongside the machine so Jeremy would be able to step up and get his leg swung around on the seat. Dutch quietly started the machine and slowly started the trip back to the cabin.

Miles was outside petting Jake when he heard the ATV approaching the cabin. Dutch and Jeremy had been gone about twenty minutes and Miles was in a bit of a hurry to get back to Minaki. He didn't want to be out on the trail after the sun went down. The temperature was dropping and they would soon run out of daylight.

Jake saw Dutch and Jeremy approaching and wagged his tail. Dutch parked in front of the cabin, got off the machine and went into the cabin. Neither man spoke at first. Miles was bewildered. He looked at both men and realized they must have had an argument or something. There was a palpable tension in the air.

Miles then looked back at Jeremy, "We're running out of daylight. We should get back soon."

Jeremy looked back at Miles with a somber look on his face. "I think I'm going to stick around here for a bit."

"What are you talking about? We have to get going. You leave in the morning, remember?"

Wincing, Jeremy slowly swung his leg over the seat. He was able to slowly get off the machine and plant his feet on the ground. He looked squarely at Miles and squinted as the late afternoon sun hit his face.

"I have some work to do up here."

Miles couldn't believe what he was hearing, "This is a bunch of bullshit! Work? What work?"

Miles's frustration was growing.

Jeremy walked closer to Miles and looked him square in the eye, "If I don't keep away from drinking right now and stay up here, I'll start again and I'll be dead for sure. At least up here I can't get any alcohol. It's the safest place for me."

Miles angrily spun around and muttered a string of profanities under his breath.

"Dutch! Hey! I need to talk to you," Miles walked briskly into the cabin where Dutch was pouring two cups of coffee.

"Yeah. I figured you'd want to know what's going on. Have a seat."

Dutch sat down and set the coffee down to share with Miles.

"Your boy out there is in a bad spot. He's run out of both chances and opportunities. You and I both know that if he drinks again, he probably gets himself in a worse situation. Can we agree on this?"

"Yes. Yes. I agree."

"Ok then. We both know how close to dead he was. So, he needs to make sure that this time he gets sober. Agreed?"

"Yeah. I agree."

"Now, I don't necessarily think that he's the best candidate to succeed in rehab right now. I think he'll play the game like he's done in the past. Say all the right things. Hell, he might even convince himself that he is doing everything right. Well, maybe he would be. But I've seen this before. It's more likely that he fails than he succeeds."

"So, what do you think he should do?" Miles contested.

"I think he should go to a hospital for the goddamn insane and stay there for a year mandatory, but that's not realistic."

"He said he has some work to do here. What the hell is he talking about?"

"He asked me for help."

"And you agreed to this? You think this is a good idea?" Clearly, Miles was challenging Dutch.

"I don't know if it's a good idea or not. All I know is this guy asked me for help. I don't know if he understands what he asked for, but I'm willing to give it my best effort. If Gabby thinks that he is healthy enough to stay here, I'm willing to try to help him. If she says no, then come back and grab him up and put him wherever. I've been a drunk and I just know that I have to try to do something for him if he stays."

"This guy is not your cup of tea. We are talking about a real personality clash here."

Dutch smiled, "Yeah, I don't think I'm his cup of tea either. But we all have our crosses to bear."

"Do you know what you're doing with this guy?" Miles asked in a somber tone.

"I don't know. But, if this guy were a member of my family, and I wanted him to have the strength to pull this off, I would prepare him as best I could. Truth is, he is running out of time and chances."

Dutch stood up and looked down at Miles.

"If Gabby thinks it's too big a risk for him to physically be out here, come back and get him in the morning."

Miles stood up and took a last gulp of his coffee. He shook his head in disbelief before saying, "Do you know how much shit my daughter is going to give me over this?"

Dutch chuckled. He knew Gabby was tough and steadfast and would give her father a run for his money.

"Yes, I do. Just have her radio me tonight or in the morning and we can discuss his injuries and what he'll need."

"I want to go on record as saying I think this may work, but both of you are completely nuts."

Miles and Dutch walked outside where Jeremy was petting Jake. The sun was much lower in the sky and the temperature had dropped.

"Before you leave Miles, I was wondering if Jeremy and I can have a private chat."

Jeremy ungrudgingly walked over to Dutch as Miles stepped away and went over to pet Jake.

Dutch squinted at Jeremy. He took a pause and sighed. When he spoke, it was very deliberate.

"You and I need to have an understanding. If I tell you to take off, it's time to go. If you want to leave, you can go anytime. I'll radio Miles and he'll come and get you within the hour. Agreed?"

Jeremy nodded, "I agree."

"Also, we will have some rules. I don't expect you to understand them, but you have to respect and follow them. No matter how obscure they seem, you need to do it. If not, I'll radio Miles and he'll come and get you within the hour. Agreed?"

Again, Jeremy nodded, "I agree."

"I will give you some tasks, some responsibilities. They will be part of your stay here. You will contribute. This is not a hotel and you are not a guest. Work is what happens here. If you can't do that, leave now. I know that you're beat up now, but I won't give you more to do than you can physically handle. If you can't handle your tasks and responsibilities, I'll radio Miles and he'll come get you within the hour. Agreed?"

Jeremy spoke firmly, "I agree."

With that, Dutch walked over to Miles as Jake jumped up. Dutch petted Jake and knelt down.

"Alright Miles. I'll take it from here. Have Gabby call me tomorrow and we'll figure out his medical situation."

Dutch stood up as Miles extended his hand. They shook as Miles glanced over at Jeremy who was now petting Jake.

"Thanks for helping him, Dutch. We were very close at one time."

Dutch in a cold voice replied, "I'll do what I can for him."

CHAPTER TWENTY-FIVE

As Miles got on the four-wheeler, he shook his head at the situation. All the plans leading up to Jeremy's departure would now be altered or cancelled. He would also have the monumental task of explaining to Gabby where her patient decided to start his rehab. He was not looking forward to the rest of his evening.

The sun was close to setting as he wound his way around the shoreline of Beaver Lake and into the thick woods that separated Dutch's cabin from Minaki. It was a quicker ride back as he could go a little faster without Jeremy. He pulled into his driveway and saw Gabby's Jeep in front of the garage door. He quietly entered the house where he saw Gabby at the dining room table.

"Where have you been? I've been looking for Jeremy. I have to set things up so John knows what flight to book for arrival in Minneapolis."

Miles sat down and took his hat off and rubbed his head.

"Well, there won't be a flight to Minneapolis. At least not right now."

Gabby didn't say a word. She simply stared at her father with a sour look usually reserved for a parent looking at a misbehaving child and not the other way around.

"He's decided to stick around for a bit."

Again, Gabby stared straight at her father. She was still confused and visibly pissed. She had just spent the last week getting Jeremy back on his feet and knew there was a long road before him with his rehab and recovery. Miles didn't know what to say. He stared straight back at her. After about 10 seconds, Gabby finally spoke slowly.

"Where is my patient?"

Miles flatly answered.

"He's spending the night at Dutch's place."

Gabby's eyes widened. She literally could not believe what she was hearing. Gabby stood abruptly and grabbed her purse from the back of her chair. She put on her coat and walked towards the door without a sound. Miles stood up and faced her as she breezed past on her way out.

"Where are you going?" he asked.

She paused at the door and with increasing emotion sternly spoke.

"I'm heading home to have dinner with Robby tonight. I'm going to bed early. You see, I have to get up at the crack of dawn tomorrow to go check on the status of my patient who has been kidnapped for the second time in a little more than a week. You see, he's out in the wilderness with a slightly crazy old man and a dog in a log cabin with no electricity or running water. Have a good night."

With that, she closed the door quietly. Miles thought to himself "I would have felt better if she had slammed the door."

Upon arriving at home, Gabby dug out a skillet, put in two pounds of ground venison, and began to brown the meat. One of her favorite meals and Robby's was tacos. Cooking and spending time with him this week was almost non-existent because of all the time she spent at the clinic with Jeremy.

And now all the travel and rehab plans were for naught. While she cooked, she dug out John's phone number and called him in Florida. She explained how the flight was going to be delayed and that she would give him more travel info as the situation evolved.

John was confused by this. "Didn't he get out of the hospital today? You cut him loose, right?"

"Yes, I did. Truth is, he is making some bad decisions already and I plan to take action in the morning."

"Jesus, he's not drinking again, is he?" John asked in disbelief.

"No, not like that. I'll call you around noon and explain. Hopefully, this whole situation will be sorted out by this time tomorrow."

"Thanks for calling and keep me posted."

Robby entered the kitchen where Gabby was slumped in her chair. She was exhausted. It had been an extremely long week.

"Ah Tacos! That sure smells good Mom."

"Yeah sweetie. It does smell good."

Robby sat down and looked at his Mom. He realized how tired she looked. She had a look of worry on her face.

"Are you ok? It's Grandpa's friend again, isn't it?"

"Yeah. It's Grandpa's friend."

Robby paused for a moment and then asked; "Is he going to get better?"

Gabby stared at the floor.

"I hope so. I sure hope so. Your grandpa doesn't have a lot of friends."

Robby had an inquisitive look.

"He has all kinds of friends, Mom. Everybody knows Grandpa."

Gabby turned to Robby. She needed him to understand something.

"Yes, a lot of people know Grandpa, but those are people that look to him for guidance or help. They respect him, depend on him, and think he's a good guy, but Jeremy is his friend from when he was young. It's different. Friends look to each other for strength. They share their victories together and they also share memories. Once you get older, you'll figure it out. When you make friends with someone when you are young, the bond is totally different."

As Miles cleared the table after Gabby left, he thought about calling John, but decided to do that in the morning. He went into the living room and sat in his chair. He grabbed the remote at first and then put it down, deciding to just sit quietly in the chair. No noise in the house. He tried to quiet his mind. All the things that were planned for Jeremy were now cancelled. He wondered what the future held for Jeremy. Would he be back in a day or two, or would the time at Dutch's place prove to be the right thing? Miles had seen so many failures when it came to people he knew who struggled with addiction. Way more disappointment than success. And, if there was success, the road was usually long and very crooked. All he could do was hope and pray that maybe Dutch could rescue his friend from alcohol's powerful grip.

CHAPTER TWENTY-SIX

As the sun began to set out at the cabin, Dutch served up a bowl of stew to Jeremy. They sat facing one another at the table lit by kerosene lamp.

"This is the first real food I've eaten in a week. Gabby served me a bunch of mush to see if my guts would work."

'Well, have you taken a decent shit yet?" Dutch asked.

"Yeah, I guess so." Jeremy was somewhat embarrassed discussing his bowels.

"I mean on a toilet. Not in your pants like the night of the accident."

Jeremy dropped his spoon and a look of disgust spread across his face.

"Look, I had no idea I did that. Nobody told me. Do we have to talk about that anymore?"

Dutch smiled slightly and then spoke very calmly.

"Look. I'm only going to say this once. There is no subject that is off limits or out of bounds. I will bring up any question I want because you asked to be here. So, the thing you need to realize is that there are no secrets here. None. Also, I saw you had a cell phone."

"Yeah. I got it back from Miles after I was in the clinic with Gabby."

"I need it."

"Why?"

"I don't want any distractions or contact with the outside. I'll safekeep it for you. But right now, I don't want you to have it."

Jeremy somewhat reluctantly handed his phone to Dutch and he slid it into his shirt pocket.

"What if someone calls me? What if I have to talk to somebody?"

"Then I'll call Miles and he can pick you up within the hour and you can talk to as many people as you want. But our work will be done here."

A look of confusion turned into a frown. Dutch pretended not to notice. He reached up on a shelf along the wall by the fireplace and grabbed a yellow legal pad and a pen. He tossed them on the table next to Jeremy's empty bowl.

"The first assignment tonight is to make your first journal entry."

"What journal? I don't have a journal. I don't really like writing much."

"You do now. This is your journal. You see, you will write what's going on in your head at the time. It might be about what you did that day or something that you recall from the past. It might be about your hopes for the future. It's up to you. But you will fill at least two pages every single day that you are here. You will also read. I have many books, and I can suggest a few titles, but you will read when you are here."

"Ok. I suppose we'll do calisthenics in the morning too?" Jeremy's tone was sarcastic.

"Well, you're not ready for that yet, but you will try to become fit. Just walking looks like enough for you right now. Just try to build a little stamina. You're in terrible shape, and I don't mean just from the accident. Alcohol has taken its toll."

At this point, Jeremy realized he wasn't just staying up in the wilderness to hide from drinking. He was being put on some kind of path. A path laid out by someone who could be considered a bit of a madman. Despite the slightly smaller stature and wrinkles on his face, Dutch looked like he was chiseled out of stone. His gravelly voice resonated with a deep baritone sound. His eyes seemed to be looking into you, not at you. After giving Jeremy the writing pad, he started for the door, then turned to Jeremy.

"I'm taking Jake down to the water and then bringing some wood inside for the night. After you get done with your journal entry, clean up the dishes in the sink."

Jeremy nodded. "Am I doing dishes every night?"

"No. I'll do them tomorrow night, seeing as you're cooking dinner."

After Dutch and Jake left the cabin, Jeremy wondered what to write. He decided to scribble details of the pain he felt. Just trying to walk. Just trying to do normal things. He felt weak and had no stamina. He wrote about how his new host could probably run a marathon and then split wood for an hour. He was hoping that he could just get himself back physically. That was what his main hope was. The pain was physical and the hope was to get some strength back and clear his head of the alcohol cravings.

As Dutch went down to the shore, Jake walked along his left side. He pushed his wet nose against Dutch's leg and they both sat on a patch of long grass that the sun had cleared of snow. Dutch looked out at the still frozen lake and contemplated the next several days and how to handle Jeremy. He knew that Jeremy was playing along for now, but that wouldn't last. He would be acting like an immature little kid soon, testing limits, and seeing how much he could get away with. Dutch also realized that if Gabby said that he was not good enough to physically handle being at the cabin, Jeremy would be gone soon anyway.

After bringing in some wood, Dutch quietly walked past Jeremy as he was still writing. He went into a small adjacent room and lit another lantern. It was a smaller space with a bed and some storage bins. Dutch used this as a spare pantry. He removed the bins one by one and made the room somewhat presentable. He then called Jeremy in. He had just finished writing and carried the legal pad with him.

"You finished your assignment?"

"Yeah. It's kind of surprising how much came out."

"Some days it's like that. Give me the pages."

"Don't I get to keep them? It's my journal. My personal thoughts."

"I just want to keep them for you. You'll get them back. And, don't worry. I'm not interested in reading it. It's your private writing. I just want you to start out with a fresh set of ideas every day. I'll get these back to you."

Jeremy nodded and tore the sheets off the top and handed them to Dutch. Dutch took them and then led Jeremy into what would be his room. They stood at the foot of an immaculately made bed. The creases were precise and the top spread albeit faded and shabby, was evenly stretched about 6 inches below the pillow.

"This is your rack. It's a good bed. We'll deal with the other stuff later. I know you don't have a lot of clothes, but I think Miles can help with that."

"I feel like I could sleep right now."

"You've got some dishes to do before bed."

'Oh yeah. Those can't wait til' morning?"

Dutch gave Jeremy an unapproving blank stare.

Embarrassed, Jeremy nodded his head and realized he said the wrong thing.

"Yeah. We'll get those done tonight."

Dutch then went over to the fireplace and loaded up some hardwood that would sustain the fire deep into the night.

Jeremy started on the dishes and was talking over his shoulder to Dutch at the fireplace.

"Not to complain or anything, but what do you have for entertainment around here? I don't see any TV or anything. You got a radio?"

"I do, but I rarely listen to it. My only indulgence is occasionally listening to my records."

"You have a vinyl collection? I used to love the sound of vinyl. There's nothing like it. I can't wait to see what you've got."

"Maybe I'll dig 'em out tomorrow. It's been a while." Dutch sighed. He seemed tired. Jeremy nodded at the sink, skeptical about ever seeing Dutch's vinyl collection.

Dutch then settled into his chair by the fireplace with a book while Jake laid down at his feet. Jeremy looked at the other chair by the fireplace, but decided to go into his new bedroom. The lantern was still lit and it started to sink in where he was. His surroundings seemed surreal. He was now living with a hermit in the Canadian wilderness. He carefully laid down on the bed after removing his shoes. He looked at the pine boards on the ceiling and tried to imagine the warmth of the Florida Keys sunshine. It seemed so far away from here. Here Jeremy realized that he had forgotten about his chest pain for a few minutes. It hurt again as he rolled onto his side slightly. With heavy eyelids, Jeremy slowly nodded off. It was the end of his first day at Dutch's.

CHAPTER TWENTY-SEVEN

A bright light blinded Jeremy. A deep baritone voice behind the light spoke.

"Wake up, cupcake. Daylight in the swamp."

"Jesus!" Jeremy exclaimed, wondering what the hell was happening. It seemed as though he had just fallen asleep, but eight hours had transpired. It was 5:30 a.m.

"It's time to start the day, Jeremy. Get the fire going."

Jeremy realized then that it was so much colder than normal. Previously, he had been in a nice warm hospital bed for more than a week, but now he was in a cold wooden prison and the warden was Dutch. Jeremy rose out of bed very slowly and carefully putting both feet on the floor. His eye was bothering him and his ribs hurt. Physically, It was not a good morning.

Dutch turned to leave the room and then spoke while starting a pot of coffee on the stove.

"Once you get the fire going, make your bed."

Jeremy winced as he was being barked at by Dutch. Gingerly, Jeremy knelt by the fireplace and began to crumple up some paper along with small twigs. He struggled with a wooden farmer's match until it lit and he could see the flames starting to catch. Dutch glanced over to the fireplace and noticed that Jeremy built the fire too close to the front of the hearth. He smiled as he realized what was about to happen.

"Let me know if you need any help Jeremy." Dutch held back the chuckle that was fighting to escape.

"God, Dutch. It's a fire. I think I know how to do this." Jeremy was clearly annoyed and muttered to himself.

As the flames in the fireplace rose, smoke began to filter out into the room and travel up the front of the fireplace mantel. Dutch pretended not to notice and kept his head down as he prepared a skillet to cook breakfast. As the room began to fill with smoke, Jeremy realized his fire was a calamity. As the flames grew and the twigs and small bits of kindling caught fire, more and more thick smoke began to infiltrate the room. It didn't take long for Jeremy to realize that he was out of his league. The smoke got in his face, irritating his eyes, causing him to cough a bit which was extremely painful on his tender ribs. He tried to stifle his groan of pain, but it was impossible. It hurt too much. Defeated, he stood in front of the fireplace and turned towards Dutch.

"I think I have a problem over here." Jeremy reluctantly admitted.

Now, Dutch was becoming enveloped in smoke as he stood in front of the stove. He made no mention of the smoke and glanced at Jeremy as the entire room was becoming uninhabitable. Dutch paused and faced Jeremy seemingly oblivious to the thickening smoke.

"What problem is that?"

Both men stared at each other. Dutch did his best poker face while Jeremy felt a sense of being played a bit. In a frustrated tone Jeremy said, "Help me. I don't want to burn the place down."

Dutch's poker face turned into a dismissive glare as he walked past Jeremy, bumping into him slightly. He knelt, grabbed some fireplace hardware, and pushed the collection of burning wood back further into the firebox. The heat was directly under the chimney pipe now and the smoke stopped coming out the front of the fireplace.

"All you did wrong was build it a little too far forward. It wasn't drawing right. You'll learn."

Dutch stood up and walked over to the door, opening it. He then walked to the opposite side of the room and opened a large window. A slight breeze cleared the room and soon the smoke was dissipating quickly.

Dutch faced Jeremy who stood quietly in front of the fireplace with an embarrassed look on his face.

"Don't get sour this early in the morning," Dutch reprimanded, then walked back towards the stove.

"I'll start breakfast while you make your bed."

Jeremy walked into his room without making a sound and started to straighten up his bed. He spent a few quick moments pulling up the sheets and blanket. He then walked out to the main table where Dutch was setting plates down. The smell of bacon and eggs filled the small space as the burnt odor of the fireplace smoke vanished. Dutch brought out a bowl of diced potatoes before the plate of eggs and bacon. Jeremy smiled as he sat down realizing just how hungry he was.

"Man, you sure know how to cook. This looks great."

Jeremy dug in immediately and began to devour his breakfast. Dutch sat down quietly and calmly sipped his hot coffee at first, and then began to eat. It was quiet for a moment until Jeremy spoke up.

"Are you going to dig out your record player today?" Jeremy asked with a mouthful of food.

Dutch nodded, but raised a finger.

"First things first. Before we get the vinyl spinning, we must hook up our electricity. That means working on the solar panels and connecting those new batteries that Miles brought up here with you yesterday. But, before that, we need to check your bed and get your morning walk in."

Looking puzzled, Jeremy asked, "What do you mean check my bed?"

Dutch wiped his mouth with a napkin, then stood up, and motioned for Jeremy to join him in the room where Jeremy slept. When he walked in, Dutch saw a rumpled pillow with wrinkled blankets covering a lumpy sheet. It was obvious that Jeremy had merely pulled the main blanket up and covered the wrinkled sheets.

"Was this the way the bed looked when I showed it to you last night?"

"Not exactly. I mean I folded the top up. What do you want me to do?" Jeremy was getting annoyed and defensive.

"I will show you how to properly do this."

Dutch tore everything off the bed and flung it on the floor. He took the bottom fitted sheet and stretched the corners over the mattress and then used his hands to spread out any wrinkles on the sheet. It was smooth after he did that. He proceeded to put a flat top sheet on and made sure both sides had equal overhang. He brought the top of the sheet even with the top edge of the mattress. He then folded perfect forty-five degree angle hospital corners with the top sheet. He meticulously smoothed out all the wrinkles of the sheet before tucking in the sides. Then the blanket, slightly lower than the top sheet, equal overhang on both sides. Then he tucked in the bottom with hospital corners near the foot at perfect forty-five degree angles. Jeremy pretended to pay attention, but he was in reality just patronizing Dutch. Jeremy saw little reason for such a display. Dutch then straightened out the pillow and folded the excess pillowcase underneath the pillow and then smoothed out all of the wrinkles. Dutch then stood up and looked Jeremy in the eye.

"Just like that. Any questions?"

"No, I think I got it." Jeremy sarcastically replied.

"Ok. Good." With that Dutch grabbed all the bedding off of the mattress and balled it up in a huge pile on the floor.

"Now you do it. Just the way I showed you."

Jeremy felt the heat building with frustration. The bed was just fine in his estimation and he was the one sleeping in it after all. Why did Dutch want to torture him over something as silly as a made bed. He kept his cool and tried to remember how Dutch did it.

Dutch exited the room and barked out from the table, "When you're done with the bed, you can do the breakfast dishes."

Jeremy was having trouble focusing. Had he actually agreed to do all this work yesterday? He wasn't sure. His frustration with Dutch and doing all these chores were things he hadn't anticipated. Out of pride, he would shut his mouth. He grumbled to himself as he tried to smooth out the sheets and blankets the best he could.

Dutch was feeding he fire with more wood and gave a few breakfast scraps to Jake. He then walked outside and looked at the framework for the solar panels that were attached to the roof on the south side of the cabin. Dutch had some wires to replace and the work would require a ladder and a few tools from the shed.

As Dutch was looking for his ladder, Jeremy came outside and found Dutch.

"I need some hot water to do the dishes. Where is the hot water faucet?"

Dutch barked back, "There isn't one. You heat cold water on the stove and then pour it in the sink out of the kettle."

Jeremy muttered to himself, "Jesus Christ, are we living in the stone age?"

Dutch heard the muffled complaint, but pretended not to. He barked back again, "How did your bed go?"

"It's done." Jeremy snarled.

"Did you do the corners like I showed you?"

"Yes."

"Are both sides equal with sheet and blanket."

"Yes."

"Good. Let's check it out."

A cold chill went through Jeremy as he knew damn well he didn't do it like Dutch showed him. What difference did it make anyway?

Dutch walked into the bedroom and immediately saw that the bed was uneven and the corners were all wrong. He pulled everything off the bed and threw it onto the floor. He then walked out into the main room and grabbed a chair. He pulled it into the room and set it next to the bed.

"You sit here and watch. I'm going to show this to you again, the right way." His voice was calm but firm.

Jeremy sat in the chair and fought the urge to speak out. He watched as Dutch lined up the sheets and blankets, checked for equal length and smoothed out all the wrinkles. The perfectly formed corners were like sealed envelopes. The bed was meticulous. Dutch worked quickly, but thoroughly.

"Do you have any questions?"

In a sullen tone, Jeremy replied, "None."

"Good. Now you do it."

With that, once again, Dutch tore everything off the bed and balled it up in a big messy pile on the floor before he walked out.

CHAPTER TWENTY-EIGHT

Gabby got up around 7 a.m. and started to take inventory of the bag she planned to take up to Dutch's cabin. She knew that Jeremy had no medication for pain and the drops for his eyes were back at Miles' house. She gathered a number of items including soap, a toothbrush, a comb, and some deodorant. She also grabbed a medical kit in the event Jeremy needed a new dressing for his chest. It had only been a couple days, but the dressing might need replacing due to sweat and dirt. The last thing she wanted was for Jeremy to get any kind of infection. She got into her Jeep and went to Miles' house where he was just getting ready to leave.

"Good. I'm glad I caught you. I need you to get an ATV ready at the shop so I can go up to Dutch's place to pick up Jeremy," explained Gabby.

"Is he ok? Did they call you?"

"No Dad. Nobody called. I am just going up there to do the right thing because nobody else seems to be doing that."

Gabby was obviously still pissed off.

Without much discussion, Gabby and Miles headed to the shop and silently loaded up an ATV with gear. Alone, Gabby started out for the cabin. Miles wanted to go along, but realized early on that his presence was not welcome. As Gabby went on the trail towards the cabin, she realized how much snow had disappeared over the past 10 days. There were spots of bare ground showing up and the remnants of the blizzard were becoming harder to find. It was a clear and sunny morning and the trip up to Dutch's took less than a half hour. She pulled into the yard in front of the cabin as Dutch was climbing down the ladder near his solar panels. Dutch smiled as she got off the machine.

"Hello, young lady." He walked over to her. She met him and

gave him a hug.

"Hi. I found out that you're running a hotel out here. Thanks for neglecting to mention the new arrangement to me."

"I think you'll find it's more like an asylum." Dutch explained.

"Where is our patient?"

"He's inside sulking. It hasn't been a great morning for him."

Gabby went inside the cabin and found Jeremy sitting in the chair beside the fireplace with Jake at his feet. Jeremy didn't look at the door. Gabby walked around the chair to the front alongside the fireplace where she could see his face. Only then did he glance up.

"You came here to pick me up, didn't you?"

"I came here to try and talk some sense into you. We have a plan for you, Jeremy. It's a good plan. I think it could work. You should give it a chance."

"You know, you're probably right. If I go to rehab right now, I would go to all the meetings, talk to counselors, and drink their Kool-Aid. It might work. I would have a good chance of staying sober. I don't doubt that. The trouble is, right now, I don't trust myself. I'm not sure I can pull it off right now," revealed Jeremy.

Gabby sat in the nearby chair and leaned in.

"What are you so scared of? Are you scared of being successful? Are you worried that you couldn't handle it?"

Jeremy looked down at the floor, shook his head, and grimaced.

"Dutch brought me up to where the accident happened. I saw this completely destroyed snowmobile, debris everywhere, and burnt wreckage. Something inside me just snapped. It was like looking at my own gravestone. I was screaming at Dutch and screaming at God, and I was in such pain that I realized that I had to try something other than traditional rehab. Been there, done that. Unsuccessfully."

"Did you decide to run away?" Gabby questioned.

"No. It's hard to explain. It felt like I have to avoid one problem by solving another one first. Does that make sense?"

"I don't know Jeremy. Maybe," Gabby answered softly.

The two sat silently for a full minute, maybe longer, while Jeremy petted Jake. Gabby knew depression, self-loathing, and disgust were classic reactions of people in recovery. She realized then that time at the cabin with Dutch was going to be part of the healing process for Jeremy.

Jeremy finally spoke.

"I really do want to get sober, I do. But I think I have some growing up to do and maybe this is the right place for that to happen."

Gabby realized at that point she was not going to be able to talk Jeremy into coming back with her. This was a curveball she had not expected. This was a pride thing and while she didn't agree completely with what Jeremy said, she saw some of the logic in it.

"You're not willing to come back with me today, are you?"

"I don't think I'm quite ready for that yet. I don't trust myself," Jeremy admitted.

"Ok. But we still have to check out your injuries. Come over by the table so I can look at your dressing."

Jeremy rose from the chair cautiously and slowly limped to the table. He sat down carefully. Making the bed repeatedly and doing the dishes within an hour was the most physical activity he had done since the accident. It was barely 9 a.m. and he was exhausted. Gabby began to peel the tape off in order to check the wound from the chest tube.

"This is improving. Do your best to keep it dry and clean. I'm going to redo this."

Gabby got to work on taping and cleaning up the wound area.

"How is your roommate? You two getting along?"

"You mean psycho? I had to make my bed three times this morning and I still don't know if I got it right. That and the dishes. Dishes done in water heated on the stove." Jeremy begrudgingly revealed his morning assignments.

Gabby laughed. She thought about the times she spent out here as a little girl with her dad and grandfather.

"He's a good cook though," Gabby pointed out.

Jeremy's eyes widened as he turned to Gabby. "Oh shit. I forgot. Last night Dutch said that I'm supposed to make dinner tonight. What the hell am I going to do?"

"He has something for you to cook, I'm sure. Just ask him where everything is."

"I didn't see a grill. I could do some burgers on the grill, but I didn't see one outside."

"Don't worry. You'll think of something," Gabby reassured him.

Jeremy looked down and shook his head. He wasn't so sure.

"Oh yeah, and I brought you a few things." Gabby handed a bag to Jeremy. It had some toiletries along with a few washcloths and a couple towels. Gabby then left Jeremy to put his shirt back on and put his belongings away. She stepped outside to speak with Dutch.

Gabby spoke without looking at Dutch. "You realize what is happening here don't you?"

Dutch, still fighting with the wires for the solar panels turned and looked at her.

Gabby continued. "He's hiding."

Dutch replied as he went back to working on the wires, "I know that."

"So why are you letting him hide?" Gabby asked.

"Because while he is hiding, I think I can make him face his problems and find a few answers. He will still need rehab and support, but I can help him here a little first, and I can damn well make sure he doesn't drink out here."

Gabby leaned against the cabin, "Can you show me where it happened?"

Dutch turned to her with a raised eyebrow. "Are you sure you want to see that?"

"After what Jeremy told me inside, I feel like I might understand this better if I did."

Dutch hesitated slightly before saying, "Ok. Let's go."

Dutch and Gabby rode out to the crash site. The trail that Dutch and Jeremy took the day before was still visible. It took only a couple minutes for them to arrive. Gabby got off the ATV and followed the footprints in the melting snow. She arrived at the burnt tree and snowmobile wreckage. The only identifiable items were pieces of the shattered fiberglass hood. She said nothing.

"I found him over here." Dutch walked over to the first tree where Jeremy had been suspended in the branches. Gabby walked around and looked below the tree. She could still see some pink snow where blood had dripped down from Jeremy's wounds and frozen that night. It was now diluted from the melting of the snow during the warm weather. She knelt beside the tree and began to sob. Dutch knelt beside her and put his arm around her. Gabby composed herself and stood up.

"If Jeremy would have died here it would have destroyed my dad. He feels responsible for this, you know."

Dutch looked Gabby in the eye. "I know he does. Jeremy needs to make that right by getting well."

"Do you think you can help him? I mean, why are you doing this? At your age? This is a guy you normally wouldn't give a second thought."

Dutch stepped back and looked at the sky and sighed. After a moment he turned back at Gabby.

"You know, when I was in the service, and I was overseas, I got really close with the guys in my unit. We were together for a long time. Some of them all the way back to basic. We went through a lot together. Those guys were like brothers to me. And I lost all of them. Some were killed in action, some made it through the war and got sick, and one drank himself to death."

Dutch's voice trailed off for a moment.

"And, I felt helpless. I couldn't make a difference. All my training as a medic and I lost a bunch of them in one day. I was in the hospital myself and when I got out, I was discharged. No contact with their families. Nothing. I felt useless. The couple that did make it after the war were so far gone by the time I got in touch, I couldn't be much help. When the last guy was gone, I prayed to God that one day I could help someone who needed it, another chance to make good. That I could do something for somebody even though I had let my friends down. So the years go by and this guy Jeremy ends up here near death and then he asks me to help him stop drinking because he says to me, "I just want to live." We don't get to pick our opportunities. They pick us. How could I possibly say no?"

Gabby smiled and nodded her head. She understood Dutch's logic. He was seeking redemption.

Dutch then asked, "Medically, is it safe for him out here?"

Gabby pondered the answer.

"I think his biggest struggles are mental right now. We may have to medicate him if he stays up here."

Dutch was hoping they could avoid medicating Jeremy for his alcohol addiction.

"I have a few ideas on how to help him mentally."

"Ok, I'm listening." Gabby replied.

"I had him start a journal last night. I thought that would be a good outlet for him so he can organize his thoughts. Give him some structure. Second, I'm getting my solar panels operating so we can have a little power out here. Then we can have some music. He's interested in my old records. That would be good."

"I agree. What else?"

"He is going to be reading when he's out here. I want him to get some good ideas into that head of his and they have to be from someone other than me. Can you bring a few books out if I give you some titles?" Dutch inquired.

"Absolutely. Anything else?"

"It looks like Jake has taken a liking to him. Having to care for an animal would be good too. I think I'll put him in charge of Jake's feeding and walking habits for a bit."

"That's a real good idea. A sort of therapy dog. Now, how are you going to handle this? I mean your approach."

Dutch smiled. "Well Gabby, I've always subscribed to the Bobby Knight approach to coaching."

Gabby gave a disapproving look and asked, "Exactly what approach is that?"

"If you want results out of competitive people, you need to piss them off a little bit." Dutch let out a devilish grin.

"Is that why Jeremy made his bed three times today?"

Dutch faked surprise, "You made that connection?"

Gabby felt little less reluctant about the whole situation, but this approach was so unorthodox she couldn't help but be concerned. The chance of relapse out here was almost non-existent, but the mental aspect of isolation and the oil and water relationship between these two men could be a potential train wreck in the making. She wanted to present a united front to Jeremy regarding the care he would get. He needed to understand that this was a first phase, and that a formal rehab facility would follow this self-imposed isolation. As Dutch and Gabby began their trip back to the cabin, she became at peace with Jeremy's decision to try this approach. She didn't necessarily agree with it, but she understood it. Jeremy saw strength and discipline within Dutch and he longed to be a part of it.

Gabby and Dutch got back and saw Jeremy in the doorway with Jake. Gabby could see that the dog enjoyed Jeremy's company.

"Looks like you made a friend out here."

Jeremy smiled and petted Jake. "Yeah, he listens to my problems. He's better than a bartender."

"Yes, he most certainly is."

Jeremy stepped forward and then asked Gabby, "Well, are you going to wrap me up in a straitjacket and haul me out of here, or am I going to be able to stay?"

Gabby pondered for a moment. "You're a grown man Jeremy. You'll do what you want. I just want you to promise me that you'll let me help you when it's needed. I trust Dutch. He's rock solid. Just be open minded. He might have you doing some things you don't comprehend. Give yourself time to understand."

"Anything else I need to do?"

"Yes. You are going to need some self-awareness. Because

you are giving up drinking, your brain is going to go through changes. You need to account for these changes when you start to feel depressed or anxious. It's a sign that your mind and body are healing. There are medications to help and that may be a road to go down at some point, but for now we can try some of the things that Dutch and I discussed. You have already started."

"You mean writing in a journal?" Jeremy wondered aloud.

"Exactly. That is one of the things you'll be able to use to better understand your growth. And, you will grow. But you need to acknowledge that there will be growing pains and these will most likely be unpleasant. Does that make sense?"

"You sound like an expert."

"I'm not. I've just seen a lot. Both good and bad. Can you promise me that you'll let others help you?"

"Well, Gabby…I'd like to think that's why I'm here."

"Ok then. Is there anything else I can get for you?"

"There is. Dutch took my phone. John needs to know what's going on and my folks think I'm headed to rehab right now. I need to call them. Can you help with that?"

"Yes. We can patch a call through on the radio to your folks and I can help if you'd like on that one. I can also call John up and explain what's happening."

Jeremy smiled when she talked about calling John. She seemed confused.

"What's so funny?" Gabby asked.

"John is probably going to call bullshit on this and think I'm ducking out on rehab. I think he's going to have a tough time understanding all of this. Don't be shocked if he thinks that I'm playing an angle out here."

"Does he want what's best for you?"

"That guy has been wanting me to quit drinking since the first week we fished together. That was years ago. I have put that guy through a lot with my shenanigans and he still sticks by me. I pay him to take me fishing, but he's become a whole lot more than a fishing guide to me."

"Ok. I'll take that into account when we talk. I should get

going."

"Hey, can you do one other thing? I could use a few more clothes. I came up here with what was on my back."

"Yes, I think my dad is coming up here this afternoon with some things for you. He's already on that."

"Thanks." Jeremy's eyes showed genuine gratitude.

"I'll stay in touch with you and Dutch and I can come up here within an hour if you need me. Just take care of that eye with those drops and make sure that dressing stays clean and dry."

Gabby then went over to Dutch and gave him a kiss on the cheek.

"Please take care of him."

Dutch smiled and nodded at Gabby. She then climbed aboard the ATV and fired up the engine. She turned the machine towards Minaki and hit the throttle. It became increasingly quiet as Dutch carried some tools over towards the ladder. Jeremy approached him.

"Anything I can help with?"

"No, not right now. I've got more to do up high. You can help with the ground work later. By the way, how are you feeling?"

"I feel tired. I mean like sleepy." Jeremy's eyes showed his lack of shut eye.

"That's good. It means your body is healing. You need to go rest right now. I was thinking that we'll do something this afternoon. Head inside and lay down on the couch or recline in the chair. Stay by the fire. It will be good for you."

Jeremy put up no argument. He turned around and slowly shuffled into the cabin and sat in the chair by the fireplace. Jake laid down next to him. Within minutes Jeremy's eyes closed and he was quietly snoring.

Dutch was trying to figure out a routine for the two of them as things progressed. While he tinkered with the solar panels his mind was putting together a plan on how to establish a schedule that would push Jeremy both physically and mentally while still giving him time to rest and recuperate as needed. There needed to be balance. Jeremy would have to be pushed to make progress.

Dutch would somehow balance meals, physical therapy, reading time, journal time and eventually some free time. He would also need to make sure he contributed along with the chores. Jeremy was scheduled to cook tonight's dinner. He had overheard the conversion about Jeremy wanting to grill, so he rounded up a grill to put over a small wood fire. At least Jeremy would be able to cook a little within his comfort zone.

Jeremy slept right on into the early afternoon. He awoke in the chair with Jake resting his nose on his leg and wagging his tail slowly. It was as if Jake wanted to wake Jeremy up to play. As he rose slowly from the chair, Jeremy groaned as he had again stiffened up. He needed to stretch his underused muscles before they would fire on command. Jake was eagerly leading him out the door as he spotted Dutch getting the batteries hooked up to the solar panels. Dutch looked at Jeremy with a bit of astonishment.

"Well, looks like you're not dead after all. You passed out for over three hours."

"Really? I had no idea. I felt so beat. Sleeping in that chair seems better on my sore ribs."

Dutch knew what he meant. He had suffered fractured ribs as a young man and knew how difficult it was to get any sleep.

"How about a little walk? Let's get a baseline for your stamina."

"Sounds ok to me. Where are we headed?"

Dutch motioned towards the ATV tracks and the two started walking at a very slow pace. After about 200 feet, Dutch held Jeremy up and motioned for him to sit down on a fallen log. Dutch then snapped off a branch from the log and pulled out a large knife and began whittling the branches off the limb and rounded off the larger end with the knife. It was a little more than four feet long. He then handed it to Jeremy.

"Use this for stability. It's good to have a walking stick."

Jeremy grabbed the stick and used it to help himself rise off the log and continue walking.

"Thanks. Having a cane might be a good thing."

"This is better than a cane." Dutch was smiling.

"Oh yeah? Why's that?"

"This is a little longer. If a bear decides to go after you, this would be better to ward off the attack."

Jeremy didn't know if he was joking or not.

They walked silently for a minute or two when Jeremy turned to Dutch and spoke up.

"Where's your walking stick?"

Dutch kept walking facing straight ahead. "I don't need one."

"What if a bear attacks you?"

"I'm not worried. You're here." Dutch chuckled, kept walking, and never broke stride.

The two walked for another 100 feet or so and then stopped again. Dutch pulled out a piece of orange ribbon and tied it to a tree branch. Jeremy had a puzzled look on his face.

"What's that for?"

Dutch answered back, "I wanted to mark this spot as your stopping point for today."

"I'm a little tired, but I can go a little further. Let's go." urged Jeremy.

Dutch stayed in one spot and shook his head.

"Best to be conservative when you start out. Remember, this is the halfway point. You have to make it back to the cabin."

Jeremy frowned a bit at this comment, but took Dutch's suggestion to heart. He turned around and started back towards the cabin. As they progressed back, Jeremy's legs felt heavier and heavier. He was breaking a sweat as they got back within sight of the cabin. The round trip was only a little over 200 yards, but it felt like a mile to Jeremy. He was laboring as he got closer to the cabin and then sat on a small bench by the tool shed. He looked up at Dutch and realized he probably bit off more than he could chew. His face was beet red and sweat was collecting on his forehead. Dutch went inside and came out with a tall glass of water. When he handed it to Jeremy, he drank it all down in one gulp.

"Thanks. You were right to turn around when we did," Jeremy

admitted.

"Let's see if you can do that tomorrow with less effort. For now, let's get you back inside. I have a couple things for you to look at."

Dutch walked into the cabin. Jeremy followed behind and collapsed into the chair by the fireplace. Jake followed in as well. Dutch walked across the room to his bookshelf and pulled a couple volumes out and brought them over to Jeremy.

"Here are some reading choices. Pick one."

Jeremy looked at both and settled on a copy of Jordan Peterson's *12 Rules For Life*.

"Is this like a 12-step book?"

"No." Dutch replied. "It's more of what and what not to do."

As Jeremy opened the book, Dutch sat down on the couch and engaged Jeremy in conversation.

"Look, this isn't some kind of cult thing. I have a bunch of books on my shelf. They are all available to you. I just wanted to suggest something to get you started. The other thing about reading is that I don't necessarily agree with all these authors. I don't expect you to either. I just want you to get a variety of perspectives. In other words, I'm not telling you what to think. I'm suggesting what you should think about. That's all."

"You like books. I mean a lot. Don't you?"

"I like to learn. I like to think I can learn from reasoning and the mistakes of others. It really helps. The emotional brain can only learn from experiences. The rational brain can learn from many different sources. Your brain is going to be going through some changes. Try to practice self-awareness and understand that some things are just in your head and don't pose a real threat or problem."

"Gabby said the exact same thing to me."

"That's because it's true. You are going to face some shit in your head. Just realize that its all part of getting better. It's like weight training, but your brain is the muscle. If it hurts, it's probably helping."

Jeremy began to page through the book and glanced at some

of the pages. Dutch walked over to his ice box and pulled out a couple frozen packages.

"You're in charge of dinner tonight. Can you grill over an open fire?"

Jeremy's head turned quickly, "Sure! I can grill. What are we having?"

"I shot a moose last fall. They make good burgers. Ever eat a moose burger?"

"This will be my first."

"I'll start to thaw these out. I'll get some wood together for the fire outside and we can get things ready for later. I have a feeling that Miles will be up here soon to bring you some clothes. Maybe he can join us."

Jeremy looked at the hanging grill that Dutch had outside for over the firepit. It was something he'd seen in magazines, but never used. He was used to his $2000 gas grill that he used on the patio next to the pool at his condo. This was a primitive set up, but he told himself that he could make this work. After he arranged some wood in the firepit, he decided to rest a little more. He couldn't believe how tired he was from that short walk. He was glad that Dutch had known to cut the trip short when he did. It was all Jeremy could do to drag himself back to the cabin. He collapsed in the chair by the fireplace once again.

CHAPTER TWENTY-NINE

Miles rolled into the yard on his ATV with a duffle bag and some supplies for Dutch. It was mostly fresh veggies and lettuce to help supplement Jeremy's new and improved diet. There were some vitamins and also some special coffee that Dutch liked. The bag also had several pairs of jeans and other clothes for Jeremy to wear. Laundry day was only once a week at the cabin, so there needed to be several changes for Jeremy.

When Miles walked into the cabin, Dutch was at the counter getting plates and silverware ready for dinner and Jeremy was still passed out cold from his most recent nap. Miles playfully began to tickle Jeremy's nose and Jeremy started to swat at his face in his foggy slumber. He eventually rose, recognized Miles, and grinned. Miles grinned back and started his interrogation.

"How was your first full day?"

"I've had better. I'm just so tired. I can't believe how much this air up here makes me sleepy. Are you staying for dinner? Apparently, I'm grilling moose burgers."

"I wouldn't want to miss that." Miles chuckled.

Jeremy went outside and put together a fire for cooking. Dutch got the table ready and Miles simply sat back and relaxed. He was obviously curious how this odd couple got along during the last 24 hours.

"How did Jeremy handle himself today?"

Dutch sat in a chair at the table, took a sip of coffee, and then sat back.

"He did ok. I didn't challenge him much today. Just keeping him from falling asleep was tough enough. I'm trying to set up a routine for him though."

"Sounds good. And how did you handle yourself today?"

Dutch gave a disapproving look at first. He knew that Miles didn't want him to be a complete hardass, but also knew that discipline is what Jeremy needed. He had even asked for it.

"I wasn't on him much today. I kind of set the tone with him yesterday at the crash site. I think he knows the fucking around portion of our programming is over. I need to keep him focused on the goal."

"And what is that goal?" Miles squinted at Dutch studying his facial expression.

"He said he just wanted to live. I'm trying to give him the reasons. That's what he needs to learn. If the reasons are good enough, he'll use his resources to find a way to get sober and stay sober."

Just then, Jeremy walked in ready to start grilling.

Dutch spoke up, "What are we having with the burgers?"

Jeremy was clearly stumped. His mouth fell open with confusion. He really didn't think about any sides and didn't even know what was available. He looked at Dutch with a blank stare. "I don't know what else we have."

Dutch replied, "I have some asparagus. You can cook that on the grill at the same time. Would that work for you?"

"Oh, yeah. That's perfect." Dutch then went into his ice box and retrieved a wrapped package of asparagus to thaw out.

"Put this near the fire and it should thaw quickly enough."

Dutch went outside and set up the hardware for the cooking grate over the fire. He could see that the fire was bigger than it should be. He knew the potential for everything burning if cooked too fast. He decided to find out where Jeremy's head was in this.

"Do you need any help with the fire at all? You've cooked over wood before, right?"

Jeremy thought the old man might be setting a trap for him. It was the same kind of question Dutch asked before the cabin got smoked out in the morning.

"How about if I need some help, I will give you a shout?"

Dutch nodded. "Fair enough."

Jeremy had the grilling tools ready along with the moose meat and asparagus. Everything went on the grill at the same time.

The fire seemed hot, but that just meant that the burgers would be done sooner. Dutch and Miles were in the cabin talking and could smell the food cooking outside through a cracked window. Jeremy flipped the burgers and rolled the asparagus while Jake sat next to him, hoping for a scrap. This was the first time he could remember grilling in years without having a drink in his hand. It felt odd to him, but the smell of the cooking meat and wood smoke was in its own way, intoxicating. After several minutes, Jeremy used the spatula to gather everything up on a large plate before he brought it inside. He put a small amount of salt and pepper on the meat and set it on the table.

The three men all sat at the table and spoke very little. Jeremy had a strong appetite and gulped down his food without speaking. It had been a long day and he was more than a little worn out. His ribs ached, his shoulder was still sore and his hip was giving him some fits. His eye was getting irritated from the smoke of the fire and he would need his eye drops after eating.

Dutch and Miles talked over dinner but Jeremy was uncharacteristically quiet. Jeremy finished his burger and then put his dish in the sink. It was Dutch's turn to wash the dishes tonight. Jeremy then went over to the fireplace, put a log in, and sat in the chair. Jake got off the floor by the table and ambled slowly over. Jeremy stroked the hair on Jake's head and the two sat in front of the fire in silence.

Miles spoke up, "Looks like Jake has a new friend."

"He's a good boy. I think he knows I'm not doing too good." Jeremy continued to pet him. "Animals can sense when someone is struggling."

Dutch wiped his mouth and got up from the table and walked over towards the fireplace. He threw another log on the fire and decided this would be a good time to put a positive end on what Jeremy was thinking of as a tough day.

"I don't know. I think today was a pretty good day for you."

Jeremy looked at him like he was batshit crazy. He was exhausted, sore, and while trying not to let it show, feeling a little sorry for himself.

"How do you figure?"

"Come with me." Dutch walked towards the entrance of Jeremy's room. Once again, Jeremy struggled to get out of the chair and Jake followed. Miles took an interest as well. Dutch lit a kerosene lamp in the bedroom.

"Well, you just made dinner for the first time in a long while for three people and it tasted damn good. You got some exercise today for the first time in who knows how long. But, the most important thing you did today is that you didn't drink. Don't take that as a given. You celebrate those days because each one is important."

"But the cherry on top is this," continued Dutch as all three men and Jake were now standing in the dimly lit room with Dutch staring directly at Jeremy's bed. "You have a perfectly made bed to sleep in tonight. A bed you made yourself. The corners look crisp, the folds are precise, and the overhang on both sides is perfectly equal. It took you three tries, but you did it. It could pass a military inspection."

The three men all paused and looked with admiration at the bed Jeremy had made.

Dutch turned to Jeremy. "No matter how shitty your day is. If you start by making your bed, at least you accomplished one task successfully. You start your day with that. You can build on it. Even if the rest of your day goes down the toilet, when you go to bed, you are a least reminded that you did one thing right that day. Sometimes, that's all you'll need to help you sleep that night. It gives you hope for the next day."

Miles looked at Jeremy and he could see the wheels turning in his head. Dutch turned around and walked back in the kitchen and began to clean up the dinner dishes. Jeremy sat down on the edge of his bed and remained quiet. Miles looked at him and asked, "What's on your mind, buddy?"

"I can't really say, Miles. I guess I'm still trying to get used to having a clear head."

"I'm going to head back to town Jeremy. Is there anything else you need?"

"I'm sure there's something. I will have to talk to my parents in a day or so and get them up to speed on what's going on up here. Can you help me with that?"

"Sure. I'll talk to Dutch and we'll set it up by radio."

"Thanks, Miles. I'll talk to ya later."

Miles left Jeremy in his room with Jake on the floor at the foot of Jeremy's bed complete with forty-five degree hospital corners.

CHAPTER THIRTY

As daylight started to stream in through the small window of his bedroom, Jeremy could smell the strong aroma of coffee coming in through his doorway. It was early of course, and Dutch was sitting at the table reading a newspaper that Miles had left behind. Jeremy slowly swung his stiff legs out of the bed and had to push with his left arm across his chest against the bed to sit upright and put his feet on the floor. His body was not used to the activity of the previous day and he was paying the bill for it now. His sleep wasn't as good the night before as his mind was more active and he had taken several impromptu naps the previous day. It was hard to quiet his thoughts after he rolled over in bed during the night and woke himself up. A myriad of thoughts that dealt with his handling of things. He wondered what rehab would be like when he left the cabin. He wondered about his parents. He worried about what would happen if he drank again. This was all middle of the night brain activity that drunken Jeremy never gave a second thought. Now he had things on his mind, and it wasn't the little details. It was big stuff, really, really big stuff.

Jeremy put on some clean sweatpants, shuffled out to the kitchen, and poured himself some coffee. He silently sat down across from Dutch. Jake sauntered up and sat next to Jeremy, leaning heavily against his leg.

"Feeling kinda stiff this morning?" Dutch asked and didn't even glance up from his paper.

"Yeah. I think I did a little too much yesterday." Jeremy sipped his coffee while petting Jake.

"You sounded like a one hundred year-old man getting out of bed." Dutch folded his paper up and glanced at Jeremy. Dutch removed his reading glasses and put them on the table. "You're in worse shape than I thought."

"I couldn't turn my brain off last night. I woke up and couldn't fall asleep for the longest time."

"Yeah, that happens. Your head has been so pickled for such a long time that when your brain wakes up you aren't sure what to do with it. So, your head is filled with all kinds of unorganized stuff. It's like a filing cabinet tipped over and your thoughts and fears are spilled out all over the floor."

"It's a little overwhelming." Jeremy stared straight ahead, obviously tired from his poor night of sleep.

Dutch stood up and walked over to the stove and poured himself another cup of coffee. "Trust me. It's going to get worse before it gets better. You have some long sleepless nights ahead. As your body starts healing more, you won't be as tired and you'll struggle to sleep. Just remember that it's normal, and it's temporary."

Jake stayed close to Jeremy as he walked back to the bedroom and went through the meticulous process of making his bed. Equal sides, corners exact, and pillow centered neatly. After a trip to the outhouse, Jeremy came back in with a couple pieces of wood for the already glowing fire. He quietly sat in the chair next to the fire as Dutch cooked up a breakfast of steak and eggs. It was venison steak from a whitetail buck he had shot the previous November, so Jeremy didn't recognize the aroma.

"What kind of meat is that?"

"Deer meat," Dutch replied. "It's healthier than beef. Much leaner."

Dutch put two breakfasts on the table simultaneously and sat down. "C'mon and have a seat."

Jeremy joined him, immediately and as he dug into the eggs, he soon realized that his sense of taste had improved. This food was delicious. Either Dutch was a master chef or Jeremy's taste buds woke up from a decade long sabbatical.

Dutch finally broke the silence after a few minutes of the men eating. Something had been bugging him and he had to know something.

"Jeremy, how old are you?"

"I'm fifty-five. Why?"

"How in the hell did you make it to fifty-five years the way you drink? I have been around some real professionals and most of them die before they are forty years old. Usually, their livers or their pancreas gives out or they have a heart attack. Some just end up in a car wreck or motorcycle accident. How are you fifty-five?"

Jeremy wiped his mouth and finished chewing, answering Dutch thoughtfully.

"That's a good question. Fact is, I didn't drink like this all the time. And, the other thing is, I was just plain lucky sometimes. I've been in those car accidents. This scar on my chin is from that. I've fallen down stairs, gotten the shit beat out of me, fell out of a boat, and rolled some golf carts drunk multiple times. But up until I won that lottery money, I was a married weekend warrior. I had a home life, a job, responsibilities, and standards that people applied to me. I followed that. On the weekends, I tore the town up though. Tailgate parties, business dinners, fraternity reunions, pub crawls with friends. My wife went along with it for a while. But, as our friends started having kids, our group got smaller. Less guys to blend in with. My wife Natalie wanted a family too. I was willing to go along with it, I guess. She was a career woman and really successful, but by thirty-four or thirty-five she wanted to pivot and do something else and be a mom. It was around then that I won that money. That was a few years ago. I thought that money was the answer to all our issues. No more work, all that time to do whatever I wanted. Turns out it was my license to party even more. I spent a ton of time traveling for sporting events and concerts. Natalie went along at first and it was fun, but she got tired of it real fast and wanted to be home more, so I just kept going on without her. I'd be gone for weekend games and not come back until Monday or Tuesday all hungover and nasty. She said either we become a family or we were going to call it quits. I didn't want to become this old boring guy so I told her whatever she decided was fine with me. Well, she decided. We were divorced within a year."

"Ah, this is much worse than I thought." Remarked Dutch. "You're the worst kind of rich drunk. You're like a trust fund baby. You won your money. You didn't grind out a successful empire or build a business. You didn't earn it. It's as bad as inheriting it, maybe worse. Oh boy. She take you to the cleaners with the divorce settlement?"

"She never wanted a dime. She told me that the money I won was the worst thing to ever happen to us and wouldn't take any of it. I made sure she got the house, and until she met someone else, I paid the taxes and expenses. She met someone else a little over a year later and the guy proposed to her. She was pregnant almost right away and has a son now."

"She was a pretty smart girl. Good looking?"

"Oh Dutch, she is still beautiful. She's so much happier today. I still love her, but she's better off without me. We stay in touch. Her husband is a really good guy too."

Dutch looked closely at Jeremy.

"Maybe you thought you didn't deserve a girl like her. You sabotaged yourself?"

"I was reading that book you gave me. The guy in the book said you don't want to be the oldest guy at the frat party. Shit. I'm embarrassed to admit it, but I was that guy for the last 15 years."

"Well Jeremy, part of fixing you being a fuckup is acknowledging that you're a fuckup. You can't fix a problem if you don't know one exists."

"Yeah, but how in the hell do you face your mortality? I mean it's better to be young and vibrant than old and grouchy, right?"

"How young and vibrant did you feel when you came home to your wife like a bag of shit after those drunken weekends? Did you use your youth to your advantage? Let me tell you something. For most people, getting old is a privilege. You may get to raise a child to do good in the world. They keep you young. They give you satisfaction and a sense that the future is going to be a better place because of them. If you get lucky enough to live as long as me, you might still have an opportunity to build something of value in your life that takes effort. It takes responsibility. You could feel the satisfaction of it later."

"Shit. Look at what responsibility did to Miles. He's worn out. Burnt out. He's not having any fun. I've tried to avoid that. My life was all laid out by my wife that led to a predictable grave. Fuck that. Look at Miles. He's dead inside."

Dutch was getting visibly pissed and he raised his voice.

"Responsibility didn't leave him dead inside. Grief did. Leaving school did. His girlfriend dying did. Losing his parents did. Losing his son in law did. The best thing he ever did was raise Gabby. It gave him purpose and he did one hell of a job. So many people benefit from Gabby being around. That's what happens when you get it right."

Both sat silently. Jeremy got up to walk to the sink and began to wash the dishes from breakfast. Dutch turned to Jeremy and addressed him in a sharp tone.

"Congratulations. You've managed to avoid responsibility quite well. Nobody would ever mistake you for Miles. He's reliable, responsible, and he sets a good example for others."

Dutch turned and walked out the door leaving Jeremy standing at the sink. It was difficult for Jeremy to hear that he basically wasted the last 30 years of his life. It was even harder for him to acknowledge that Dutch was right.

CHAPTER THIRTY-ONE

The regime designed by Dutch ensured that Jeremy was kept very busy. Breakfast was prepared by Dutch most mornings with Jeremy washing the dishes afterwards while the two men would alternate dinner responsibilities. There would be time at the woodshed cutting and splitting wood for the fireplace, and water was carried from the hand pump to the cabin. The men took daily walks together and Dutch would move the ribbon each time Jeremy increased his distance. It was remarkable how Jeremy's strength and stamina increased the more time he spent in this remote area.

Eventually Dutch had the solar panels working and there was enough electricity in the tiny rustic cabin to power the record player. Dutch retrieved a dusty box from the bedroom containing his collection of old albums. Excited to finally hear some music, Jeremy began to paw through Dutch's collection with childlike enthusiasm. The collection included albums from many bands that were popular during the mid to late 1960s. Jeremy found LPs from The Animals, Buffalo Springfield, Cream, The Who and The Rolling Stones.

"This is an awesome collection you've got here, and these jackets are in near mint condition," marveled Jeremy, as he continued to flip through the pristine collection albeit more gently now. "My folks listened to some of these artists when I was growing up, but they were more into jazz during that era."

"Oh, I listened to some of that too." Dutch replied. "I've got some John Coltrane, a few from Miles Davis and some Dave Brubeck. Keep looking."

As the platter on the turntable began to spin, Jeremy handed Dutch The Stones *"Let it Bleed"* and soon the haunting melody of *Gimme Shelter* began to drift through the small speaker in the front of the old Dansette record player. Dutch sat in the chair closest to the fireplace, put his head back and closed his eyes. The music acted like a time machine with each man having his own frame of reference. It had been too long since music had played at the cabin. Too long for Jeremy and much too long for Dutch.

Jeremy continued his journal entries and wrote down his activities from the day and random thoughts about what was rolling around in his head. The routine was getting comfortable. The structure gave Jeremy things to look forward to each day. As he approached the end of his first week at the cabin, he decided to quit shaving and let a beard begin.

With the increase in strength and stamina, came new problems. Sleep at night became more and more difficult. Jeremy would be tired at the end of the day, but wake after midnight and feel anxious. His mind would constantly go over events in his head from his divorce, to problems with his parents, to his health worries, and then circle back to the divorce. Eventually, he would decide to get up and use that time to try reading more. He finished the Jordan Peterson book and was now reading a version of the story of the Battle of Britain that Dutch had given him a few days earlier. It was an old book, printed back in the 1950's with a blue green hard cover complete with gold lettering. The pages were yellow and musty. The book talked about the struggle between the Royal Air Force and the German Luftwaffe during the late summer and early fall of 1940.

Despite his early morning reading, Jeremy's anxiety level was increasing. His feet would sweat and after several nights he realized there were layers of dead skin peeling off the bottoms of his feet. He was not used to this and became concerned. How would he handle himself once he left the cabin? This resulted in more worry and in the lonely darkness of night in that cabin in the Ontario wilderness, Jeremy started to think that drinking was going to be the only way to calm himself down. He was terrified. On the seventh day at the cabin, he decided to ask Dutch for help with the night situation since it was getting out of hand.

As Jeremy sat at the table with Dutch, his shoulders were

slumped. Dutch would sometimes wait for Jeremy to initiate a conversation, but this time he could see that Jeremy was more withdrawn and seemed distant. Dutch knew something wasn't right, so he just came out and asked; "What's on your mind?"

Jeremy fiddled with his coffee cup, hesitated and finally, he just admitted it out loud.

"I sure could use a drink."

Dutch smiled in spite of himself because he knew this moment would happen. Hopefully, he could make an important point for Jeremy. Jeremy saw that Dutch smiled a bit and got pissed.

"This fun for you? You enjoying yourself?"

"No. This isn't fun. And, I'm not enjoying myself. What I'm seeing is progress, believe it or not."

"You have got to be kidding me," Jeremy was getting agitated at the inference that this was going well. In his mind, he was a guy barely holding on with no confidence. His conviction was fading.

"No. I'm not kidding. What you're going through now is something that everybody goes through eventually. You've gone almost two weeks without a drink and you can't even see how you've improved. I went through this stage a long time ago and it wasn't easy. You think you're the first guy to go a couple weeks without booze and your thoughts get the best of you? Are you special?"

"Look Dutch, this is the longest I've probably gone without drinking since I was seventeen years old. I can't settle my mind down. I can't shut it off. We can go for walks and cook and read books but I dread that goddamn bed every night. The skin is peeling off my feet because I lay in bed and sweat. I can't relax and just close my eyes. I think about almost dying, I think about my failed marriage, I think about my parents. I think and think and think and think and I'm FUCKING SICK OF IT!"

Jeremy slammed his fist on the table, rattling the dinner plates, and startling Jake. The dog retreated away from the table and went over by the fireplace.

Dutch, as usual, got calmer as Jeremy became more agitated. He moved closer to Jeremy and looked him dead in the eye and spoke quietly and deliberately.

"You think your problem is drinking. It's not. Sobriety is your problem. You need support from people or a group that has your interest at heart. You need somebody to help teach you how to deal with shit that comes up when you stop drinking. You're not drinking for no reason. You're drinking to manage your emotions and help grease a way through your problems. Once your drinking is removed and all these thoughts and problems that have been festering in your head come up, you have no coping skills. You feel like you can't trust yourself. That's why you're up here now. You're hiding."

Jeremy's eyes widened as he sat back in his chair. Dutch had just described perfectly what had been going on in his head that he couldn't put it into words himself. It was like a light went on.

Jeremy muttered slightly above a whisper., "Holy shit."

Dutch knew this point would come and he wanted the message to stick when it happened. He looked Jeremy in the eye and spoke even slower, "Do you want help?"

"Yeah Dutch. Help me get through this."

"Ok then. I want you to finish the Battle of Britain book tonight. We'll talk about it tomorrow."

Confused, Jeremy nodded his head as he took Jake outside and walked him down to the lake. The snow was retreating more each day and the ice around the shoreline was receding slowly. The ice in the middle of the frozen lake was getting darker each day and as the snow melted, the water seeped through the icy top of Beaver Lake. The spring sun was doing its job. Jeremy felt bad for scaring Jake inside the cabin earlier, so he petted the dog and talked to him in a soothing voice. He then realized that the short walk felt good. His ribs were still sore, but nothing like before. His eyesight was clearing up some and the bend of his broken nose was not as pronounced now that the swelling had gone down.

Dutch started cleaning up after dinner. The previous days had been somewhat mundane, but tonight there was something electric about their conversation. It was as though Jeremy understood something a bit more. It could be that his brain fog was clearing, or maybe he was finally realizing what cogent thought was like again.

Jeremy went to his bedroom that night and put in the time to finish the book that Dutch talked about. He fell asleep around 11 p.m., later than usual. He woke up to go to the outhouse before daybreak again, but his anxiety level was not as high when he went back to bed. His feet weren't sweating and his thoughts were not racing as they were those other nights. He dozed off slowly and was soon sleeping again. Dutch could hear him snoring from his own room. He felt like things had maybe improved a bit for Jeremy and was glad he was finally getting some rest. Maybe Dutch could push him a bit more physically going forward.

After breakfast in the morning, Dutch started to pack up a few items in a backpack and asked Jeremy to get ready. Today was going to be a work day.

"What kind of work are we doing today?"

Dutch grinned and told Jeremy, "Cleanup day today."

CHAPTER THIRTY-TWO

Dutch led Jeremy outside to a small pull cart with what looked like small bicycle tires. Dutch carried the backpack while Jeremy pulled the cart. Jeremy struggled at first, trying to use his walking stick in one hand while pulling the cart with the other. Exasperated, he finally just tossed the stick into the cart. They continued on the same walking trail that they had been using every day, but when they reached the marking ribbon from the previous day, Dutch took it off the branch and put it in his pocket.

"We won't be needing this anymore." Dutch mumbled.

Jeremy was confused by the action of Dutch. Jeremy assumed they were on their way to get some firewood or maybe to clean up the remnants of a downed tree. As the two men kept walking, a sinking feeling come over Jeremy once again. He started to suspect where they were heading. Their walks during his entire time had been leading up to this.

After going another one hundred yards around trees and through a small hollow, they arrived at the infamous tree line where the destroyed Yamaha snow machine lay in pieces. Jeremy's mouth grew dry as he remembered being here the first time after the accident. It was only a week ago, but a lot had happened since then. Jeremy could feel his body temperature increase. He became sweaty as the thought of death entered his head.

Dutch was in front of Jeremy for the entire walk, but paused as Jeremy caught up. The two men stood shoulder to shoulder looking at the twisted remains of the SRX. Most of the snow had melted around the base of the charred tree. Little red and white shards of shattered fiberglass littered the ground. Twisted skis and balled up metal lay in small piles in front of the men. Once again Jeremy wondered how and why he had survived the crash.

"It's time for you to start getting this mess cleaned up," Dutch turned to Jeremy and handed him some work gloves.

Without a word, Jeremy grabbed the work gloves from Dutch and slowly walked toward the wreckage. He pulled the cart behind him and slowly picked up pieces of debris putting them in the cart. Dutch walked around the site looking for anything unusual, but decided not to assist at all in the cleanup. Dutch wanted Jeremy to understand that it was his mess and he had to handle the clean up.

After about thirty minutes, Jeremy's ribs ached and the cart was full. Dutch suggested heading back to the cabin. Jeremy began to pull the cart, but struggled from the outset. It was heavy and the ground was uneven. In addition to his ribs being sore, Jeremy had also built up a sweat bending over and picking up wreckage. He was feeling more than a bit fatigued.

Dutch tossed his backpack in the cart and began to pull. Jeremy grabbed his walking stick and started to lead the way. Dutch knew this was more exertion than Jeremy thought he could handle, but it was time to push him a little more. Jeremy followed the walking path back toward the cabin and Dutch followed pulling the cart. As the two men got about halfway back to the cabin, some movement up ahead on the trail caught Dutch's eye. He immediately stopped.

"Jeremy, STOP!"

Jeremy turned around, slightly annoyed, and questioned Dutch, "I'm fine. I just need to…"

"GODDAMNIT JEREMY! STOP NOW!"

Suddenly, there was the breaking of branches and the sound of something heavy moving through the trees. Jeremy turned around and looked ahead in time to see a large brown bear enter the clearing. The bear was approximately one hundred feet ahead of them. Dutch lowered his voice and spoke very slowly and without moving.

"Stop talking. Don't move. Maybe he won't notice us."

Jeremy's eyes widened as he saw the huge head of the bear turn towards them. Jeremy was frozen by fear. Within a second, the bear whirled around, bunched up, and started to run directly at the two men.

"Just stay there………" Dutch urged.

Jeremy felt a wave of panic come over him, "Holy Shit!"

Next an adrenaline rush came over Jeremy as he saw the huge animal bearing down on them. He could see the muscles of the bear's back and shoulders rippling. The paws of the bear slammed into the ground as the animal charged them. Without thinking, Jeremy raised his walking stick and pointed it at the bear. He let out what could only be described as a barbaric scream. At the top of his lungs.

"AHHHAHHHHHHH, FUCKING BEAR!!!!!!" echoed through the forest.

Jeremy's legs went into motion and he moved towards the oncoming beast. They were no more than thirty feet from each other with Jeremy screaming and the bear grunting as it charged.

BOOM! BOOM! BOOM!

Three incredibly loud gunshots rang out, shattering the noise of Jeremy yelling and the bear growling. The bear slammed on the breaks and pivoted off the trail, creating a huge cloud of dust and flying dirt. Terrified, Jeremy collapsed on the ground when the gunshots rang out. The crack of the gunfire rang in his ears as he balled up on the ground. His eyes were as big as saucers as he looked back through the dust and hazy smoke from the muzzle blast.

Dutch stood calmly with a huge desert eagle pistol aimed directly over the bear's head. The .50 caliber shots let out a deafening sound and the shots went right over the bear and Jeremy. The startled bear bolted away when the rounds thundered off and echoed through the thick woods.

Jeremy lie on the ground trying to collect himself with his ears still ringing. He was shaking and his voice was high pitched, "WHAT THE FUCK WAS THAT!?!"

Dutch calmly looked down at Jeremy. "Are you ok?"

"NO! DUTCH! NO! I'M NOT OK! I THINK I LOST MY FUCKING HEARING!"

"Seems to be just fine to me."

Jeremy struggled to his feet as he brushed the dirt and dust off himself. Crouched down, he was still shaking and the high-pitched tone in his voice remained. He couldn't believe the size of the pistol Dutch was holding. It had a barrel that looked as big as a drain pipe.

"When did you bring that gun along?"

"I always bring my firearm with me in the woods. Sometimes you encounter a bear."

"Yeah, Dutch. No shit," still agitated, Jeremy was trying to collect himself. "Thanks for the warning."

The two men stood still staring at each other.

"Oh no," Jeremy sounded distraught.

Dutch looked at him with concern, "What's the matter?"

Jeremy slowly came out of his crouch and turned to Dutch.

"I think I shit myself," Jeremy confessed sheepishly.

Dutch's eyes widened, "AGAIN?!?"

"What the hell do you mean again?"

"This is the second time!"

Jeremy crouched down.

"I don't count the first time. I was drunk and crashed into a tree," explained Jeremy, trying to defend himself.

"Well, I sure count it. I had to clean it up."

Jeremy attempted to catch his breath before speaking again.

"Goddamn, that bear was huge."

Dutch put the huge pistol back in his bag and then reached in an outside pocket for a roll of toilet paper.

"Here. Clean yourself up," and he tossed the roll to the still shaken and trembling Jeremy.

"Hey, by the way, what were you going to do with that stick when the bear got to you?"

Jeremy's voice was shaky as he realized that he had charged a bear.

"The first time we took a walk you gave me that stick and said

I should use it to fight off a bear," Jeremy reminded Dutch.

Dutch gave him a disbelieving look.

"I wasn't serious."

Jeremy yelled in his high-pitched voice, "WELL SHIT, DUTCH! I DIDN'T KNOW THAT!"

Dutch started laughing at the situation. It was the first time Jeremy saw him laugh and he couldn't help but chuckle himself.

Dutch was now egging on Jeremy, asking him how to hold the stick in case of a bear attack. He struggled to get the words out. He was laughing too hard. Tears rolled down his cheeks and he was having a hard time catching his breath.

Jeremy looked at Dutch with a combination of incredulity and relief. He realized that the old man had saved his life once again. At that moment, Jeremy got another whiff of his full pants.

"Oh man, this smells so bad," Jeremy admitted and began to gag.

Now this made Dutch really howl with laughter, and when he managed to collect himself, Dutch finally got out some words through his laughter and tears.

"Don't feel too bad kid. That bear probably shit himself too," chortled Dutch as he smacked Jeremy on the back lightheartedly.

CHAPTER THIRTY-THREE

After the two men got back to the cabin, Jeremy took a bath and cleaned himself up in the tub outside. Dutch had heated the water over the campfire while Jake played in the yard. It was a warm afternoon and it felt as though spring was maybe here to stay. Birds were flying around and the sky was blue. Dutch was working on the solar panel batteries when Jeremy asked about something that had not yet come up.

"Can I ask you about your sobriety?"

"Sure. What do you want to know?"

Jeremy struggled to find the words to explain himself, and then asked, "Did you have the night sweats and thoughts running through your mind like a train? You know. Like, you couldn't shut off your brain."

Dutch climbed down the ladder and sat on the edge of a log and began to pet Jake. Even though it was a nice sunny day, you could see that the thoughts in Dutch's head were bringing back some dark clouds. He looked skyward for the way to start explaining.

With a faraway look, Dutch told his story.

"I was fourth in line moving up the hill. Tom Reese was on point, Gary Millet was behind him, and some new kid just in from the world was ahead of me. I think his name was Paul. We didn't spend a lot of time getting to know new guys 'cause they got killed so fast. We were near Dak To and it was November 17, in '67. We were on a hill they airlifted us to. The NVA had a bunch of bunkers there and they suckered us into coming after them. There was a shitload of casualties because of friendly fire, NVA rockets, and mortar fire. We even had a marine pilot accidently drop a couple snake eyes into a medical area that killed and wounded a bunch of guys and medical personnel."

Dutch took a deep breath and continued, "Anyway, I was the

fourth guy when a sniper got the kid right in front of me. He was shot in the neck. I stayed low to the ground and got to him right away, but he was hit real bad. I tried to patch him up, but he was dead inside of a minute. The guys behind me, Carl Devlin, Mike Robisch, and Tony Ginello went past and I heard Tom and Gary open up on a tunnel entrance up ahead. Carl, Mike and Tony ran up to join them when all of a sudden there was a bunch of rocket fire coming down on the guys ahead of me. Shit was blowing up. There was yelling and screaming. I could hear everybody open up on the high ground. There were more guys behind me, but suddenly, we were taking fire from the rear too. We were caught in a trap." Dutch explained with a faraway look in his eyes.

"So, our guys were firing in two directions and I see Gary coming back with his arm around Tony hopping on one leg. Tony said to stay there because he had to get Carl. Carl was hit much worse. I wasn't sure whether or not to move when Bruce Crane comes up from below and says they need me down there. I tell him to stay with Gary and wait for Tony to come back with Carl. He says ok."

Becoming increasingly animated, Dutch continues, "So, I go down the hill and find a new guy with a foot wound and Denny Fricke with a bad chest wound. I get Denny wrapped up the best I can and drag him away from the fire towards our line and two guys run into me. I ask them to get him down the hill asap, because I got other guys up the hill waiting for me. They grab Denny and haul him down and I go back to check on this new kid and I can't find him anywhere. I head back up to find Gary Millet and Bruce Crane because I know Tony is coming back with Carl. I get back to where I left Gary and I find both of them dead. There was a mortar round that got 'em both. Just then, Tony gets back, carrying Carl. He lays him down and starts back up saying he has to get Mike because he got hit too."

"So, I'm working on Carl and his belly wound and it looks like I'll be able to get Carl out of there. I start to carry Carl down the hill and I find some more help. They grab Carl and another medic joins me and we head back up to where Tony and Mike are. Tony

Ginello has Mike Robisch over his shoulder and screams that we gotta get outta there. There's a shitload of NVA that are pouring out of the tunnels and heading our direction. All the way Mike is screaming that he thinks Tom Reese is still up there somewhere, "We gotta get Tom. We gotta get Tom. " I ask him, "Where is he?" Mike says he was right next to him when a rocket came through and hit next to them. He must be there. I ask Tony, "Where is Tom? Where did you see Tom?" Tony said he didn't see him at all anywhere. Mike is still screaming about Tom. This is all happening while we are trying to get down the hill with all these wounded guys."

Dutch pauses for a moment and stares straight ahead. He takes a deep breath before continuing.

"We finally get out of the hard stuff and the enemy at the base of the hill had been put down. We were just about ready to head back to the makeshift LZ so we could evac the guys that needed to get out first. I'm standing right next to Tony when an incoming round hits me right in the ankle. I fell like a bag of wet cement. Tony grabs me and pulls me on one leg to the LZ. As I'm waiting for my turn on the chopper, I'm trying to work on Carl and I find Denny and make sure his dressing is good. Mike is laying on the ground with about 20 holes in him, covered in blood, crying that we gotta get Tom over and over again. I tell him that we're gonna find him and it's going to be ok, knowing for damn sure that it isn't. Tony and the other medic try to get back up there to look for Tom, but the mortar fire is fierce. Then we get orders. Everybody off the hill because the guys at the firebase are going to light it up."

Dutch takes a deep breath, "We got back to the hospital and the surgeons are working on everybody. I'm like third from last because my wound isn't that bad. When they operated on Mike Robisch, they found several bone fragments in Mike that came from someone else. Then, one of the surgeons pulled a piece of shrapnel out that was one of Tom Reese's dog tags."

Dutch was emotionally exhausted as his story came to a close, "So, that day we lost Gary Millet, Bruce Crane, that baby faced kid Paul, and Tom Reese. I was really tight with Gary and Tom. Mike Robisch too. The balls Tony Ginello showed that day. He saved five guys from that hill. Tony came out of all that without a scratch. Running through all that fire and he never had a scratch."

Jeremy sat silently as Dutch stared off into the woods, a million miles away..... The long silence was uncomfortable. Finally, Dutch spoke once again.

"And for Tony to go through all that and make it home just to get killed in a car wreck three miles from his house? Shit. What God allows that? He was only twenty-two."

"I'm sorry Dutch. I didn't mean to drudge all this up."

"No Jeremy. It's about my sobriety. My biggest problem was, and still is survivor's guilt. I think about Bruce Crane staying with Gary Millet because I asked him to. If Bruce goes on up ahead like he was originally, maybe he makes it off the hill that day. I take a round and I'm not there for the rest of my tour. I was in a hospital so I could walk again and keep my foot. I was discharged and sent back to the world. Why was my life spared?"

"You stay in touch with the guys? The ones who made it?"

"I did for a while. I met up with Denny about a year after I got back and he was still trying to recover. His health was never the same and he died when he was only forty-six. Mike Robisch was hard to find, and when I did, he was a drunk. I didn't know how to help him. He was so broken by what had happened to us on the hill that day. Losing Tom when he was right next to him. There was nothing left of Tom to bury. Just that damn dog tag and some bone slivers." Dutch paused for a moment and looked skyward again. Jeremy could see how painful it was for him to share this.

"Well, Mike never got sober," Dutch explained. "His liver gave out before he was forty. He couldn't figure out how to live with it. So here I sit. Of the seven of us that made it to the Battle of Dak To, you see the only lucky bastard left. So, believe me when I tell you that I know what it's like to not be able to sleep."

"How do you do it?" Jeremy wondered out loud.

"I try to remind myself that I owe these guys. They didn't make it. If I had the ability to put myself back together and make a good life and I didn't follow through with it, I'd be pissing on their graves. I owe them to do well."

Jeremy sat embarrassed thinking about his problems in comparison to the burdens Dutch carried. He tried to put a positive tone into the conversation.

"Yeah, but look at you. You've got the drinking beat. You've been sober for so long that you can be proud of the fact that you beat it."

"Listen carefully to me. The amount of time sober doesn't have dick to do with how much danger you can be in. Every day could be your last day sober. You can be on the edge for years and sobriety can disappear in a flash. It's easy to think that because I've been sober for almost forty years that I'm out of the woods. But the fact is I still struggle sometimes to say no, not today. That whole thing could be reset with a few bad choices. I have gotten better at dealing with my problems sober, but I didn't get this smart all at once."

This made Jeremy wonder. "Let me ask you something. Before you had a problem with it, did you ever enjoy it? Drinking? I mean didn't you cut lose and have some fun? Is there ever a time now when you think, man, a drink would really hit the spot?"

Dutch pondered for a moment and smiled. "Yes. There is one thing I miss. On a real hot summer day after mowing the grass or sweating outside in the sun, I miss drinking an ice-cold beer."

Jeremy smiled. "Yeah. I hear ya there. But, hey, they make nonalcoholic beer. You know, several companies make it. Even Heineken makes it."

Dutch slid off the log and started toward the cabin. He turned back and looked at Jeremy still bathing in the water.

"Jeremy. I'm going to tell you this once and once only. I don't drink near-beer and I don't fuck inflatable plastic women."

CHAPTER THIRTY-FOUR

As evening began to descend on the cabin, Jeremy was doing the dinner dishes while Dutch was bringing in wood for the fire. Jake was laying by the fireplace and snoozing. The excitement of the bear incident was still fresh in Jeremy's mind. He could even remember the odor of the huge animal after it took off into the woods.

"Hey Dutch. Do you think our friend the bear is relaxing for the evening now?"

As Dutch put another log on the fire, he smiled a bit. As he settled into the chair, he stroked the fur on the top of Jake's head and commented, "What I couldn't believe is when you started going after the bear. I didn't expect that."

Jeremy shook his head, "I didn't even realize I was doing it. That bear was going to shove that stick right up my ass."

"You never know." Dutch mused. "That might have prevented the other problem you had."

"No, Dutch. I think that was going to happen no matter what."

"Let me ask you a question, Jeremy. Do you think the guy that showed up here a week ago would have the balls to go after a charging bear with a stick?"

Jeremy stopped at the sink for a moment and pondered.

"Honestly Dutch, I guess I figured that the only thing between us and that bear was my walking stick. Of course, I didn't realize you had that cannon in your bag. Otherwise, I would have circled back behind you and hid like a little girl."

"Yeah, but you didn't know I had that pistol. You were trying to do your best to survive. That says something."

"Yeah, but I guess I just don't know if that's progress or if it's just some kind of reflex. You know, a reaction."

"Self-preservation is the most basic reaction there is. It's the most important reaction," explained Dutch."It says that you're on the right path."

Dutch was getting somewhat frustrated because he was having trouble expressing his point in a way Jeremy could understand.

"Did you finish the Battle of Britain?" Dutch inquired.

"Yeah, I finished it before I went to sleep last night like you asked."

Dutch looked at him.

"And?"

"And what? The British won the battle, they shot down a bunch of Germans and Hitler couldn't invade England. End of story."

Dutch shook his head. "You don't get it, do you?"

Jeremy seemed frustrated.

"What am I missing? Enlighten me."

Dutch turned in his chair to face Jeremy so he could better explain the point he was making.

"During the summer, the Germans knew the Royal Air Force was good. They had good planes and some excellent pilots. In order to be able to defeat the Brits, the Germans knew they needed control of the air. So, they got the RAF pilots up into the skies for dogfights. They bombed British air bases. And, for a while, it was an even battle. The Brits and the Germans were matching each other, plane for plane. Each side was losing equal amounts. The problem with that was that the Brits had fewer planes and pilots to lose. The Germans had a numbers advantage. When they hit the airfields and focused on defeating the RAF, the Germans were turning the tide."

"But, in late August, some British night raids inadvertently dropped bombs on residential areas of Berlin, killing civilians. Hitler immediately ordered the Luftwaffe to start creaming London every single night. Plymouth too. It was about killing civilians now and Hitler wanted a high body count. While this was going on, the pressure was taken off the RAF so they were able to get more newly trained pilots into the fight. They also got the airfields repaired and got more new planes into service."

"So, while the cities were getting bombed and lit on fire every night, those unbelievable pilots and crews of the RAF were gaining momentum. By mid-September, the Brits were bringing down German planes at a higher rate than before. In one day, the British lost twenty-six planes, but the Germans lost sixty. This was the same night that London took a hell of a beating. Bombs even landed on Buckingham palace."

"All the war correspondents were looking at the cities and thinking that England was losing the battle. Fires everywhere, destroyed buildings, wounded, and killed civilians. What they didn't realize was that the shore batteries and anti-aircraft crews and the young RAF pilots were beating the shit out of the Germans in the skies away from the cities. It didn't take long and the raids started to weaken. Pretty soon the Brits knew they had made it."

Jeremy listened intently as Dutch summed up the entire battle in minutes.

Dutch stared at him and finally said, "They were winning the battle and they didn't even realize it."

Jeremy walked over to the table and sat in a chair and let Dutch's point sink in.

Dutch relaxed his tone a bit, but still wanted Jeremy to understand something.

"You are doing better than you think. The sleepless nights, the regrets, the 'what could I have done differently crap' is going to be there, but you are figuring out how to deal with it."

Dutch got up from his chair and walked over towards his room, getting ready for bed. He turned back towards Jeremy.

"Besides, you went after a charging bear today with nothing more than a walking stick and lived to talk about it. Put that in your journal. Goodnight."

Dutch shut his door.

CHAPTER THIRTY-FIVE

The next few days were quieter. Dutch and Jeremy would start off in the late morning and pull the cart out to the crash site. Now that Jeremy knew Dutch carried that huge pistol, he didn't worry about bears or any other animals ruining their day. By the third day, Jeremy had enough strength to pull the loaded cart nearly halfway back to the cabin before he ran out of steam. He would make it back to the cabin, sit in the sun near the woodshed, and drink water. As Dutch pulled the cart into the yard, he would unload the snowmobile wreckage under a shed roof and then cover it up. Jeremy wondered why he wanted to conceal the twisted pile of debris.

"Hey Dutch? Why do you keep hiding that stuff under that tarp?"

"I don't want Miles to see it yet. I might have Doug come out and pick it all up. It would be good to get it out of here."

"I know that machine was old, but why did Miles keep it? Why didn't he have a newer one? He has enough money for a new one, right?"

"This one belonged to his dad and his dad has been gone a number of years. This sled meant a lot to him."

"Oh, sentimental value. I get it."

"No." Dutch explained. "Not just sentimental value."

"Ok. What else?"

"Miles' dad, James was a carpenter around here in the summer. For the winter, he would go down to Wisconsin and Minnesota and bartend at different resorts during the tourist season when people were riding these things. He won this machine in a race one time."

"Oh, shit. You mean they were going at each other for the title to their sleds?"

"This time, yes. Mostly it was for bragging rights, but

sometimes it was for money and sometimes it was for a lot of money."

Jeremy nodded his head.

"I've seen that on trips to Wisconsin. The Polaris guys are bitching at the Ski Doo guys and the Yamaha guys are pimping the Arctic Cat owners. It's a religion in some places."

"Yes. Well, in the late 70's, it was really bad. Anyway, James had a homemade sled that was fast as a damn rocket. He built it himself and he knew what he was doing. He knew how to ride, and he knew how to lake race against other sleds. It looked homemade and some of the bar customers were giving him crap about it."

"Now, James knew about the new factory sleds and what they could do. His sled was almost as fast as this SRX, but not quite. He went down to the lake one night on the ice and watched the owner of this sled race a few guys and beat everybody. This was the fast sled. What intrigued him was how the guy was riding the sled. He was all crouched up behind the windshield, right up to the handlebars. He had too much weight forward. James figured it was costing him speed, especially on his hole shot, just at the beginning. What you needed to do was to get as much weight back as possible. Get your arms extended and get the back part of the track in contact with the surface as much as possible. This translates to more speed, especially your hole shot."

"The next night in the bar, this Yamaha owner comes in bragging about his SRX and how hot it was. James chuckles a bit and this guy sticks his chest out and starts giving him shit about the homemade sled and how it could never stand up to the new technology and all that crap. James baited him in perfectly. The SRX owner challenged him to a race and James said he would only race for the pink slip. The guy balked and said the homemade sled wasn't worth as much so it wasn't even. So, James evened it out by saying he would pay the guy's cabin bills for the week for his group if he lost. Well, everybody laughed at that and thought James was nuts. They shook hands and met on the ice after closing the bar."

"There was probably 200 people down on the lake in front of the resort that night. James came out and got on the line and the other guy came out with this SRX. James looked over and saw just what he wanted to see. The guy was all the way forward, hiding behind his windshield. They had some random guy drop a flag and both sleds took off. It was a quarter mile long and James had a huge jump out of the hole."

"The SRX finally got traction and started to catch up, but James ended up beating the guy by a sled length. The guy just totally flipped out. James knew that the SRX was a faster sled, but it wasn't being driven properly. The SRX guy was just beside himself for losing the race and his brand spanking new Yamaha. He signed the slip over to James and then, incredibly, he asked James to sell him his sled. The homemade one. James couldn't believe it. He said he had to think about it. Well, he throws an offer of $6000 at him and tells him the offer is good for the next ten minutes. James tells the guy to have a nice night."

"The next night the guy comes in and offers him $1000 more and says that's his best offer. Seven thousand dollars for a sled that James built all by himself with borrowed tools and his own knowledge. He took it. He then rode this SRX and won several races for money over the next two winters. That money is what got Miles started in college and was the original nest egg that grew into the money that put Gabby through med school at Madison."

"Jesus," Jeremy couldn't believe what he had just heard. "So, let me get this straight." Jeremy started, "This snowmobile that I totaled in a drunken stupor, helped pay for the education of the doctor that helped save my life because I totaled this snowmobile in a drunken stupor."

Dutch pondered the sentence for a moment, before replying, "Yes. That pretty much sums it up."

Jeremy's head dropped at the realization of what this snowmobile meant to Miles' family. Hard work and smarts enabled them to succeed. They didn't have a lot of money. The

Yamaha that James left to Miles was a symbol of his family's character traits and it was destroyed by an act of carelessness and drunken stupidity.

Dutch's voice lowered a bit as he gave Jeremy a direct look, "I think you can appreciate why most people would be a little pissed off by this." Dutch got up and headed towards the cabin, "C'mon inside. Let's call for a carryout dinner tonight."

Jeremy was totally confused. He knew there were no places in Minaki that delivered, but he followed Dutch inside the cabin. Dutch went over to the radio set and called into Minaki. He got Carl on the radio and asked for a phone patch to Gabby's cell phone. Carl obliged.

"Hello? Dutch? This is Gabby. Is everything ok? Over."

"Yes. We're ok. We wanted to invite you to dinner tonight if you would bring it with you. Over."

Gabby laughed, "Let me guess Dutch. You want a couple of large pizzas from the Cider Barn?"

"You have a tremendous gift of reading minds young lady. Hold on. Over."

Dutch quickly turned to Jeremy, "What do you want on your pizza?"

Jeremy was completely stunned by this. He was caught totally off guard by the idea of getting pizza delivered into the Canadian wilderness.

"Uh, I guess sausage and mushroom. Oh.... and black olives."

"Gabby, I'll have my usual and Jeremy wants sausage, mushroom, and black olives. Oh, and bring some tomato bread for Jake. Over."

"Ok, Dutch. Should I bring Dad with? Over."

"If he wants to come, sure. Bring Robby if you want too. Order enough for everybody. Over."

"Thanks Dutch. We'll be up there around six or so. Over and out."

Jeremy smiled. It was an unexpected treat to not have to cook or do dishes tonight. He smiled and gave Dutch a pat on the shoulder.

"Thanks, Dutch. Pizza is a really great idea."

Dutch smiled back at Jeremy and patted him on the shoulder, "Don't thank me, Jeremy. You're the one that's buying."

Dutch smiled for an extra second, then took his hand off Jeremy's shoulder and headed back outside to pump some water.

Jeremy smiled as he realized he had been duped. He had been eating all of Dutch's food for the past 11 days. It was only fair that he stepped up and provided something. The old man had gotten him yet again.

A couple hours later Dutch and Jeremy could hear ATV's coming up the trail from Minaki. Miles was on one machine and Robby was driving the other with Gabby on the back. As they pulled in the yard, Robby got off his ATV and ran right over to Dutch and said hello. Dutch tousled Robby's hair and Jake came up to lick his face. Robby hadn't seen Dutch or Jake since the beginning of hockey season and it was clear they had a connection.

Gabby came over to Jeremy and her eyes were wide, "Holy cow! You look a lot better than the last time I saw you. You have better color and you look like you gained some weight. Is that a beard I see?"

"I guess I'm trying to fit in around here. Consider it a souvenir of my spontaneous Canadian visit."

Gabby led Jeremy into the cabin.

"Take your shirt off. I want to see how your scar is."

"Yeah, Dutch changed the dressing a few days ago."

"I know. I told him to."

Gabby looked carefully at the sight where the chest tube had been. It looked to be healing nicely with no sign of infection.

"You talked to him?"

"Yes. He radios me almost every evening with an update on your condition. It was something we agreed to do when you decided to stay here."

"So, you know about what has been going on?"

"You mean the sleepless nights and the skin peeling off the bottoms of your feet?" Gabby asked.

"Yeah. There's that."

"We talked about it. Sounds like you have been doing a little better this week. I mean sleep wise and with fighting off your anxiety."

"I don't know if I'd call it fighting off the anxiety. I think I might be figuring out a way to deflect it a bit. Did you bring anymore books?"

"No, but I did receive an email for you from your mom and dad that they asked me to give you. I printed out for you so you could have it."

"Thanks. Hey, I'm really hungry. Let's eat."

Within a few minutes, everyone was sitting around the small table in Dutch's cabin. Jake was munching away on a piece of tomato bread while Gabby, Miles, Dutch, Robby and Jeremy all sat around eating pizza, drinking lemonade and sharing stories about the past week.

"So, Jeremy." Miles started. "Show me this new weapon you use to hunt brown bears."

Gabby looked at her dad and Jeremy with her mouth open and wondered what they were talking about.

Dutch immediately shook his head, trying to hide the fact that this incident went unreported to Gabby during Dutch's daily radio reports.

"What are you talking about?" Gabby asked while squinting.

Miles was laughing as he gave the headline.

"Well, this bear came out of his winter nap and decided to introduce himself to Jeremy here. While hiking."

Wide eyed, Gabby was jokingly chastising Dutch.

"Why am I just hearing about this now? Are you putting my patient in some kind of danger?"

Dutch and everybody chuckled as the shock registered on Gabby's face. Gabby faced Jeremy.

Exasperated, Gabby asked, "Jeremy, what happened?"

With a straight face, Jeremy answered, "Uh, medically? The bear scared the shit out of me."

Everybody laughed. Even Robby started to laugh as the trickle truth finally gave way to the whole story.

Robby looked at Jeremy, "You pooped your pants!?!"

Jeremy pasted as dignified a face on the situation as he possibly could but answered quietly, "Yes Robby. I pooped my pants."

"Geez." Robby retorted. "I haven't pooped my pants since I was like three or something."

"Well, Robby, apparently, it's kind of a regular thing for me up here. Anyway, we can all aspire to keep a clean record and clean underwear much like yourself, young man. Hey, is this really table talk anyway?"

Everyone had a good-natured laugh at the bear story and the pizza was a great way to bring the group together. The days had been running into one another for Jeremy and this really broke things up and lifted his morale. After everyone had finished their plates, Dutch walked over to the garbage and Jeremy pulled him aside.

"Hey Dutch. Can I ask you a favor?"

"What is it?"

"Can you give me my phone? I want to get a few pictures of everyone tonight and I just want to enjoy this."

Dutch nodded in agreement. He retreated to his bedroom and got Jeremy's phone. He rejoined the table and got some pictures of the group and Miles asked if he had any Florida pictures he could show them. Jeremy started to scroll through some pictures that showed fish from John's boat and pictures of Jeremy's condo in Islamorada. Robby was surprised at the pictures of the condo and patio area.

"Holy cow. You have your own swimming pool?"

"Absolutely, Robby. And if you manage to keep your non-poop streak going you can come down anytime, stay at my place, and swim in my pool."

The pictures were mostly taken at bars and some pics were with John and Jeremy together. Gabby saw those pics and asked Jeremy who the guy was with him.

"That's my buddy, John. You talked to him on the phone."

Gabby smiled. "He's kind of good looking."

Miles saw some pics of Jeremy's boat and looked over it carefully. "You keep it on a lift to avoid the saltwater, Miles?"

"Oh yeah. The salt is really rough on the seals on the engines and lower unit."

Dutch asked if anybody wanted coffee and everyone but Robby raised their hands. Robby got a frozen piece of chocolate cake that Dutch had stashed. After the cake, Robby and Jake went outside to play in the remaining daylight after dinner.

Dutch and Miles sat at the table talking about the coming spring and summer. Gabby pulled Jeremy aside and led him outside where Jake and Robby were playing on the hill approaching the shoreline of Beaver Lake.

"Let me ask you Jeremy, how does Dutch seem to you?"

Jeremy didn't know how to answer. He had known this man for little more than ten days. It was a confusing question because he wasn't sure if something was right or wrong.

"I don't know. He's really smart. He tells some amazing stories. Sometimes he scares the hell out of me. What should I be noticing?"

"His son is supposed to come up here in a few weeks with his grandson. Has he mentioned that at all to you?"

"No, but I can ask him about it. Would that be ok?"

"Yes. But do it without making a point of it. If it comes up in conversation, fine. Don't just blurt it out."

"Ok." Jeremy hesitated. "Gabby, is something wrong?"

"No, I don't think so, but just keep your eyes open."

CHAPTER THIRTY-SIX

Jeremy went back into the cabin where the fireplace was going and there was good chatter around the table. Both Jeremy and Dutch were tired, as it was well past their regular bedtime. Robby, Gabby and Miles were getting their jackets on after dark and had to ride their ATV's back with their headlights on the whole way.

After clearing the table, Dutch sat down and enjoyed a little more coffee before retreating into his room.

"Did you get some good pictures of everybody tonight?"

"Oh yeah." Jeremy pulled his phone out. "I think you might have accidently smiled in one of them."

Dutch looked at the myriad of the night's pictures, then scrolled back earlier. He went into the Florida pictures and kept going further and further back. It was a mix of fishing pictures, bar photos, and the occasional selfie with some woman in a bar. Confused, Dutch finally had to ask something.

"Are these girlfriends of yours?"

"I wouldn't call them that. Sometimes it's two ships that pass in the night. That kind of stuff."

"I see. Do you have any pictures of your parents in here?" Dutch had yet to see any.

"I think I do. I must."

Jeremy took the phone and scrolled back through hundreds of photos that were on his phone. He couldn't find one single picture of his mom or his dad. Nothing from Boca Raton, no old pics unloaded from an old computer, nothing.

"I swear I had at least one in here."

Dutch looked at Jeremy and spoke quietly, "I know that I said your dad probably thinks you're an asshole. But I guarantee that he has a picture of you on his phone, or a picture of you in his wallet. You should have the same."

"You're right. You're right," admitted Jeremy.

Jake came over and sat next to Jeremy and leaned hard against him.

"Dutch, do you have a picture of your son?"

"Well yeah, sure I do." Dutch pulled out his wallet and there was a photo of a couple with a young boy.

Dutch pulled the picture out.

"This is my son Jason, his wife Ann, and my grandson Kyle. This was taken when they visited here a year ago."

Jeremy looked carefully at the photo and smiled, "I can see some of Kyle in you."

"That's what people tell me, but I don't see it."

Dutch took the pic back and slid it in his wallet. As he did, Jeremy caught a glimpse of an old faded picture.

"Hey. Wait. What's that one right there?"

Dutch knew Jeremy spotted the old photo. He reluctantly pulled it out and handed it to Jeremy. It was from Vietnam. Three young men were in the photo. The two on the ends didn't have shirts on and the one in the middle had short hair. It was a young Dutch Woodson with two of his buddies from his unit. They wore army fatigues with dog tags hanging around their necks. Dutch, the one in the middle was smiling, but the two on the ends were laughing. The one on the right was holding a beer and a cigarette.

"Oh man, is that you in the middle?" Jeremy looked at the pic in disbelief. Dutch looked so young. The other guys in the picture were much taller. The one on the left was extremely well built and muscular. "Were these guys from your unit?"

Dutch took the picture from Jeremy and stared at the image for a moment.

"Yeah. That's me. The guy on the left is Gary Millet and the guy with the beer is Tom Reese. These were my best friends in the world over there."

Jeremy looked at the pic again.

"You guys look totally bad ass. Gary looks like a monster."

Dutch raised his eyebrow and looked at Jeremy.

"He was a monster. We were in a bar in Manilla on leave. He got into a fight with a guy over a girl in that bar. It took six MPs to pull him off the guy or he would have killed him. He spent the night in the stockade, but they let him out the next day."

Jeremy could tell Dutch had thoughts of Vietnam racing through his head again. Dutch took the pic and laid it on the table and sat back.

"This picture was taken about eight weeks before they were killed. I look at the photo and realize that's all the older they got. I try to picture them as old guys like me. I imagine them talking about their careers and their knee replacements. Spending their winters in Arizona or Florida. But they'll forever be twenty years old. Never more than twenty years old."

At that point, Jeremy really wanted to backtrack and ask Dutch more about his son, but he could see that now was not the time. Dutch was lost in thought, staring straight ahead and Jeremy could see that it was getting way too late.

"Listen, Dutch, I'll finish straightening up the kitchen. Why don't you hit the sack? I think we can finish the cleanup work out by the crash site tomorrow."

"Yeah. Sounds good."

Dutch didn't make eye contact and quietly retreated into his room and closed the door. Jeremy felt bad for Dutch. It had been a terrific night and it ended on a somber note thanks to Jeremy.

Anxiety crept in once again and Jeremy began to overthink. Why had Jeremy asked so damn many questions? Why had he pushed Dutch for details when the details were clearly painful for this man? Why hadn't Jeremy done more to maintain his own friendships? His thoughts were racing once again. The truth was hard to admit, but now he was facing it head on. For longer than he cared to admit, alcohol had been his only real friend, and it was a toxic one.

John was Jeremy's friend and he had taken him for granted, he just hadn't seen it. In his alcoholic haze, Jeremy thought of John as only his fishing guide. His ticket to the trophy fish. He paid John to fish. He paid him well and occasionally if Jeremy got his tit in a wringer, it was John to the rescue . . .

Then there were the college guys like Miles who he hadn't spoken to in decades. . . There were guys like his old buddies Tom Siemen and Kurt Schiltz, who should both be a larger part of his life rather than guys who took the occasional all-expense paid trip to Florida to offer Jeremy financial and legal advice, and of course, to let loose a little.

It was starting to become clear, maybe a little too clear. As an alcoholic, it was easier to keep your distance so others don't figure out your secret. You don't want them to see your shame, your selfishness, your self-loathing. Jeremy did not want the people who once knew him so well to see what he had become, a drunk, and a selfish one at that. Jeremy wanted to become a better friend. But how?

The next morning, Dutch slept in. Jeremy's internal clock was getting set for daybreak and today was no different. It was odd for Jeremy to be up before Dutch and he chalked it up to the evening going longer than normal last night. After Jeremy got a fire started, coffee going, and breakfast cooking , Dutch came out of his room and sat at the table. Jeremy could see that Dutch looked slightly more tired than usual, and thought about suggesting they both take it easy that day. Maybe the crash cleanup could wait until tomorrow.

"Hey. What if we just did some chores around the cabin today? We could finish crash cleanup tomorrow morning."

"Nah," Dutch countered. "I'm sick of seeing that place. I would think you are too. Let's just go back out there and get it wrapped up."

"Are you sure? I can catch up on my journal entries and I was hoping to use my phone today to call my parents."

Dutch looked at Jeremy and smiled, "I don't think your phone is going to work out here. The cell reception is awful. You need to get higher to get a signal from the tower in Minaki. If you want to call your parents, we can set it up with the radio. I can contact Carl or Miles and they can help set it up."

Jeremy relented, "Alright. I just want to catch up with them and figure out what we're going to do once I check out of the Jackpine Savage Hotel here."

Dutch would normally show some sign of contempt for this flippant comment. He instead just drank his coffee and petted Jake who was begging at his side for scraps from the breakfast that Jeremy placed on the table.

The two sat and ate breakfast without much discussion. Jeremy sensed that Dutch was preoccupied by something. Jeremy thought he would give Dutch a break and take care of the dishes despite the fact he had cooked breakfast.

"Why don't you check out the lake ice and see if there is any progress this morning? I'll take care of the dishes before I start reading another book."

Dutch turned to Jeremy.

"What did you finish last?"

"I found an old Hemmingway book. *Men Without Women*. I read that in a day and a half."

"Yeah. I like short stories."

Dutch started to walk out of the cabin with Jake when he turned back to Jeremy.

"That's another discussion you're going to have to deal with."

"What's that?" Jeremy inquired.

"Women. I'm guessing by your lack of discussion on the subject that you don't have anyone in particular since your divorce."

Jeremy kind of smiled because he knew this subject was going to be breached at some point. He knew in his previous experiences with addiction and recovery, relationships were a delicate thing. Most people were discouraged from getting involved with someone until their recovery had gained some momentum, and it was on a path that would be considered somewhat safe from an outside influence such as a romantic partner. Dutch knew about Jeremy's divorce, but didn't know much else.

"I do my best to keep the ladies at bit of a distance the last few years," explained Jeremy.

Dutch smiled as he suspected the reasoning.

"Because of your money? You don't want some gold digger planting her flag?"

"That is the biggest reason. My financial guy, Tom Siemens told me to really watch out for that."

"That sounds like good advice. But you're going to be prone to those kinds of things if you use tiki bars as your main venue. From what Miles told me you cut a pretty big wake down there in Florida. If you're a regular in all those places like you seem to be, eliminating that part of your life might open an opportunity to meet someone that isn't a piece of shit skank that's looking for a meal ticket."

Jeremy laughed at the conversation. He couldn't help it. He was getting romantic advice from a guy twenty years older than him who lived alone in a cabin over ten miles away from the nearest woman.

"Yeah, you're probably right Dutch. I guess that's one part of life I'll have to figure out as I go along. So, what do you think is the best course of action in the relationship department?"

"Simple. You find some gorgeous sober woman who has more money than you and do whatever it takes to keep her happy."

"Oh yeah, Dutch. That's realistic. That is such a huge part of the female population."

"Hey, I didn't say it would be easy. You might have to make some concessions. You might have to settle for someone who's not a virgin."

Dutch turned and walked out the door.

After finishing the breakfast cleanup, Jeremy looked at the bookshelf and pondered what he would read next. As he perused the books on the shelf, Jeremy looked for something more inspirational. He searched for self-help books, but found none. The books were either history, how to books, or biographies. The Jordan Peterson book was the only one that seemed out of place, but that was the first one he read. Most of the books were old. The biography of Chuck Yeager seemed interesting, so he grabbed it off the shelf. He remembered some of the Yeager story.

One of Jeremy's favorite movies when he was a kid had been the 1984 classic "The Right Stuff." He sat in the chair and began to read about General Yeager and his exploits.

CHAPTER THIRTY-SEVEN

Things were quiet around the cabin that morning when finally Dutch came in and suggested they make one last trek out to the crash site. Jeremy and Dutch walked through the woods and made it to the site much quicker than previous days. Jeremy was becoming more active and his physical stamina had improved in the nearly three weeks since the night of the crash. As they walked around the crash site and Jeremy picked up the pieces, Dutch stood alone looking out to the northeast where the hills flattened out and there were more open fields. It was an area that Dutch used to hunt more when he first moved out here over 20 years before. There was a moment where the old man felt a bit melancholy. He used to cross those open fields easily, but the aches in his legs and back had limited his walking distance with age. He was as fit as any 76-year-old man could be, but he knew his decline had one direction.

"I think that's it," Jeremy spoke loud enough for Dutch to hear him 50 feet away.

Jeremy had his hands on his hips as he inspected the area around the tree for any additional small pieces of shattered hood or windshield. The cart was only three quarters full, but there were many small pieces. All the snow had melted around the trees and the brown dead grass would soon give way to the green sprouts of the new spring.

"Let's take a quick look over here." Dutch motioned to Jeremy. He led him to the tree where Dutch had discovered Jeremy so badly injured that night.

"Just give it a quick look and see if anything else is over here."

Jeremy strolled over to the tree where his body was once hung up. He looked around the tree and saw nothing. As he was about to turn away, he stopped cold, and caught the glimpse of something white laying in the matted grass. He crouched down, reached for it, and was completely shocked.

"What is it?" Dutch inquired.

With an astonished look on his face, Jeremy reached down and picked up the white item. It was his busted off tooth. It didn't even occur to him that it might be there, but once the snow had melted, it was easy to spot. The tooth had cracked off his jawbone the moment his skull hit the trunk of the tree. No blood was left except for the pulp that hung out in a pink strand from the base. The familiar wave of anxious heat went through Jeremy's body as he realized once again the violent collision that took place here. He had a visceral reaction to finding his tooth and it pissed him off.

"Jesus, Dutch. How in the hell did I live?"

"I don't know." Dutch responded. "Maybe you were supposed to live. Maybe somebody thinks you still have a purpose. I wasn't one of those people who would think that, but maybe I was wrong."

"How much of my life has been a waste of time?" Jeremy shook his head in disgust.

As Jeremy looked into his hand at the busted tooth, Dutch walked up behind him. Dutch let out an audible sigh and realized that it was time to get Jeremy out of the woods and back to the cabin.

"C'mon. Let's get going."

Jeremy stood up and took one last look around the spot where he nearly died. He took a couple deep breaths and closed his eyes. His ribs still ached when he inhaled as his lungs pressed against the newly healing fractures. When he opened his eyes, he turned and followed Dutch to the cart. There were only a few charred branches and some busted tree limbs. Other than that, you'd never know anything horrible had occurred there. He never wanted to see that spot again. As the two men left the site, Jeremy put his tooth in the small right front coin pocket of his jeans.

After getting back to the cabin and unloading the cart, Jeremy thought it would be a good time to make the phone call to his parents. He was feeling positive about getting the crash site cleaned up and he knew that his folks would want an update on his condition. Jeremy approached Dutch about setting up the radio relay with the phone.

"Hey, can we try to make that call to my folks?"

Dutch was a little more tired than usual and was hoping to lay down for a bit before it was time to get dinner started.

"Let's try in an hour or so. I'm going to close my eyes and rest my back."

Jeremy was a little annoyed as he was looking forward to making the call, but he also knew that Dutch probably needed some down time. As Dutch went for his nap, Jeremy retrieved his phone from his room. It still had a decent battery charge from the night before and he decided to go outside and see if by chance there was any signal reception from the tower in Minaki. As he stepped outside, he was astonished to see one single bar of reception on his phone. He had expected nothing. He knew it would be a weak signal and unlikely to be sustained through a call, so he looked for a higher spot to stand. There were no hills or high spots to increase his elevation. As he was about to give up and go back inside, he realized he could simply climb on top of the woodshed. There was a small ladder in the back to get him onto the roof of the old shed.

"Perfect." Jeremy muttered to himself.

Jeremy lifted the ladder up and placed it against the shed roof. He carefully went up the ladder and then stepped off onto the roof. It was a 4/12 pitch, making it a flat surface and easy to walk on. The sun had dried the surface making the footing stable. Looking out he could see the deteriorating ice of Beaver Lake down the hill. Jeremy reached for the phone and upon pulling it out, saw that his new vantage point gave him two bars of reception. It worked! Jeremy smiled as he could now place the call and not have to bother Dutch who was resting comfortably inside the cabin.

As Jeremy began to dial the phone number, he stepped

forward on the roof to get a better look of the lake. It was a magnificent view. As he turned around while dialing, his feet suddenly gave out from underneath him. He had stepped on a rotten board and a large hole was blasted through the roof by the weight of Jeremy standing in that one weak spot. As he disappeared through the roof, his phone fell from his hand and his body dropped clean through the hole and down onto the rows of neatly stacked firewood. As his feet struck one of the rows of wood it tipped over and his tailbone then hit another row. He let out an audible bellow as his rear end connected with the oak and maple hardwood. Two rows of firewood toppled as his body bounced off one row and rolled down in between a partially depleted row and another full stack. The back of his head hit some wood and he briefly saw stars. He lay in a contorted position on the floor of the shed semi-covered in firewood. He thought he might have blacked out for a moment, but then shook off the fog and the shock of the fall.

As he lay on the woodpile, he took inventory of himself. His damaged ribs appeared to be ok. He didn't seem to be bleeding. His tailbone throbbed from the hard landing, but he seemed to be alright otherwise. He felt fortunate for a moment, but then looked around and saw the neatly stacked wood was now toppled and strewn about. His head turned towards the opening of the shed and he was a shocked to see Dutch standing just a few feet away from him, glaring at him laying amongst the toppled firewood. Dutch then spoke.

"Do you know what sodomy is?"

Jeremy was still disoriented, but the shock of that question hit him almost immediately. He looked at Dutch with fear and realized he was holding a large piece of firewood in his right hand.

"Uh..... I, uh...." Jeremy had a difficult time speaking.

Dutch calmly continued, "Sodomy is the practice of shoving something into someone's typically unwilling rectum for the purpose of sexual gratification or punishment."

He smiled at Jeremy as he completed the sentence. Jeremy's

mouth was wide open as if was about to speak, but no sound could come out. He felt paralyzed. Dutch then spoke as he continued his demented grin.

"Confused? No problem. I will use it in a sentence to give it some context. Sodomy is a versatile word. We'll use it as a verb. That might give it some clarity and understanding for you."

Dutch then raised the piece of wood in his hand and glanced at it in an admiring way.

"If I see you on this woodshed roof again or doing something else this stupid, I'm going to sodomize you with this splintered piece of firewood."

He glanced back at Jeremy with his Cheshire grin. Jeremy didn't speak. His mouth stayed open but still he made no sound. After a few seconds, the smile disappeared from Dutch's face as a look of disgust then took over. He tossed the piece of wood onto the floor of the shed. He turned to walk out and quietly muttered, "Come inside and we can rig up the radio for your phone call."

Jeremy slowly got up off the toppled woodpile and shuffled his feet out the door and into the cabin. Remarkably, other than a sore tailbone, he was fine.

CHAPTER THIRTY-EIGHT

The phone call went well. Dutch left the cabin so Jeremy could discuss things with his parents privately. He spoke to both his mom and dad and they were pleased to hear him in such good spirits. The topic of conversation turned to when was he going to come back to the states to do his rehab. This was something that Jeremy and Dutch hadn't discussed and there was no firm timeline.

"I'm not sure Mom. I know I am doing better than when I got here. I've learned quite a bit from Dutch, but we haven't really talked about when I'm leaving yet. Maybe I'll know more in a few days."

Jeremy's mom was worried about the wilderness aspect of this therapy her son was getting, but she trusted Gabby and knew that this was the longest Jeremy had gone without drinking for decades. She was concerned, but grateful as well.

"We appreciate you calling Jeremy. Just please keep us updated more. We worry about you and love you."

"I love you too, Mom. I'll talk to you soon."

Jeremy ended the call and felt good. He got up from the chair and realized his tailbone wasn't that bad and he really got lucky. It all happened so fast though. Dutch then returned to the cabin with Jake.

"Jeremy, I'm hoping you can take Jake for a nice long walk. I need to radio my son. He's supposed to be coming up here this summer and I need to start making plans for when he gets here."

"Sure. No problem. C'mon boy."

Jeremy was relieved at Dutch's tone. His demeanor from the woodshed incident was totally gone and he acted as though nothing had even happened. Jeremy realized that the older generation was like this. It was a bit like his dad. No grudges. Just a bump in the road and you keep going.

Jeremy and Jake began walking towards the lake. A breeze had come up and pushed the remaining lake ice away from the near shore and the late afternoon sun was reflecting off the clear blue water. There was still a chill in the air from the low water temperature, but it could be that summer would actually show up sometime. The warmth of the sun felt good on the back of Jeremy's neck. He sat in the brown matted grass near shore. Jake laid down next him letting the sun soak into his brown fur. As Jeremy closed his eyes, he could hear the water rippling on the shoreline. He could hear birds singing. The slight southern breeze made a comforting sound as it passed amongst the tree tops. Jeremy laid in the grass next to Jake and they both fell asleep.

Dinner was some grilled trout that Dutch had caught through the ice around Christmas. He served it up with some fried potatoes and baked beans. Both men had good appetites and the tension and awkwardness of the woodshed incident was completely gone.

"What were you reading today?" Dutch asked.

"The book on General Yeager."

"I love that one quote of his." Dutch smiled.

"Which one?" Jeremy had only gotten about fifty pages into it, so he wasn't sure what Dutch meant.

"When he says, "The first time I saw a jet, I shot it down." The balls on that guy," Dutch chuckled.

After Jeremy finished the dinner dishes, Dutch came out of his room carrying a manilla folder filled with pages. He placed them on the table in front of Jeremy. Confused, Jeremy wondered what was up.

"What's this?"

"These are the pages of your journal writing from each evening since you arrived here. I told you that I would keep them for you. I think it's time you glanced back and got some reference about where you were when you started compared to where you are now. It's been a little less than three weeks, but I think you'll notice a difference in your writing."

"Did you read any of it?" Jeremy asked.

"No. Not at all. I said I wouldn't. It's your private journal. But, based on what you were doing when you got here and what is happening now, you seem to be going through some changes. It's like you are searching for something. What does it seem like to you?"

Dutch wanted to know what his pupil was after.

Jeremy sat back and thought hard about his answer. It took him a bit to find the right words, but he then spoke.

"I'm trying to figure out what normal is. I thought I knew what a normal day, or a normal week, or a normal problem was, but I was so messed up. I just want to be a regular guy, but I'm not sure what normal is anymore. Why can't I be normal? So many other people can have a problem, get a little frustrated, find a solution and move on. Why can't I drink like a other people? Why can't I have two beers and call it quits. Why can't I drink one day a week and be fine? Why not me?"

Dutch nodded in agreement. He understood where Jeremy was coming from and had felt the same way from time to time.

"Why not you? Why not me for that matter? I'll tell you why. It's because we're different. Our normal used to be like everybody else's normal. But somewhere along the way, something became different. Something changed us. Maybe it was brain chemistry. Maybe it was grief. Maybe it was guilt. But we became different. Not worse. Just different. Because of that, we have to live differently to survive."

Jeremy was getting out some of his frustration. He could hear Dutch's argument and agreed with it, but he hated the truth it carried.

"It just doesn't seem fair. Why can't everybody be able to enjoy the same fruits of life?"

Dutch laughed out loud, "Fair?!? What the hell is fair? Is Parkinson's disease fair? Is war fair? Is cancer fair? Why should addiction be fair? Nothing else is."

Dutch shook his head at the silly suggestion that fairness was an issue to address. He then walked over to his bookshelf and pulled out a paperback copy of a Carl Hiassen book called Tourist Season and sat in the chair next to the fire.

"I'm going to read about your Florida Keys. Maybe I can figure out why all of you act so nuts."

Jeremy opened the folder on the table and began to page through his writing from the time he arrived. After a while, he pulled out his notepad and began to scribble a new entry.

CHAPTER THIRTY-NINE

The next two days were uneventful. Jeremy did get on the radio once to talk with Gabby and Miles, but it was a brief conversation about his improving health and talk about a possible timeline for getting back to town and possibly scheduling his rehab. Jeremy didn't feel ready yet, but it seemed as though he needed to start thinking about it. Jeremy went into the woodshed and restacked the two rows of wood that toppled over when he fell through the roof. He wanted to repair the roof too, but he wisely chose to leave that to Dutch. He wasn't about to get up there again.

On the late afternoon of his twentieth day at the cabin, the wind picked up and finally drove the last of the ice on Beaver Lake into the distant shore. The lake was now totally open. It was a warm and sunny afternoon, nearly seventy degrees. Dutch and Jeremy walked down to the lake and admired the water. It was a fantastic sight after the long winter. Dutch walked to the water's edge and began to undress.

"What the hell are you doing?" Jeremy asked, almost laughing.

"I'm baptizing myself. I do it every spring the day the ice goes off. It's like being born again. Shed the old skin."

With that, Dutch tossed his underwear onto the pile of clothes on the shore and trotted into the lake and dove in.

"WHHOOOOO! THAT WILL WAKE YOU UP!" Dutch barked in a high-pitched screech.

Jeremy laughed and marveled at the old man jumping into the freezing cold water in his birthday suit.

"How cold is that water?" Jeremy yelled out to Dutch, who was now about 50 feet from shore. He stood up and the water was at his chest level.

"About 35 degrees I reckon. Just above freezing," Dutch yelled back.

"Shit. I guess you gotta do what you gotta do." Jeremy mumbled as he started to pull off his shirt and jeans.

He got down to his birthday suit and then ran into the water and jumped in as fast as he could. Jeremy dove under and then emerged almost instantly and screamed at the top of his lungs.

"OH MY GOD!"

Dutch chuckled at the sight of Jeremy standing in the icy water. Jeremy's skin felt like it was being poked with a thousand needles. His feet and ears hurt from the cold water. He looked at Dutch who was laughing at him.

"You don't do this every spring, Dutch. You did this just to get me to jump in," Jeremy said indignantly.

"If I knew it was going to be this funny, I would have cut a hole in the ice a week ago and talked you into this."

Dutch was having some fun seeing Jeremy shaking.

Jeremy was shivering as he turned and started to walk back to shore. The sun felt good as he walked out of the frigid water. He picked up his clothes and started up to the cabin to dry off. Dutch followed soon behind. Jeremy found a towel and began to get dressed as Jake wagged his tail while sitting next to him. Dutch walked in with a towel and was drying off his arms and torso. He had already put his pants on outside.

"Well, winter is over," Dutch declared.

"I can't believe you tricked me into that." Jeremy shook his head.

"Hey, seriously. I do that every year the day the ice goes off."

"Aren't you afraid of getting a heart attack?" Jeremy asked.

"So what? I die in the lake? Who cares? You gotta go sometime. I could think of worse ways to go," Dutch shrugged his shoulder with a degree of indifference.

"Are you nuts?" Jeremy exclaimed. "You go through a whole brutal cold winter just to die when the weather breaks and is starting to get nice? That's the worst thing you could do."

"You know kid, that's the most sense you've made since you got here. You're not that dumb after all."

Jeremy decided to grill some venison steaks outside that

night. They ate around the firepit as it was a warm evening and there were no bugs outside yet. The sun was setting as the two had their feet up against the rocks of the pit. They sat in the orange glow of the fire drinking ice tea as the darkness of the evening descended. Jake sat next to Jeremy as Jeremy stroked the fur on his head.

"When is your son coming back for a visit?" Jeremy inquired.

"Next month I figure. He waits until Kyle is done with school and gets a break in his sports schedule. The lake will be warmer then and the fishing picks up."

"It almost feels like summer now," Jeremy commented.

"It takes me a while to get used to the heat. I'm kinda tired. I'm going to turn in early. That was a good dinner." Dutch got up from his chair and slowly made his way to the cabin door.

"Thanks Dutch." Jeremy sat in the chair outside while Jake stayed next to him. He looked up in the sky and as it got darker, the stars became brilliant. It was hard to see this many stars in Florida because of all the city lights. The only way you could see this many stars was out on the ocean at night. It was at this moment Jeremy began to realize that there was a unique peace to this place. It was a peace much like the ocean. It was always there, but he had been too distracted and overlooked it. This peace was something he had neglected for too long. It was the ability to go out in a boat and just enjoy the ocean and the stars and the calm it could bring. Jeremy made his second decision at that moment. Besides being a better friend, he would dedicate time to savor the peace that seeing the stars oculd bring.

After putting the fire out, Jeremy and Jake retreated to the cabin. It was perhaps his best day so far. He made dinner, went for a chilly swim, and was able to focus on something that gave him solace. He made no journal entry that night and just went to bed. It was the best sleep he had in a long time.

CHAPTER FORTY

There was a strange sensation as sleep slowly melted away. Jeremy opened his eyes and a more brilliant light entered his window. He was confused. It was late. Normally, Jeremy would rise just after sunup, but this was at least two hours later. Also, there was a lack of smell. If Dutch got up before him, the coffee aromas would envelop the cabin. That was missing. Something was off. He got worried. Was something wrong with Dutch?

Jeremy quickly threw the sheets back and walked out of his room and went into Dutch's room. He was not there. His meticulously made bed lay empty. No breakfast was cooking, no coffee, and Dutch was not around. As he walked out of Dutch's room his gaze caught a sight on the dining table that made him stop dead in his tracks. A cold chill ran through him and he took a step back. He could feel his hands getting clammy. He walked over to the table and sat down. Sitting in the center of the table was a brand new two-liter bottle of vodka.

At that moment, there was no sound. Jeremy sat in front of the bottle looking carefully at the label. It was a bottle of Absolut, a Swedish brand. He had consumed hundreds of gallons of this vodka in his lifetime. He knew what to mix it with. He knew how much it would take him to get buzzed. He knew how much it would take for him to pass out. He knew where the bottle of Absolut was in nearly every bar between Homestead, Florida and Key West. He stared at the liquid inside the bottle. Even though the bottle was sealed, he swore he could faintly smell it. Vodka has an odor. Don't let anyone tell you otherwise.

For a moment, Jeremy couldn't feel his face. His sweating palms were resting on the table. He gradually pushed himself up out of the chair and slowly walked back into the bedroom. He closed the door and began to make his bed, just like every other morning. He went over it in his head. Equal sides. Make sure the corners are correct. Center the pillow. He talked himself through it. It took all of his concentration to accomplish what had become a normal and simple task. Jeremy could feel his heart beating inside his chest. It was pounding hard. He could also feel that heat building up inside him. It started in his core, went up through his shoulders, and then went to the back of his head. There was an anger building. He finished the bed and quickly put his pants and shoes on.

Jeremy could hear some activity outside the cabin. It sounded like the splitting of wood. Jeremy flung the bedroom door open, marched to the table, and grabbed the bottle by the neck. He went out the main door and quickly turned the corner around the back to the wood shed where Dutch was standing up round logs for splitting. Jake sat in the late morning sun observing.

"What the fuck is this!?!" Jeremy demanded in a terse manner.

"Looks like a great big bottle of vodka to me," Dutch responded in a deadpan, matter of fact tone.

"What is it doing here?"

Jeremy was getting confrontational. And, as usual, when Jeremy got agitated, Dutch became calmer. It was annoying to Jeremy. He wanted an argument. Even a fight perhaps. This bottle was an invasion of something pure to the cabin. This was supposed to be a place where he was safe from alcohol. Safe from drinking. It was an oasis. It was the reason Jeremy came here in the first place. This was blasphemous. Introducing a bottle of vodka to this sacred place was an atrocious act and put him at risk. Why would Dutch would do such a thing? Dutch put down his splitting maul and took off his gloves. He walked over to Jeremy and took the bottle out of his hand.

"Maybe you don't remember, but a little over three weeks ago you got on a snowmobile in a blizzard to drive through my neighborhood on the way to Red Lake to get this," Dutch paused for a moment and looked Jeremy in the eye, "I'm curious if you still want it."

Jeremy felt the heat in his neck go down. He contemplated what to say next. He then remembered something Dutch said to him just recently.

"We're different. Aren't we?" Jeremy said.

"Yes. We are," Dutch replied.

"Yes, I still want it. But I know I can't have it."

The two sat silently for nearly a minute. Then Jeremy turned to Dutch and asked, "Why in the hell did you have to bring that bottle out here. I wanted to stay here because this place is safe. Why would you put me at risk? Hell, why would you put yourself at risk? Having that shit around here. It will cause nothing but trouble."

Dutch smiled at Jeremy.

"The bottle isn't the problem kid. You and I are the problem. Just because there's no booze around, that doesn't mean we're safe. It's easy to be virtuous when you don't have the opportunity or capability to do something bad. That's not sobriety. But, if you have the capacity to do something wrong, but you instead choose to do it right, that's real virtue. That's real sobriety."

Jeremy sat quietly trying to make sense of this. Dutch continued his soliloquy.

"There are going to be all kinds of opportunities for you to drink. Think about it. When you fly back home, there are always a couple bars in the airport terminal. God knows how many bars and liquor stores are in the Florida Keys. Every time you go to the grocery store. You'll always be just an aisle or two away from the wine. What the hell are you going to do? Hide up here? For how long? Indefinitely?"

Dutch paused for a moment and then put his hand on Jeremy's shoulder.

"We are tested every day."

Jeremy shook his head. He knew that Dutch was right.

"I just thought that this would be a safe place," Jeremy muttered.

"It might be Jeremy. But your life isn't here. Your life is with your parents. It's with your friend John. It's with Miles. That's your life. Not stuck up here in a cabin with a grouchy old man."

Jeremy pleaded with Dutch, "Wait, we still have to fix the roof of the woodshed. We still have to get the pier in. There is still a shitload of wood that needs to get stacked so it can dry for next winter……"

Dutch cut him off, "It's graduation day. You need to get your real rehab started. Besides my son will be here in a few weeks to help me with the little projects. It's time for you to move on."

Dutch walked back to the cabin carrying the huge bottle of vodka.

Jeremy watched Dutch pass by and then lifted his head and yelled out, "Where are you going with that vodka? You should get rid of that."

"Oh, I'm going to hang onto it."

"What for?"

"You never know. I might get some hot little babe up here as a visitor. She's going to need most of this bottle if I am gonna have half a chance with her."

Dutch made the radio call to Minaki. This time, Miles answered, "Hey Dutch. What's going on? Over."

"It's time to come get your boy. Pick him up."

CHAPTER FORTY-ONE

Around lunchtime, Miles pulled into the yard on the ATV. Jeremy gathered up his journal entries and the clothes he borrowed from Miles and put them into a duffle bag. He looked around the room that he had occupied for the past three weeks and felt anxious about the next step he was about to take. Dutch was right he thought. It was a bit of a graduation day. He still felt like he could have more to do here, and wished that he could just recapture the peace he felt the night before looking up at those stars. Just when he was starting to figure this place out, it was time to leave.

The three men sat around the table and enjoyed a bowl of venison chili. They talked about the hole in the wood shed roof and had a good laugh. Miles had informed Gabby that Jeremy would be leaving, and she was coordinating arrangements with John to meet up with him at the Minneapolis airport. From there, John would accompany Jeremy on the flight to Atlanta. Jeremy's parents would be at the rehab clinic during check-in so they could see him. John was setting all of that up.

Dutch was pleased to hear that there was a firm plan in place for Jeremy.

"Looks like the ball will be rolling soon." Dutch looked at Jeremy.

"We'll fly to Minneapolis this afternoon and you'll connect with a flight there. You'll be in Atlanta by ten p.m. tonight when you will check into rehab," Miles laid out the timing.

"I want to take a walk down by the lake once more. Do we have enough time?" Jeremy asked.

"Sure," Miles answered.

Jeremy walked out the door and Jake followed him. He took a few treats for the brown dog and Jake paid close attention to Jeremy when his hand went near his pants pocket. Jeremy and

Jake stood on the shore, both looking out at the blue water and calm waves reflecting the midday sun. Some newly arrived birds floated a few hundred feet out. A couple of loons. Jake turned his head and had a look of curiosity. Jeremy took a deep breath in and could still feel the dull ache of the mending ribs, but it was clear that things were improving. The smell of the lake was intoxicating. It was a cleaner smell than the ocean off The Florida Keys. A freshwater Canadian shield lake was one of the purest forms of freshwater in all the world. Jeremy knew he would want to return to this place someday.

As Jeremy walked back up the hill toward the cabin, he could see Miles securing his duffle bag to the ATV's cargo rack. Dutch stepped outside and was talking to Miles. They were shaking hands, and it was time for Jeremy to say goodbye to Dutch.

"Hey Miles, can you take a picture of Dutch and me?"

"You bet. I'd be happy to."

Jeremy handed his phone to Miles and he stood next to Dutch. As the two men stood together, Jeremy felt Dutch's hand come around and tightly grip his shoulder. It made Jeremy smile. Dutch also had a proud grin and Jake was in front wagging his tail. When Miles handed the phone back to Jeremy, he saw that the photo encapsulated his time at the cabin, and the relationship between the two men. The crystal blue lake behind them that had once been ice was a perfect background.

Dutch turned to Jeremy and extended his hand. Jeremy grabbed his hand to shake it and instead pulled the old man in for a hug.

"Thanks, Dutch. I owe you so much."

"Do what they tell you, ok?" Dutch muttered.

"Ok," Jeremy's voice cracked.

The men broke their embrace and Jeremy gave a quick squeeze to Jake while giving him the last treat from his pocket.

"That is one great dog." Jeremy told Dutch.

Dutch nodded in agreement.

Miles fired up the machine and got on the seat. Jeremy then jumped up and rode on the rear part of the seat with his back against the duffle bag.

"When I come back for a visit up this way, I'll keep an eye out for you, Dutch." Jeremy smiled a devilish grin.

Dutch shook his head and smiled.

"You've waited a long time to say that, haven't you?"

Jeremy grinned, "Yes, I have."

As Jeremy and Miles made their way back to Minaki, Jeremy had a wide range of emotions going through him. He was grateful to be alive. He also felt that he owed a debt of gratitude to so many of different people for giving him a second chance. Jeremy felt a deep connection to this place and these people. Miles navigated the four-wheeler along the trail and it seemed like a very short trip back to town. When the machine pulled into the town shop, Gabby was waiting for them along with Doug. As the two men got off the four-wheeler, Gabby approached and grabbed the duffel bag. Jeremy gave her a smile and Doug gave him a whack on the back of his shoulder.

"You look a heck of a lot better than the last time I saw you." Doug announced.

"Yeah, I stayed at the Dutch Woodson spa and resort. Everybody comes out glowing after that experience," Jeremy replied with a sarcastic grin.

Gabby laughed at the spa comment. She knew what a curmudgeon Dutch could be. Because of the nature of Jeremy's surprise departure, a lot of logistical things had to fall into place for Jeremy to make Atlanta by that night and Gabby needed to speed things along.

"John is going to meet us in Minneapolis so he can accompany you on your flight to Georgia," Gabby explained.

"Us?" Jeremy inquired.

"Yes. I'm going with you and Dad on the flight to meet him." Gabby replied.

"Ok, how soon before we depart?"

"We need to leave here in 90 minutes if we are going to make it to the connecting flight." Gabby answered.

"Alright then." Jeremy got a serious look. "I need to sit down with you for a few minutes now and discuss a few things. I am going to need your help. Ok?"

Gabby nodded in agreement. Something was on Jeremy's mind and she knew it was important.

Miles gave Gabby and Jeremy some time to meet in the town shop office while he headed to the airstrip and hangar to preflight the plane and make sure it was ready for the trip. It would just be the three of them with no cargo and it would be a quick turnaround.

Jeremy sat with Gabby and discussed several things. He wanted to know if the old SRX that he had totaled could be replaced, and if so, how to go about buying it. He also wanted to find out about Dutch's family. His son and his grandson specifically. Jeremy knew that Dutch wouldn't accept money from him, but yet he wanted to do something for his family. Something that would be a show of appreciation for both saving his life and helping him get started on the right path. Gabby took a few notes and made a few suggestions.

Jeremy realized that once he arrived at the facility in Atlanta, his focus would be on his work there and earning his sobriety. He didn't have a lot of time and he still had more questions. What were Miles' long term plans? He wanted to know specific details about Miles and what his hopes were for the future. Gabby didn't have a lot of answers and their conversation grew more intense, but he knew he could trust Gabby to handle things and find out answers to these difficult questions.

"I called your parents and they said that they would meet you in Atlanta to check-in tonight." Gabby said.

"Good. I'm glad they know what's going on. How did they seem?"

"They sounded relieved. I don't think they understood what you were doing out at a wilderness cabin for the past three weeks. I'm not sure I understand it either. But, they are flying in from Fort Lauderdale, and said they are going to meet you and John at the Atlanta airport when your plane arrives. They'll rent a car and drive you to the rehab facility." Gabby explained.

"Good. Good." Jeremy nodded.

He was pleased with the way things seemed to be falling into place.

"I need to make a few phone calls before we take off. Can I rely on you to handle a few things for me?"

Gabby sounded concerned, and rightfully so. She was concerned that because of his new destination and rehab assignment, Jeremy's anxiety levels might be getting the best of him. She was worried because there seemed to be a such a sense of urgency in Jeremy's voice. The sense of urgency was actually determination, and in truth, Jeremy was surprisingly focused. He knew that if he wanted to get the ball rolling, he would need Gabby to step some things up. Being in rehab meant that he could not focus on anything else, and in less than 12 hours, he'd be checking in.

Meanwhile, Miles readied the plane and packed a few snacks on board. He knew that Jeremy would be caught up in a lot of activity in a short period of time and figured that they would not have enough time to stop and eat somewhere. As he finished his pre-flight checks, Carl came over and checked to see if Miles needed any help.

"No thanks. I just have to get our passenger ready for his flight," Miles replied.

"Are you ok Miles?" Carl noticed that Miles seemed even more quiet and reserved than usual.

"I'm just worried Carl. I've seen people go off to rehab before and you hope for the best, but in reality, you don't know what's going to happen. I'd like to think that this is going to turn out ok, but in truth, I don't know if I'll see this guy again."

Carl nodded, knowing that Miles was right.

As Jeremy finished up with his phone calls, he left the office and found Gabby outside getting a few things packed into her Jeep.

"We should probably get going. Dad is getting the plane ready," Gabby said.

"You're right. Did you get ahold of John?"

"Yes." Gabby replied. "His plane arrives in Minneapolis about a half an hour after we land. Your connection to Atlanta is about 60 minutes after that."

"So, we'll have some time in the airport before John and I leave?" Jeremy inquired.

"Yes. We'll have to get to your departure gate, but we should have about an hour or so."

Gabby collected up the bundle notes from the brief meeting with Jeremy and grabbed a bag to take on the plane. She and Jeremy then traveled in her Jeep to the airstrip where Miles was finishing his final walk around before departing.

"Remember to send me a bill for all these flights, Miles. I know that this isn't cheap." Jeremy commented as they entered the plane.

Jeremy settled into the passenger seat next to Gabby in the back and got a backpack of medication for his eye and some meds to help him sleep.

"Hey!" Miles chirped from the cockpit. "Where are you sitting?"

"Back here with the civilians I suppose?" Jeremy replied.

Miles laughed. "Get your ass up here and sit in the right seat up front. The view is awesome."

"Cool!" Jeremy hurriedly unbuckled his seatbelt and rushed up front to join Miles. Gabby laughed at Jeremy and his childish reaction getting to ride "shotgun."

CHAPTER FORTY-TWO

As the plane lifted off and gained altitude, Jeremy looked out with wonder at all the water and remote lakes that passed beneath as they took a southern heading. They soon flew over the vastness of Lake of the Woods that stretched all the way from Kenora to the Minnesota border. The two men sat in front laughing and enjoying the ride. It was the first time in many years that Jeremy had flown and was not either drunk or extremely hungover. It was a clear and beautiful day as they got up to 20,000 feet and then all too soon began their descent to Minneapolis/St. Paul airport. Miles gracefully touched the wheels down and headed towards the private hangars where a car awaited to transport them to the American Airlines terminal. They would then meet John and await the flight to Atlanta.

Once the car met them at the hangar, Miles, Gabby, and Jeremy rode to the terminal just as John's plane was in on approach from Key West. Miles and Gabby used their law enforcement and medical credentials to get through TSA and join Jeremy for the meeting with John. As the three of them awaited John's plane arrival at the gate, Jeremy paused for a moment and gave Miles a serious look. He then spoke quietly.

"I want to see you as soon as I get out of rehab. So, am I coming up here, or are you going to come to my place?"

"One thing at a time, Jeremy." Miles replied. "We both know you have some work to do. I will be there for you if you want me to be."

"Ok, then." Jeremy nodded.

After the Airbus 320 pulled up to the gate, Miles got up and walked with Jeremy towards the door as the passengers were exiting the plane. John was the fourth person out and as he spotted Jeremy in the gate area, his eyes widened.

"Holy cow! Look at you!" he exclaimed.

Jeremy immediately came over and gave him a hug. "Thanks for coming to get me brother."

John hugged him back and Jeremy winced a bit as he guarded his mending ribs.

"Oh shit! I'm sorry man. They still hurt, huh?" John asked.

"Yeah. They're better, but its gonna take some more time."

Jeremy introduced Miles to John and they shook hands. Almost silently, Gabby came up from behind and extended her arm out to John.

"Good to finally meet you, John."

"This is Doctor Gabby." Jeremy introduced her to a clearly smitten John. John tried to hide it, but Jeremy could tell that John was quite impressed with Gabby's looks.

"Easy there Captain. She's my personal physician and somewhat of a niece to me now," Jeremy quipped.

The four of them retreated to a food court area near the gate where the flight to Atlanta would be boarding within the hour. They all grabbed a bite to eat and sat at the table. Jeremy asked if his house was ok and John assured him everything was fine. Gabby caught John up on medical situations and let him know that she had been in contact with Jeremy's parents and the rehab center concerning medical care and prescribed medications that would be part of the picture upon arrival.

Miles was mostly quiet during this time, enjoying the stories that Jeremy told of Dutch and the cabin. John couldn't get enough of the cabin tales Jeremy spun.

"I wish I could have seen the bear encounter," John chuckled as Jeremy kept up the pace of conversation.

The four of them finished eating and Jeremy turned to Gabby and gave her a big hug. He smiled as he embraced her. She quietly spoke into his ear.

"Do what they tell you. Ok?" She reminded him.

"I will," Jeremy answered with conviction.

Jeremy then turned to Miles.

"I know I'm heading out for now, and I don't know when I

will see you again, but I'd like to think this is the beginning of something." Jeremy said.

"I don't know exactly what you mean, but I think I could see myself coming down there for a visit. Sound good to you?" Miles asked.

"Sounds good to me, buddy." Jeremy embraced his tall friend.

As Jeremy and Miles finished saying their goodbyes, John grabbed his backpack and started toward the gate where the Atlanta flight was beginning to board. Gabby walked over to John and gave him two envelopes and squeezed his hand.

Gabby then retreated back and with her dad watched as John and Jeremy entered the walkway to get on the plane boarding for Atlanta.

As the two men walked down the winding hallway to the plane, Jeremy started to joke with John.

"You like her, don't you?" Jeremy smiled as John walked straight ahead.

"She's gorgeous. I hope I didn't let it show," John said.

"Well John, I'm an alcoholic with diminished capacities and even I could see you acted like an eighth-grade boy with her," Jeremy jested.

John looked at him with slight worry and embarrassment.

Jeremy put his hand on John's shoulder, "Don't worry, I'll lie and put in a good word for you."

CHAPTER FORTY-THREE

The flight to Atlanta was a fast two hours in the air. As the two men got off the plane, Jeremy's parents were waiting just outside TSA. Jeremy gave his mom a hug and shook his dad's hand. His mom looked at Jeremy's face and shook her head at the sight of his beard.

"You look so old with that."

"Actually, I feel much younger with it. Maybe I'll trim it a bit."

Jeremy turned to his dad and asked him a question. "Hey, do you have a picture of me in your wallet?"

Jeremy's father gave him a curious look and answered, "Of course I do."

Jeremy's dad pulled out his wallet and actually had three pictures of his son. One was a sixth-grade school picture, another showed the two of them together at Jeremy's wedding, and the third was of Jeremy floating in their swimming pool at the condo in Boca Raton. Jeremy smiled while looking at the photos, and realizsed once again that Dutch had been right.

The three of them didn't spend a long time in the airport as it was getting late and they wanted to get Jeremy checked in to rehab that night. Jeremy's mom bombarded him with questions about the accident, how he was feeling, and what took place at the cabin. Jeremy didn't share many stories from the cabin, but he talked about his journal and the books he had read. He also talked about Jake and how having the dog around helped him. More than anything, Jeremy was glad his folks were a part of the process.

Jeremy came to realize that there were a lot of people who wanted him to succeed in this endeavor and he didn't want to let those folks down. He had a long habit of disappointing people. His drinking and the lies he told to cover it up were not doing anybody any good, especially himself. He felt like even though he was a couple thousand miles from the cabin, Dutch remained in his head.

As the car pulled up to the front entryway of Placid Lakes Recovery Center, Jeremy grabbed his backpack and started to the front door. Both of Jeremy's parents sat in the car for a moment when Jeremy asked, "Do you want to come with me to the front desk?"

Jeremy's mom was tearing up and she shook her head no. She had lost her composure when she realized they had arrived. Jeremy's dad got out and walked alongside him.

"I'll go in with you," he said.

A quiet man about 60 years old was sitting at the front desk. He smiled and stood up, "Welcome to Placid Lakes. Can I help you?"

"Hi. My name is Jeremy Fine. I'm here to check in."

The man at the desk extended his hand. "Glad to meet you, Jeremy. I'm Dale Holmgren. I'm the intake director. Your doctor informed us you were coming tonight."

Jeremy then turned to his dad and spoke; "I think the rest is up to me. Thanks for coming."

Jeremy extended his hand to his father, but instead, Mr. Fine embraced his son and said quietly, "Do this the right way. Don't let yourself down."

Mr. Fine turned and walked out the exit as Dale Holmgren and Jeremy went back to check in with the nurse on call. He had to be examined medically and certified that is was safe for him to be there.

CHAPTER FORTY-FOUR

Over the next thirty days, Jeremy attended meetings, took classes, participated in activities all while under the care of the counselors and staff of Placid Lakes. He continued journaling, read intensely, and interacted with the other patients in group sessions. He found many similarities in the stories of the people there despite their different backgrounds. It didn't matter if you were a man, woman, white, black, Hispanic, Asian, or any other race. The beginnings of their alcoholism may have been different, but they all seemed to converge into the same hopeless abyss.

Upon completion of one month of in-patient treatment, it was suggested by his counselors that Jeremy continue his treatment in a different capacity. Jeremy had been free of alcohol for eight weeks at that point, and he was showing excellent progress in his sobriety. He was asked to take a more active role in group sessions and share his unique perspective because of his weeks at the cabin with Dutch. Self-imposed isolation prior to formal treatment was definitely outside the box when it came to recovery. It was a unparalleled step for Placid Lakes, because this approach created a new wrinkle in patient treatment. The unconventional method that Jeremy started on his path to sobriety was going to be critiqued and reviewed to see whether it was something that could be beneficial for future patients when treating this ugly addiction. When the counselors spoke to Jeremy about this, he laughed at their suggestion that Dutch's method should be considered for other patients as a test.

"There is no way that this should ever be done again," Jeremy said with a smile. "First of all, it wasn't about the isolation. It was about the man who saved me. You'll never get another guy like Dutch Woodson. God broke the mold when he made Dutch. His demented view of justice, sense of humor, and strength of character would be impossible to duplicate. You guys would be foolish to go down that road."

Jeremy continued in treatment and enjoyed taking a more active role in meetings. He was able to get in contact with John back in Islamorada regarding some changes he had in mind for his house. He wrote letters to his parents, Miles, Gabby, and even Dutch was sent a couple notes detailing his path in recovery. Jeremy was always glad to get a couple short messages from Dutch through Gabby, and Jeremy always answered Dutch back as soon as he possibly could.

After six weeks at Placid Lakes, Jeremy was feeling much better physically. His ribs no longer ached, his sleep patterns were still a struggle, but he was finding ways to deal with this. He looked forward to meals especially, and began to take more of an interest in cooking while he was in recovery. His new and intense focus on health and nutrition was a way to redirect his addiction in a positive way. He continued to journal, read, and started to exercise as his body healed.

Behind the scenes, Gabby was helping to take care of some of the details that Jeremy had gone over with her. She started to find ways to plan for Miles to spend some time with Jeremy in Florida once he got out of his rehab stint. She emphasized to her father that this friendship was now *his* responsibility as he re-initiated it by kidnapping his friend. Miles understood that spending time away from Minaki was going to be an adjustment, but because of his increasing age, Miles would be forced to face the harsh realities of his job. Very soon, he would struggle to continue the stressful and physically demanding pace that he had maintained for so many years. Gabby continued to carry out a checklist of items that Jeremy suggested and maintained contact with John in Islamorada to see that some of the more involved wishes would be carried out.

CHAPTER FORTY-FIVE

Two months had passed since Jeremy entered rehab and by that time, he had lost some weight, healed from the accident, and gained a new perspective on what life could be without alcohol. Sixty days in Atlanta under intense treatment was something that Jeremy could never have envisioned prior to the accident. The accident was clearly the event that he could point to and say, "That is where I hit rock bottom." Jeremy knew that it was nearing time to depart Atlanta and that a new road lay ahead of him. This caused some anxiety, but at the same time he saw possibilities with a clarity he had lacked during most, if not all, of his adult life.

At the sixty day mark, Jeremy decided to leave rehab and embark on his plan for a sober life after treatment. His counselors felt that the time might be right for him to transition. He would need to continue to work the steps of the program and attend meetings regularly to find support and encouragement and to maintain a healthy and sober life. Ninety meetings in ninety days was the goal that was put before him. This would give him the structure he needed once he left Atlanta. As Jeremy walked out to the main door of Placid Lakes, Dale Holmgren extended his hand to Jeremy.

"Good luck Jeremy."

"Thanks Dale. I appreciate what you all did for me," Jeremy replied.

As Jeremy grabbed his bag with his journal and photos, both Jeremy's mom and dad walked to the entrance. They had visited several times during his treatment, but this was a special day. Their son was completing rehab. Jeremy realized he had the same uneasy feeling in the pit of his stomach that he had the day he walked down to the shoreline of Beaver Lake with Jake to take a last look before leaving Dutch's cabin on that day two months ago. It was graduation day all over again. This time he felt more prepared and physically strong enough to lead a fulfilling life without drinking.

The Fine family drove to the airport and boarded a flight for Miami. It would be a short trip, under two hours. Once in Miami, they would rent a car and drive the hour and thirty minutes to Jeremy's house on the bay side near mile marker 84 in Islamorada.

The flight was uneventful and they arrived in Miami on schedule. Jeremy's mother was so relieved to see Jeremy relaxed and bright, more than she had seen in years. He asked a bunch of questions, mostly about their health, and Mrs. Fine assured him that things were good. They took the Miami Mover train to the rental car center where Jeremy's dad got the keys from the rental desk and then went to the lower level to pick up the vehicle for the drive south.

Jeremy checked his phone for voicemail messages and there were none. No texts and no emails either. All was quiet. He had hoped to hear from Gabby today upon his exit from rehab, but she might be busy in Minaki today. Nonetheless, he expected to see John when he arrived home.

CHAPTER FORTY-SIX

As Jeremy's dad pulled down the street towards the house, a new gate welcomed them.

"Oh good! They got it installed." Jeremy exclaimed.

Jeremy wanted a security system installed for the property and was hoping it would be operational by the time he got home. The system would prevent uninvited guests from his former life to show up at all hours. It was a problem in the past as late-night booty calls would sometimes show up unannounced. That was a part of his life he wanted to eliminate in sobriety. There were some people that he simply would not want to hang out with anymore.

As they pulled into the driveway, he could see John's truck parked, and was glad to see that John was there. As Jeremy and his parents exited the car, they could hear a kid yelling and laughing from the house. Confused, Jeremy walked inside and noticed that all the changes he talked to John about had happened. The kitchen had been redesigned, the furniture replaced, and many new pieces of artwork were added. He loved how it had turned out. John had a decorator come in and redo the interior to change the house and give it a fresh, bright new look. He could still hear the kid yelling and realized it was coming from outside on the pool deck. Jeremy walked outside and was shocked to see Robby splashing and playing in the pool.

"Holy cow! Robby! When did you get here?"

Just then, John and Gabby came from around the corner of the patio. Both had big smiles on their faces. John gave Jeremy a big hug and slapped him on the back. Jeremy couldn't believe that Gabby was there too. She gave him a hug as well.

"Well, how's the patient doing?" She asked.

"Oh, wow. It's so good to see you here. I feel really good."

Jeremy smiled as he was still getting his bearings. Both of

Jeremy's parents came over and greeted Gabby. They had talked on the phone numerous times, but this was the first time they actually met in person. They were obviously indebted to her for helping save Jeremy's life after the accident.

"We'll never forget what you did that night to save our son." Jeremy's dad said as he hugged her.

Jeremy's mother was getting teary-eyed at the meeting.

"Let's take a look at the place." Jeremy stated as he clapped his hands together.

As Jeremy started to walk to the far end of the house where the bedrooms and two extra bathrooms were, he turned to Gabby. "Did you pick out a room yet? When did you get here?" Jeremy asked.

"Oh, I'm not staying here at your house Jeremy. I wouldn't just move in," she answered.

"Well, you are not staying in a hotel down here. You should be my guest."

Gabby smiled and reached out to John and grabbed his hand. "I actually came down a couple days ago and am staying at John's place."

Jeremy's eyes widened as he looked at John who simply grinned. Jeremy then looked back at Gabby and realized what had taken place. He smiled broadly at both of them and shook his head.

"I see." Jeremy was caught off guard by the turn of events.

Gabby then spoke up, "John and I talked so much on the phone after we met in Minneapolis. And, things kind of went from there."

She saddled in close to John and it was apparent that they were now a couple.

"Now John, you better treat her well." Jeremy had a jokingly lecturing tone in his voice.

"Yes. I understand Jeremy." John could only smile.

They walked around the house and John showed Jeremy what the contractors had done to the house in order to make all of the changes. He especially wanted the end of the house towards the gulf side to be updated with a new patio off a large bedroom with a private bath. Jeremy wanted Gabby to see it and walked her inside.

"This is the space we talked about. What do you think?" Jeremy asked.

"I think it's perfect," she said.

"How is your dad?" Jeremy asked.

"You don't need to ask me Jeremy. He's right up the road at the Ocean View. He wanted to be here when you arrived, but he was famished and went up to get a sandwich. He walked up there. Why don't you go up there and pick him up?"

"Everybody came down? This is awesome! I can't believe how great this is!" Jeremy was thrilled as he went out to the garage to get his golf cart and head down the street to the O.V. to meet Miles. Everyone else stayed back at the house. Robby played in the pool while Mr. and Mrs. Fine relaxed. John and Gabby sat at a table near the pool drinking iced tea and preparing for the two old college friends to return.

CHAPTER FORTY-SEVEN

As Jeremy drove the short distance to the O.V., he was elated. He couldn't believe that Gabby and Miles would both be down here to welcome him home. He felt thankful for the good fortune of having friends. He chuckled to himself thinking about John and Gabby getting together. The new work on the house was better than he could have hoped. So much had happened since he had left here drunk in the middle of the night nearly three months before.

He pulled into the parking lot of the bar near the rear entrance, outdoor bar, and the pool area. Miles was watching a baseball game on the TV as the bartender handed him a sandwich which he had ordered to-go. Miles turned his head as he saw the golf cart pull in and smiled immediately. He walked towards the cart and the two friends hugged each other. Jeremy laughed as Miles lifted him off the ground when he hugged him. His ribs had completely healed, otherwise this would have been a definite problem.

"Oh man," Jeremy exclaimed, "I can't believe you're here."

"I wouldn't miss it buddy," Miles replied with conviction. "I'm glad you did the work to get back here."

"I've got a lot of work left to do. I still need to find a meeting to make today, and I need to find a sponsor. I want to get a new routine set up. I've got a lot of good shit planned. Are you able to stay awhile?" Jeremy asked.

"I kind of semi-retired to be honest. Gabby shared a few things with me that you had talked to her about. I wanted to discuss them with you," Miles replied.

"She was right. There are a number of gigs down here and you have a place to live. Let's head back to the house." Jeremy and Miles jumped into the golf cart and went back down the road past the new gate and to the house.

When the two men re-entered Jeremy's home, everyone was sitting in the main living room. Everyone stood up when Miles and Jeremy entered. Jeremy wanted to get to the back part of the house where the new patio was to show Miles. The two walked past everyone while Jeremy talked. He really didn't notice everyone.

As Jeremy entered the newly redone room, Miles stood and looked in amazement at the view of the gulf.

"This is yours buddy. Your room in our house. I had the bathroom remodeled too. You have your own patio and deck area. You can move in whenever you want and you are free to come and go as you please." Jeremy smiled as he could see the astonishment on Miles's face.

Miles stared at Jeremy and finally said, "I investigated that job out of the Marathon airport, you know. The one you told Gabby about. I might go over there and talk to the guy."

"You'll be able to fly quite a bit. That's for sure, and the pay is pretty good." Jeremy stated.

"I actually have a pretty decent nest egg put away. I'm not sure I would have to work. I would like to stay busy though."

Now it was as if Miles was thinking out loud. But, after a moment, Miles turned to Jeremy and wiped the smile off his face.

"I have to talk to you about something."

CHAPTER FORTY-EIGHT

It was clear from his tone that Miles was serious. The two men walked out by the pool. Robby was gone and it was just Jeremy and Miles. Everyone else was inside the house in the living room. Jeremy could see everyone sitting down talking, but didn't know what was going on. Jeremy was confused as Miles started to speak.

"I know you've been through a lot buddy. You've done great. It's no small feat what you've accomplished over the last three months," Miles looked solemn.

Jeremy nervously smiled and replied, "Thanks. I appreciated that."

Miles then continued never losing eye contact, "You have to stay strong. We're here to help you in any way we can. We want you to succeed, no matter how hard it is."

Just as Jeremy was about to speak, he caught a glimpse of something that he hadn't expected. From the other side of the pool, near the entrance by the boat lift, he could see Robby coming with a dog on a leash. He was confused, but as Robby approached closer, he could clearly see the dog was Jake. Jeremy immediately smiled, stood up and called to him. The leash slipped through Robby's hands and Jake rushed to Jeremy and jumped up, putting his large brown paws on his chest.

"Oh my god!" Jeremy exclaimed. "This is awesome. I can't believe this. Where is Dutch hiding?"

Just then, he glanced back at Robby and realized that Robby had tears in his eyes. Jeremy was confused. Robby then turned around and went back through the entrance leaving the pool area.

In total bewilderment, Jeremy turned to Miles and could see that a stone look of sadness had overtaken Miles' face. Jeremy looked at Jake who had settled down and now sat at his feet.

It was clear that something was terribly wrong. Jeremy looked directly at Miles and without the two men speaking, Jeremy knew that Dutch was dead. A feeling of shock hit Jeremy and he sat back in his chair. He could feel the air go right out of him. All the happiness of the day disappeared in an instant. It felt like a giant hole had been ripped in his chest. Jeremy put his hands over his face and closed his eyes. He could feel Jake's body lean against his legs, putting weight against him. It was as if Jake was trying to console him.

Gabby slowly opened the door to the pool area and quietly pulled up a chair next to Jeremy. Jeremy could feel tears forming as Gabby put her arm around him. Miles sat quietly. Jeremy was lost for a moment. He felt like he was almost floating, when he decided to wipe his eyes and take a couple deep breaths. Realizing that the man who had saved his life was now gone was a shock he was not prepared for. Dutch had seemed like an indestructible man. A man who had weathered so much. A man who had mastered the art of living and defeating his personal demons. How could such a man die? It didn't make sense. Once Jeremy caught his breath, he could finally ask the question.

He whispered quietly, "What happened?"

"Dutch had cancer." Gabby gently answered. "It was in remission for a number of years, but it came back. He thought it was gone, but about the time of your accident, his symptoms returned. It was in his prostate at first, but spread very quickly. It went to his spine. He knew he was sick, but he chose not to get treatment."

"When did you know?" Jeremy asked.

Miles answered, "When we got back from Minneapolis, Dutch called me and we went and picked him up and got him to the clinic. Gabby did some tests and he had a scan done in Kenora. It was everywhere. He insisted we not say anything to anyone. Especially you. He wanted you to do your rehab and not change the plan at all. He swore us to secrecy."

"So, what happened? When did he go?" Jeremy asked. His eyes were red as he stroked Jake's soft brown fur.

"About 10 days ago." Gabby answered. "His son and grandson came up and spent the last weeks with him. I was up there almost every day checking on pain meds and keeping him comfortable. He died in the chair outside by the firepit facing the lake. Jake was next to him along with his son."

Jeremy stood up and wiped the tears from his face. He could see inside the living room through the window and everyone was standing and looking. Everyone knew. They knew Jeremy would take this hard and they were concerned for him. Even Jeremy's parents, who had never met Dutch, understood how important he was and what he had done to save their son when he was at his lowest point. Without Dutch, Jeremy wouldn't be alive today. John and Robby stayed inside, knowing that Miles and Gabby were the ones to handle giving Jeremy this difficult news. Miles stood up and put his hand on Jeremy's shoulder.

"Dutch gave me something to give to you." Miles said and handed a sealed envelope to Jeremy.

Gabby and Miles stayed behind in the pool area while Jeremy and Jake walked out of the pool deck and onto the walkway facing the gulf. The warm afternoon sun and breeze off the ocean helped dry the tears off Jeremy's face. Jeremy sat on a bench near the canal entrance as Jake sat next to him. Jeremy slowly slid his finger under the sealed flap of the envelope and tore it open. He wiped the last remnants of tears away as he pulled a letter out and began to read.

Dear Jeremy,

Sorry I couldn't be there for your new start, but it couldn't be helped. I guess that sometimes we must do the best we can when we're around and have faith that things will work out once we're not. I guess Nelson Henderson said it best, "The true meaning of life is to plant trees, under whose shade you do not expect to sit."

Despite your intrusion onto my property that miserable night, I'm glad we met. You gave me an opportunity to step up and help someone when I felt I had some unfinished business. I was still fighting some of those demons. I'll always be grateful to you for that.

I am going to need something from you. I want you to make Jake's remaining years good ones. He stuck with me during those endless Canadian winters. His old bones don't like the cold anymore. He deserves a good retirement and I'm asking you to see to it. Make sure he never sees another flake of snow.

The only other thing you need to do is take care of yourself. Because, if you're not your best, you're no good for anybody else.

I wish you the best kid. Keep making your bed. Take help from others. Offer help to those that can use it.

Dutch

Jeremy sat back and looked out into the ocean. Jake rooted his nose under Jeremy's wrist as a prompt to pet him. He stroked the top of Jake's head and looked at the dog. He softly spoke, "Looks like it's you and me buddy."

After a few days, Jeremy's parents headed back to Boca Raton. Gabby left soon after with Robby, but not before checking out the local schools and looking into openings on the medical staff at Fisherman's Community Hospital in Marathon. It was apparent that John and Gabby were a thing now and it looked like Gabby was seriously considering relocating. Robby was excited about the prospect of living near the ocean.

As for Miles, he decided to try rooming with Jeremy at the house. Minaki had found a replacement for Miles. Actually, two men had to be hired to do the same job that Miles did. He would take it easy for the time being, learning how to navigate the waters of the Florida Keys and spend time trying to build a new life in a new place. It would be an opportunity to live in the sun and be close to Gabby once the move was done. He could be that retired grandpa that everyone envied. Who knows, he might meet someone too.

Jeremy started fulfill his goal of ninety meetings in ninety days. Initially, he said very little. At the beginning of his second week, he finally stepped up, introduced himself, and spoke to the group. It was a group he seemed to like and Jeremy connected with a few of the others afterwards. He was still searching for a sponsor when he spoke that night. After clearing his throat and getting over his initial anxiety, he addressed his fellow alcoholics.

"I had great parents growing up. I attended a terrific college. I made some life-long friends. I enjoyed a promising career. I was married to a beautiful woman. I won millions of dollars. But it wasn't until I was drunk, half frozen, hanging from a tree branch in the middle of a blizzard with shattered ribs, a collapsed lung, a broken nose, and my right eye hanging out of my head that I was able to find out, I am truly a lucky man."

ACKNOWLEDGEMENTS

Thanks to Dr. Jeff Bird. Also thanks to Rick Mai. Appreciate the assistance of Brian Ruechel. Jim "Pop" Daniel also for his expertise. Thanks also to Dr. Shane Brahm, OD.

A special hats off to our inspirational friend and expert snowmobile rider Renuka Vishnubhakta. Always wear your helmet my friend.

The biggest thanks to Linnea Strutz Jackson for her editing skills and ability to help tell this story.

ABOUT THE AUTHOR

Ken Jackson

Ken Jackson has been a lifelong resident of St. Germain, Wisconsin. He authored his first book in 2003 and has published a number of projects that deal with fishing and Wisconsin history. He and his brother Tom and their families run Jackson's Lakeside Cottages on Little St. Germain Lake.

Ken and his wife Linnea raised a son and a daughter and live on the property that his great grandfather purchased in 1920. When he is not at the resort or writing, he can be found in the boat chasing muskies and bass.

BOOKS BY THIS AUTHOR

Don't Fish Angry

Vintage St. Germain - Volume 1

Vintage St. Germain - Volume 2

99 Summers

Fishing The North Country - Presque Isle

Fishing The North Country - Boulder Junction/ Manitowish Waters

Fishing The North Country - Mercer- Turtle Flambeau Flowage

Fishing The North Country - St. Germain - Sayner

Fishing The North Country - Minocqua

Fishing The North Country - Cisco Chain - Land O' Lakes

Fishing The North Country - Eagle River - Three Lakes

Fishing The North Country - Hayward - Chippewa Flowage

Made in the USA
Monee, IL
28 March 2025